THE DESERTERS

M.G. Lamb

DSI Press

DSI Press LLC
DSI.Press.Lamb@gmail.com
Evergreen Park, IL 60805

The Deserters. Copyright © 2025 by Michael G. Lamb.
All rights reserved
Published under the pen name M.G. Lamb.

While some events and historical figures may be referenced, the narrative in this novel is a product of the author's imagination. Any resemblance to actual persons, living or dead, or actual places or events is purely coincidental or used in a fictional context.

Summary: *The Deserters* is a World War II-era historical novel about two teenage draftees who desert under very different circumstances. Their paths cross in war-torn France, where themes of morality, love, resilience, and faith unfold amid the horrors of battle. Contains explicit sexual content and scenes of extreme violence.

ISBN 979-8-9986470-0-0 1-World War II fiction, 2- military desertion, 3- historical war novel, 4- France WWII, 5- wartime love story, 6- antihero soldier, 7- PTSD, 8- moral conflict, 9- coming-of-age in war, 10- mature historical drama

To Joanne

"Dulce et decorum est pro patria mori."
—*Horace*

Prologue

September 1944 – Belgium

His body trembled and the ground shook as Joey Kowalski cowered in his foxhole, the shallow grave he had clawed in the dirt for himself. He closed his eyes tight like a terrified child and curled into a ball as though that could stop the bombardment surrounding him. The Americans had started the ear-splitting barrage with 25-pounders that shattered the ground and heavens. The Nazis were on the run, they were told. This morning's opening salvo was supposed to begin an American assault. And then the enemy opened up with their own dreaded 88s, exploding shrapnel everywhere over Joey's position and drowning the screams of the wounded. It was the beginning of a counterattack the Allies were not expecting.

In 1940, the US military was a global pipsqueak with fewer than 460,000 soldiers, a fighting force nineteenth in size worldwide. But a looming storm finally unleashed its horrors on Yankee shores and soon an unprepared nation stumbled and then charged into a worldwide battle at two vast and unthinkable fronts, swelling its forces to a monstrous sixteen million men. Of those, ten million would be reluctantly, and many unwillingly, drafted. Barely eighteen, Joey Kowalski, with the unlikely dream of a Kowalski going to college, was snatched away from home and loved ones in the frantic conscription of US soldiery. On a raw September morning in 1944, in the rain-drenched purgatory of the Hürtgen Forest, where shells cracked trees apart like firewood and men clutched their hands in prayer in mud-filled holes, the love of God was nowhere for Joey and his beleaguered comrades.

PART I

"Sneak home and pray you'll never know
The hell where youth and laughter go. "
--Wilfred Sassoon

Chapter 1

August 1943 – Chicago

It was dusk. The sky, a bruised purple, faded to black. The storm had subsided somewhat, and the crowd of people huddled like idiot silhouettes against the harsh glow of the parking lot's sodium lamps, their drooping figures outlined in the alien light.

Zosha Kowalski clung to her son Joey and wouldn't let go. Rain still drizzled on the cheap, black umbrella the boy held above their heads.

"Okay, Mom," Joey said, squirming himself from her arms. Tall and lanky, skinny as the umbrella he held, Joey looked around nervously at the dozens of boys in wet black suits waiting to go to war.

Joey Kowalski, his mother Zosha, and sister Dorothy stood in a parking lot with a crowd of umbrella-hidden strangers inhaling the sour breath of diesel fumes next to a line of parked buses. The crowd's unintelligible murmurs drizzled the asphalt like a hive's uneasy hum.

Joey, as though in a trance, stared mesmerized at the slick rainbows of oil which glimmered like a kaleidoscope on the wet pavement next to the depressing black wheels of each bus. He had a habit of drifting away. His high school teachers said he had an attention problem. The nuns in grammar school said he had too much imagination. But like his younger sister, Dorothy, his aptitude for equations and numbers was undeniable and earned him a college scholarship. To the astonishment and quiet pride of Zosha, her two children had emerged as mathematical prodigies at DuSable High School, and higher education was their destiny. But the war, indifferent and unrelenting, had abruptly changed everything.

When the rain finally stopped, the umbrellas slowly disappeared, revealing the heads, one by one, of a new batch of young Army recruits emerging like worried flowers from the pavement. A US Army sergeant shaped like an olive-green fire plug barked out orders to the crowd, his steely voice slamming through the damp air like a ball-peen hammer. "Those designated for bus A, board now!"

Joey looked at the scrap of paper pinned to his bony shoulder. Poorly scrawled, it read, *A*.

"Joey." Zosha gripped Joey's arm tightly. "Remember to say your prayers. The Lord will protect you."

"Sure," Joey said unconvincingly.

"I mean it," she implored. "I could never have gotten through all we have been through without God's help."

Joey nodded. "I know."

Draftees were given two weeks to put their lives in order before reporting to their induction center. It was a time of farewells as Joey Kowalski said goodbye to his family and friends. His emotions were more bittersweet than he imagined he was capable. Long ago, after the sudden deaths of his father and little brother, Joey had steeled his broken heart to never have feelings again. Feelings were for the weak and he willed himself to be impregnable against such pain ever again. But now he knew he had only lied to himself and was learning he wasn't as strong as he had imagined.

He had said goodbye to Mr. Brennan, his music and band teacher at school. He would miss this mentor who helped him learn the clarinet and taught him to love music, especially the syncopated new jazz of Duke Ellington and Benny Goodman. Joey could only smile fondly at the school's diminutive music director who had the face and neck of an ostrich. "Ah, young ones," Mr. Brennan would cackle. "Listen closely," his eyes twinkling with the spark of musical passion. "This rhythm, this syncopated jazz, it's like a sly fox tiptoeing through a henhouse. It's about the unexpected, the offbeat. Play it straight, and you're a predictable rooster. But bend the time, shift the accents, and you've got a whole barnyard dancing to your tune." Wide-eyed Joey was enthralled from that moment on and was determined to be the greatest jazz clarinet player of all time.

He shook hands and said goodbye to Clarence, his best friend since they were children. Clarence hugged Joey unexpectedly.

"Are you crying?" Joey asked surprised at his friend's emotion.

"Come back in one piece, Joey. Don't get killed."

Joey chuckled. "Ain't gonna happen, buddy. Keep an eye on this shit-hole while I'm gone. I'll be back. See you when I see you."

And after the weeping of his mom and sister, he had said goodbye to the tiny, struggling Kowalski Five and Dime, which his mother owned, crammed with its dusty trinkets and faded candy wrappers, their night time beds tucked away at the back of the store. Joey now asked himself if he would ever walk those creaky floors again. The thought gnawed at him like the hungry rats they couldn't keep from emerging nightly through the floorboards.

The family had been a team for survival, as he willingly took on chores for his mom, stacking cans, sweeping floors, and running errands before and after school. He'd grown up in the aisles of the little store, but the opening of a new Woolworth nearby surely spelled doom. So the night before he was to leave, he had become an accomplice in something reckless, something insane, to help the Kowalski Five and Dime survive.

Two days earlier, Joey and his girlfriend Kathleen O'Brien sat in each other's arms in a pile of burlap rags in an empty boxcar at the Racine rail yard. There was no youthful passion. Joey was frozen in his own thoughts and may as well been sitting alone even though Kathleen held him tight. The wind made an eerie wailing sound as it passed through the open doors of the boxcar. The burlap made Kathleen's skin itch, but it was not her only irritation. He was leaving her for war, and this was the best he could do for a goodbye? She was feeling as alone as Joey. This was not only about him. She had feelings too.

"You can't go," she finally said.

"Huh?" Joey awoke from his thoughts.

"What about us?"

Joey could only shake his head.

"Let's get married," she blurted. "Before you go. Tomorrow." This war had shaken Kathleen's plans, and she felt her33 dreams were passing through the doors of the boxcar like the wind.

Joey had plans too; college, a good job, then they would marry. He wasn't surprised by her proposal. Kathleen had always been a spontaneous head strong girl, and he did love her.

"Phil Hepner and Susie Delaney did it the day before he left. They went right down to city hall and got married."

Joey didn't answer.

Kathleen stared ahead. This was not how things were supposed to turn out.

"I'll wait for you, Joey," she finally said, but even to her, the words sounded hollow.

Kathleen kissed Joey's cheek and left him alone in the boxcar. She wiped the dirt and dust from her polka dot dress.

The war would not end soon, and Joey knew it. He had begun to follow the news more closely. The Allies had not even landed on the European continent, which the Nazis had held in their deadly grip for over three years. Older boys he knew in the neighborhood were coming home wounded or dead. This wasn't playing soldier in the empty lots of the neighborhood. The real world was hurtling at him with lightning speed.

"Well, I guess this is it," Joey said bravely, hoisting his duffel bag onto his shoulder. His mother and sister did their best not to cry. They had done all their crying weeks before. Many of the boys waiting to be shipped off were not so young. Joey saw some that looked as old as his mother. The US military was drafting men aged eighteen to thirty-eight. It bothered Joey that Kathleen did not come to see him off, but maybe it was for the best. There would be no more mom, sister, Clarence, or Kathleen. He had been sucked into the vacuum of war and like it or not, he was on his own now.

Standing tall and awkward as a bean pole at six-three, Joey looked over the throng of heads surrounding him. He recognized some of the faces. He glowered when he saw Sammy Smythe, a bully since the first grade, a distant childhood nemesis. The episode happened years ago in the fifth grade when Sammy teased and harassed Joey at school on a daily basis. Joey's dad told him the only way to deal with a bully was to punch him square in the nose no matter how afraid you are, and that's exactly what Joey did. Sam's nose gushed blood as they rolled around the school parking lot thrashing at each other until a teacher finally broke up the fight. Sam still went on to his bullying ways but never messed with Joey again. In the world of grade-school politics, Joey had reluctantly become something of a hero to his adolescent peers.

Joey continued to scan the crowd. Behind his mom and sister, beyond the gaggle of embraces and whispered goodbyes, a man in black stood in the shadows next to a stone pillar. It was the parish priest, Father Martin. Joey saw him. The man gave a short wave. Joey nodded. The sight of the priest made Joey shiver.

Joey's last night in Chicago had been hard to believe. Did it really happen? Joey was no saint and had his share of delinquent activity growing up with petty theft and vandalism, no worse than most boys. But last night he helped the parish priest at Saint Gerard's burn down the Woolworth department store.

Father Martin knew Joey and his family well. He comforted Joey's mother, Zosha, through the tragic deaths of her husband and youngest boy. He organized the local Chicago Youth Organization, which provided sports for young boys to help keep them out of trouble. The priest made sure the school gym was left open on weekend nights for basketball and boxing.

Having been a feather weight Golden Glove champion as a youngster, Martin showed Joey how to use his long arms with straight jabs from the shoulder to keep opponents at a distance. Regardless, Joey had his nose broken twice and decided to stay away from the ring. He still went to the gym with dozens of other boys in the cold winter months to play basketball and just hang out.

The priest was short on words which most of the parishioners appreciated at mass, and he kept his political thoughts to himself. He was what the Catholic Church would call a socialist or communist, which was considered a cancer to religion, but he hated the insatiable greed of big business and the oppression and hardship they put on the poor. The new Woolworth was just another corporation putting small stores like the Kowalski Five and Dime out of business. He wanted to do something to help the Kowalski's besides pray. When Joey was in the church confessional days earlier, instead of forgiving Joey's sins, Father Martin talked him into committing a felony.

Joey grimly remembered his father's job at the stockyards where his dad and the other workers were treated not much better than the hogs they slaughtered. The millionaire owners of the Union Stockyards didn't spend a dime on his injured father's medical bills, or a nickel on his funeral. The anger and helplessness of those times stayed with Joey. He was more than happy to help the priest.

As Joey walked away from his family, he suddenly slapped his breast and coat pockets. "Oh, crud!"

"What?" Zosha said.

"My deck of cards. I forgot them." Joey had a mild addiction to card playing, especially poker and blackjack, and he had become a regular playing with his dad's friends after his father's death. Joey had learned early that a sharp mind could tip luck's balance; he remembered what cards had been played, what was left to come, and it gave him an edge.

Dorothy stepped forward and handed Joey a brand-new deck neatly packaged in cellophane. They both laughed. "Always smarter than me," Joey said to his sister, and gave her a big bear hug.

"Always," she answered. Dorothy's face began to sag. Her best friend was leaving, maybe forever, and she tried to fight back tears.

Joey made his way towards the middle of the bus and took a seat next to a window. The diesel engine coughed and shook as the bus idled. The bus floor was wet, and the seats smelled like they had been disinfected with ammonia. Joey slid the window open. He could see his sister still standing outside on the pavement with his mom.

"Do you think he'll be okay?" Zosha said. She also fought back tears. Life had taught her to always fear the worst.

"Joey's a survivor. You know that. He'll be okay," Dorothy said. "What about that fire at the Woolworth?" she said changing the subject.

"Yes. Terrible." Although Zosha would not admit it openly, the fire at the Woolworth was a godsend for her small dime store. Had God answered Zosha's prayers?

Dorothy walked away and left Zosha alone. Zosha saw Joey's face in the bus window and blew him a kiss. Joey felt the bus lurch forward as it pulled away from the terminal. He glimpsed Father Martin come up behind his mother and put his arms around her.

The bus rattled west down Madison Avenue, and the city lights of Chicago were soon behind. From the window, Joey could see nothing but the black landscape of western Illinois, and his own sad reflection. The boy next to him snored.

Joey Kowalski was no longer excited about entering the war like he had been a year ago when he tried enlisting at seventeen and war fever was pitch high, but he had not been rejected because of his age, which he should have been. He was labeled 4-F because his feet were too big for GI-issued boots.

Now a year older, he had changed his mind about the Army, and started to look forward to college. A math scholarship to Illinois State University promised to open doors his family could never have dreamed of affording. His education would be free, and engineering was his goal—a field where he could build things that mattered. In his mind, the future was clear and orderly, mapped out like one of the equations he loved solving. He'd graduate, land a high-paying job, and take care of his mother so she never had to work or worry again. She'd never have to spend another hour behind the counter at the Five and Dime. Then there'd be a wife, a family, a house with a yard. His first son would be named Henry, after his father, though he'd call him Hank, a strong name for a bright future. It all seemed so real in his head, so close he could almost touch it.

The bus hurtled its way west to Rockford, Illinois, carrying Joey and a hundred others into the jaws of pre-induction. Now eighteen years old, Joey was no longer 4-F because of the size of his feet. Boots now stretched in sizes three to fifteen and a half. The Army was short on flesh and blood, not leather.

Doctors examined each draftee. Eye exams amounted to nothing more than counting the number of eyes. Two was passing. Draftees who could not read were sent to a special school for three weeks to try to get them to a minimum fourth grade level of comprehension, more or less. Joey and the others also now bore the weight of their dog tags, eight embossed digits with their name and blood type that hung from their necks with cold uncertainty.

His clarinet, always a comfort at home, had to be left in Chicago. Its absence left a sharp pang. A sad melody clouded Joey's head. He thought about his girlfriend Kathleen, but most of all he missed his mom and the dingy southside world he had just left behind.

The bus carrying Joey parked next to a large building in Rockford. There were dozens of other buses lining the street. The induction line was long. A short boy with freckles wearing a baseball cap was in line in front of Joey. "I'm not going," he stammered over and over. "I'm not going." He turned to Joey, pleading as if Joey could help him. "I don't belong here. My auntie is sick." Joey did his best to ignore him.

The Army gave each recruit a new pair of shoes, which Joey sorely needed. Boots would be issued at the final training facility. He was told his family could ship his clarinet and send letters once the location of the seventeen-week training center was determined.

The following night, herded like sheep into the black maw of a train, Joey and a faceless horde boarded a serpent of one hundred boxcars. The air inside smelled of oil and sweat. Their destination: Camp Wolters, Texas, a name as alien and ominous as a distant star. Joey's farthest journey ever had been a one hour drive to a state park in Indiana on brief summer vacations. As a child, those soft brown, sandy shores of Lake Michigan seemed as exotic as Tahiti or Bora Bora, but were now just faded pictures. Joey drifted in and out of sleep, his head gently swaying with the rhythm of the rails that carried him further and further away from everything he had ever known.

The steel caravan traveled south down the flat spine of Illinois through a seemingly never ending emerald carpet of baby corn and waves of amber wheat as far as the eye could see. They paused several times to pick up more draftees at other induction centers along the way. At each stop they were allowed out of the train to stretch their legs. Soldiers with rifles and intimidating eyes watched the draftees carefully so nobody wandered away. The American Legion at each stop had tables filled with soda and coffee. Pretty girls handed out doughnuts and cigarettes. The terrain eventually stopped its boring flatness, rising rocky and twisted the further the boy soldiers traveled in this grim parade.

In the stifling Texas heat, Joey was one of thirty thousand draftees crowded into Camp Wolters where they would be taught how to be killers. The camp was hastily thrown together one year earlier on thirty-six thousand dusty, vacant acres in Mineral Wells, Texas. It was now a small city teeming with life with over two thousand buildings, a hospital, theaters, bowling alleys, churches, and even restaurants. The camp was also home to over four thousand German POWs captured in North Africa.

Immediately after deboarding the train, Joey became just another face in an ever-lengthening line snaking its way to the camp barbershop. Joey's mop of sandy, blond hair disappeared in less than a minute as the barber cut away, whistling while he worked. In line behind Joey was a chubby boy with a beach ball paunch and unusually long black curly hair that ran to his shoulders. The barber, who had half of a burned-out cigar in his mouth, said, "I am glad you have come to my salon, Susan!" He whistled as the hair disappeared.

The boy with the long curly locks was Isaiah Stomp from Topeka, Kansas. He and Joey had talked in line about the whirlwind of being drafted.

Isaiah Stomp had an easy, honest manner, and Joey immediately liked him. He said he was part Indian, but didn't look it. Isaiah had a wife and new baby at home. "I'm a dad," he told Joey. "How can they just take us away like this?" He threw his hands in the air.

Joey had never met anyone who wasn't from the south side of Chicago. Most of the kids talked with funny accents. After they exited the barbershop, Joey and Isaiah stared at each other, mouths agape. They pointed fingers at each other and laughed out loud.

"Ya'll look like a peeled potato," Isaiah Stomp said to Joey.

"You should talk. You look like you're about twelve." Joey looked around. "Where do we go now?"

Isaiah shrugged. "How about over that fence?" Even though they both knew Isaiah was joking, they still looked uneasily at the eight-foot-high chain-link fence surrounding the camp. The barbed wire coursing the top said they weren't going anywhere.

Chapter 2

Each man was shepherded into the armory, where they were issued an M1 rifle. It was an abrupt reminder that they were being trained to kill. The M1 was the first semiautomatic rifle in the world to be issued to infantry. It came with an eight-round clip that could be fired continuously, riddling the enemy with lead without the soldier ever taking his finger off the trigger. Joey stared at it as though it was a horrible living thing.

The rifle felt wrong in Joey's hands, heavy in a way that no stickball bat or broom handle ever had. It wasn't the weight—he could handle that—but the meaning, the violence it promised. *Thou shalt not kill.* Of the Ten Commandments religiously ingrained in him that was the big one, and yet here he was. He'd grown up navigating the sharp angles of fire escapes and the careless chaos of the street, but now he was becoming a part of some ominous drama. The armory smelled of dust and sweat, of something faintly metallic that clung to the back of Joey's throat. Around him, boys who had spent their lives hefting shovels or bales of hay looked as bewildered as he.

He never thought he'd say it, but he missed the city—the honking cars, the narrow streets and alleys, the warm, filthy pulse of it. Here, the world felt stripped bare, just sky and dirt and the bark of the drill sergeant, each command biting sharp and cold, in the Texas heat. Holding his weapon, Isaiah stood next to Joey. He shook his head with a look that said, *what the hell have we gotten ourselves into?*

Joey and Isaiah became fast friends and found they would be quartered in the same building – Barracks 32B. Men who would fight together in the same squad were housed together so they could work as a team when they were out at the front trying to kill Germans. There were thousands of sleeping quarters for the soldiers which were nothing more than plywood shoeboxes perched on stilts like oversized chicken coops. The siding was tar paper, black and thin, as if the builders had shrugged off the idea of real walls. The interior of the barracks was as unfeeling as the Texas weather: blazing when the sun burned high, frigid when the nights turned sharp. Ceiling fans helped little with the brutal summer heat. Latrines were outside. There was a single wood-burning space heater emptying into a chimney at the center of each structure. Joey didn't know what Texas winters were like, but he knew enough of the Chicago cold to think that getting near the stove was a good idea. He and Isaiah pushed by other recruits and grabbed bunks near the heater.

A squeaky voice yelled from outside. "Fall in!" The boys scrambled from their hut into the bright sunlight. The squad drill sergeant was a short, bald man built like a block of concrete. Anger was etched on every rigid line of his face. His voice was shrill, screeching like the tip of a knife scratching glass, sending chills down the spine of every recruit.

"Attention!" shrieked Drill Sergeant Mealy. He stalked slowly down the line of soldiers, stopping occasionally to scowl at a boy's uniform. He whirled and stared at a skinny recruit.

"What's your name, soldier?" The boy, trembling like a leaf in a storm, couldn't find his voice. "What's your name?" Sergeant Mealy screamed.

"West," the boy stammered. "Larry West." But his words soon dissolved into sobs.

"Little baby going to cry?" Sergeant Mealy mocked. "Button that top button!" he shouted. "You lousy piece of shit. Twenty push-ups now." The terrified boy dropped and began counting push-ups.

Sergeant Mealy walked along and stopped in front of Joey. He looked up, and his lips curled into a snarl. "What are you staring at, private?"

"Nothing, sir."

"You say I'm nothing?" Sergeant Mealy stood on his toes and yelled, spittle flying in Joey's face. "What's your name?"

"Kowalski, sir."

"You stupid Polack. You are the one who is nothing."

Joey looked straight ahead, not daring to look at this little monster.

"Look at me when I'm talking to you!"

Joey looked down, and, in his head, was strangling this little man.

Sergeant Mealy strutted along until he stopped in front of a short boy with bad teeth and a face like a rodent. The minimum height for a recruit had been five three, but with the war in full swing, it was lowered to five feet. This recruit barely made that height. Sergeant Mealy took a liking to this boy, probably because he was one of the few he could literally look down on.

"What is your name?"

"York!" the boy hollered. "Erskine York."

"Where you from, son?"

"Monroe, Tennessee. Sir!"

"I know Monroe. I grew up nearby in Livingston."

The boy with the squirrel face beamed with delight.

"You wouldn't be kin to Sergeant Alvin York?"

Alvin York was a World War I hero—one of the most recognized and decorated soldiers of the first war. Gary Cooper played him in a movie.

"Yes, sir. A cousin, sir!" Private York hollered. "And I can shoot the eye out of a rabbit at two hundred yards."

Sergeant Mealy smiled. "I think we are going to get along, York."

Under a relentless sun, the soldiers ran drills all day. Backpacks were loaded with rocks. Many of the boys passed out from exhaustion. Sergeant Mealy walked up behind Joey and stuffed extra rocks in his pack. After each mile run, they were forced to do push-ups with their backpacks on. More boys dropped from exhaustion. Joey thought he was in good shape, but he was mistaken. It seemed Sergeant Mealy was trying to kill all of them, his every command a sadistic gauntlet of agony.

Joey's friend, Isaiah Stomp, was struggling badly. Chubby and soft from years behind a diner grill, Isaiah had never been built for military life. His folks were farmers, and while he respected the work, it wasn't for him; farming required a kind of grit he'd never claimed. Cooking was his world—flipping eggs, stacking burgers, and perfecting what he swore was the best grilled cheese sandwich in all of Kansas. He couldn't stop thinking about his wife and three-month-old son back home.

The constant yelling and punishing drills left Isaiah flailing. He felt stupid and could not follow orders fast enough. His mind seemed stuck in molasses. He'd glance frantically left and right, hoping to steal a clue from the others, but he was always a step or ten behind. Every moment felt unreal, like he'd wandered into the worst dream imaginable, a dream he couldn't wake from. He wasn't going to last.

After mess, every damn one of the boys collapsed into their bunk. Joey wanted to write home but could not lift his arms. Sleep came quickly but Joey still remembered to say his prayers per his mother's instructions; a bedtime prayer taught to him since he was a baby boy. *Now I lay me down to sleep. I pray the Lord my soul to keep. If I die before I wake, I pray the Lord my soul to take.* It seemed Joey had just closed his

eyes when the bugle of reveille blasted him awake with
Sergeant Mealy pounding the lockers, barking orders.

One soldier in Joey's hut was taking to Army
life like a fish to water. Erskine York. The other men
started calling him Squirrel. He wasn't upset. He liked
the name. His ability to fieldstrip his rifle with speed
and ease while blindfolded was remarkable. He was
often cleaning and polishing his M1 long after the
members of the platoon had stacked their weapons at the
end of the barracks and gone to supper. He woke every
day before reveille and was standing at attention in front
of his bunk before Sergeant Mealy showed up. His
bragging about his prowess with a rifle was not a brag.
He qualified with marksman grades the first day on the
range while most of the boys could not hit the target if
they were standing in front of it. There were four levels
of shooting proficiency in boot camp—unqualified,
marksman, sharpshooter, and expert. York would leave
training with an expert sharpshooter badge, the highest
qualification.

Though dim-witted in ways that made the others
shake their heads, his IQ barely scraping rabbit
territory—Erskine "Squirrel" York was exactly what the
Army wanted: obedient, tireless, and unnervingly good
with a deadly weapon.

On just the fifth day, Isaiah confided with Joey that he
couldn't take it anymore and he was going to go over
the hill as soon as he got a chance.

"You can't do that," Joey pleaded. "Get that out
of your head. We have to survive."

"I can't. I can't."

"We can do this. They'll catch you for sure. You can get shot for desertion. Or you'll spend ten years in an Army prison. You're tougher than that. You will never get back to your wife and little boy. I'll help you get through this."

Isaiah settled down. He took deep breaths. "I'll try."

Experiencing near torture each day, the men began to bond by the suffering they all shared. Squirrel became a favorite for the boys to tease. He never took offence and chuckled affably when the guys played jokes on him. "Aw, shucks" was his typical response. However, his marksmanship with an M1 rifle amazed Sergeant Mealy and everyone in the squad.

The barracks smelled like sweat and disinfectants, a heady mix that clung to the air long after the supper calories were devoured and the boys were able to lounge before lights out. There were boys from all over the country, a motley crew from farms and factories, bustling cities, and sleepy towns.

The boys sprawled across their bunks; their faces half-turned toward the dim glow of the overhead light. Hezekiah "Zeke" Walker, a farm boy from Hastings, Nebraska, broad-shouldered and quiet, leaned against the wall, massaging his feet in calloused hands. Across the room, a pencil thin boy, Jack Elliott, from Flint, Michigan, picked at a scab on his elbow. His sharp, angry eyes darted between the other boys who began to loosen up and talk about themselves, and where they were from.

"Where's Elephant Butte, anyway?" Stitch Hansen, a wiry wise guy from Philadelphia, piped up, his voice loud and grating. He had been silent for most of the evening, sizing up the others, but now he couldn't hold back his curiosity. "Sounds like a place from a western movie."

Mitch Klausner, the kid from Elephant Butte, New Mexico, shot him a small grin. "Small town. Lot of desert. You ever been to a place where the only sound you hear is the wind scraping against the dust? That's Elephant Butte." His accent was thick with the drawl of the Southwest, a stark contrast to Stitch's fast-talking Philly swagger.

"Elephant Butte. That's a dumb name. You ain't lived till you've eaten a Philly cheese steak," Stitch informed everyone.

"And you ain't lived till you've eaten jack rabbit," Mitch shot back. All the boys laughed, including Stitch.

Mark Swanson, a boy from Cleveland with a lantern jaw and dimpled chin, nodded. "Sounds quiet. Ain't nothing like that back home." He looked at the ceiling for a moment, his hands behind his head. "My place back home is so noisy, the traffic from the highway's so loud you can't hear yourself talk."

Mark Swanson had Hollywood good looks and considered himself the handsomest boy on earth, and God's gift to the female inhabitants of the planet.

"This is a bore," He rose from his bunk, walked to his locker and stared into the tiny mirror that was attached, and started combing his hair which was literally a half inch long. Nobody could tell what he was doing. "Gotta look good for the ladies."

"What ladies?" Stitch asked.

"I'm goin' into town and gettin' some pussy."

"Sure you are."

"I know the guy who's on duty at the east gate. As long as I get back before he's done with his shift, I'm golden." Swanson looked around the room. "Who's with me."

Nobody raised their hand, their terror of Sgt. Mealy too palpable.

"Aw, you're all chickens."

"And you're stupid," Zeke said. Swanson walked back to his bunk and laid down, his bravado fading. Swanson earned the nickname, "Pretty Boy."

Larry West, the crying boy from the first day of camp, who had been pretty much silent since their arrival, finally spoke up. His voice cracked, as if it hadn't been used in months. "Duluth... it's cold there," he muttered, eyes downcast, his hands fumbled with the blanket at the edge of his bunk.

"It speaks," Stitch said sarcastically.

"I just want this to be over," Larry muttered.

"Anybody from Chicago?" Joey called out. Nobody answered.

Skinny Jack Elliot, from Flint, Michigan, was the son of a Ford auto worker, grandson of a Ford auto worker, and soon to be a third-generation Elliot to work for Henry Ford himself. Thin as a broomstick, barely noticeable when he turned sideways, Jack soon got the nickname, "Fatman." The squad never saw anyone who could eat as much as Elliot and just get skinnier. He never chewed. Anything on his fork he swallowed whole. He was annoyed when other grunts in the canteen stared at him in amazement.

"What you lookin' at?" the ill-tempered Fatman would growl.

Another boy from this cast of misfits was Wilbur Lafayette who sat on the edge of his bunk, his broad shoulders hunched as he worked his boots off, his fingers thick and clumsy from a life spent working the chains and ropes used for hunting alligators in the Louisiana bayou. His Cajun drawl, deep and melodic, carried through the room like a low rumble, but the boys had learned quickly not to ask him to repeat himself. His accent was so heavy, the words seemed to hang in the air longer than they should, and half the time, the boys just nodded along, pretending to understand. He was an enigma, a giant of a boy with a demeanor so quiet and intense that all the boys kept their playful jabs to themselves.

Wilbur didn't speak much. His large, flat nose and the deep-set eyes, framed by the thick ridge of his brow, gave him a look that made most men shy away. No one dared joke about his accent or his size—not unless they wanted to see his tree-trunk arms come swinging. The nickname, "Gorilla," stuck, though, not out of mockery, but out of awe. He looked the part, and

when he clenched his jaw, you knew not to push him
further.

There was a long pause, and for a moment, the
barrack was still. Then, as if the weight of silence had
been too much, Jack Elliott snorted, breaking the
tension. "Duluth, Flint, Elephant Butte... hell, we're all
just a bunch of losers here anyway, right?"

"Speak for yourself," Joey answered.

But the others nodded, a mix of agreement and
quiet resignation on their faces. They had come from
different corners of the country, with different stories,
different lives—yet, here they were, sharing the same
unpredictable destiny.

Besides Stomp, Joey became closest to the
oldest soldier in the squad, Milton Carmichael III from
Florida. At thirty-eight years old, he could've been a
father to most of these boys. He taught high school
English in Tallahassee. His favorite book was *The Great
Gatsby*. A bachelor, he was stunned to receive a draft
notice at his age. He promised his mother he would be
home soon. He earned the nickname "Pops."

Pops was surprised to learn that Joey actually
read books and was fond of Shakespeare.

"You ever consider becoming a teacher some
day?" he asked Joey.

"Nope. They don't make much money. I'm
going to study engineering. Build bridges, design
skyscrapers, and stuff." Pops nodded. No. Teachers
didn't make much money but that's not why he loved
his job. He loaned Joey a copy of *Hamlet*.

After a particularly grueling day of non-stop marching exercises, Stitch Hansen stood on his bunk and began to mimic all the comedians on the big screen and radio. He could "yuk, yuk, yuk" like the Three Stooges, and with a small comb under his nose, he was Adolf Hitler and then Charlie Chaplin. He called Gorilla "My Little Chickadee", in a perfect nasally W. C. Fields impersonation. He even dead panned a hilarious impersonation of Sergeant Mealy. "Kowalski," Stitch squeaked, "you bowling-ball-headed Polack, you couldn't blow your nose if brains were dynamite." Joey couldn't help but scream with laughter, but the hilarity was a fleeting moment before lights out, and soon the 4:30 AM reveille blared over the loud speakers, promising another crushing day of boot camp drills.

Chapter 3

Joey christened the next day's drill "Hell's Half Acre," where they were all forced to crawl across the ground beneath barbed wire with live machine gun rounds being fired over their heads. Farm boy Hezekiah Walker got kissed from a bullet through the top of his helmet, knocking it off his head. After that, the recruits, especially Zeke, crawled with their faces tight against the dirt.

It had not rained for two weeks, and the ground became red powder, choking the soldiers during their drills. The dust invaded their eyes, noses, and throats causing them to gasp for air. Sergeant Mealy decided that the training grounds used for the barbed wire crawling drills should be hosed down to create a terrain of mud, muck, and misery. The men now crawled Hell's Half Acre gagging on muddy, red slime.

One of the boys stopped crawling. It was Larry West, the crying soldier from the first day of camp.

"Keep crawling, soldier!" Sergeant Mealy hollered. "What is wrong with you soldier? Move it!"

"I can't. I can't," the boy whimpered. Sergeant Mealy put his boot on the back of the recruit's helmet and pushed his head under the muddy water. Seconds passed, and then a minute. The boy started flailing his arms. Bubbles jumped from the water.

Nearly every recruit watched, horrified. Joey nearly jumped up to tackle the sergeant. Mealy finally took his boot off the boy's head, reached down, and picked him up by the back of his collar.

"Go back to barracks. Now! Double-time."

The boy stumbled away gagging.

When the filthy men returned to their barrack, they found the boy sitting at the edge of his bed sobbing. Milton "Pops" Carmichael sat down next to him and put his arm around the boy.

"Don't worry, Larry, everybody cries. That's part of training. They want to break us." That night, under an indifferent Texas sky, the boy from Duluth, Minnesota, snuck away from camp and deserted.

Private Joey Kowalski lay on his bunk staring at the ceiling fan of their hut. The blades moved slowly. If its intent was to move air, it had failed. Kathleen O'Brien sent him a letter smelling of perfume. It was more a note than a letter. It said she loved him, to hurry home, and not much else. He passed the fragrant envelope around for the other guys to jealously sniff.

He thought about his mom and sister Dorothy all the time. He also got letters from his best friend Clarence lamenting how Chicago was boring, and nothing in the neighborhood ever changed. Clarence mentioned that there was a terrible fire at the new Woolworth. Had Joey heard?

Joey also received a letter from his sister saying that she had been suspended from school for stabbing a boy in the neck with a pencil. This made him smile. Like Joey, she excelled at math. As a freshman at Du Sable High School she was already taking senior level classes. But as Joey knew and now this poor boy discovered, her temper was savage when sufficiently harassed. The boy never pulled her braids again. The letters from home were a blessing taking Joey's mind off the brutality of each day, and he felt sorry for the boys who never received anything at mail call.

Outside the sky blackened, and the glass in the windows rattled violently. After two weeks of drought, the skies broke with lightning and thunder, bringing a deluge of rain. Joey dreaded tomorrow's drills. Pops was at his bunk reading a book. Stitch and Fatman, who had become good friends, pitched pennies into a coffee can. The perpetually angry Fatman admired and was envious of Stitch probably because they were exact opposites. While Fatman was quiet and introverted, Stitch was raucously outgoing and could fit into any crowd with breezy ease.

Squirrel stood on his toes and looked out the window at the storm. "Goodness, looks like the devil his-self is throwin' a fit. That's a gully washer fer sure. Sure am glad we're inside."

The entire hut shook. "I hope we stay that way," Swanson said.

"When this war is over, you all come to my diner in Topeka. I make the best grilled cheese sandwich you will ever eat in your life," Isaiah Stamp said. Isaiah, with Joey's help, was finally getting used to the grinding boot camp life. He had lost most of his baby fat but still lay in his bunk dreaming of the days in front of the restaurant cooktop. He licked his lips and could almost smell the grease and onions sizzling, smiling to himself as his mind traveled to the sight of a well-made grilled cheese.

"Where's Topeka?" Gorilla muttered.

Pops lifted his eyes from his paperback. "Kansas."

"Where's Kansas?" Gorilla asked again.

"It's in *The Wizard of Oz*," Squirrel answered helpfully. Pops set his book down and sighed. No geography majors here.

Joey wondered what his girlfriend Kathleen O'Brien was really doing. Her letters never really told him anything. He knew she was wild. That's what he liked about her. Would she be running off with somebody else as soon as he was gone? The question bothered him.

"Hey, Gorilla," Isaiah said. "What do'ya do in Baton Rouge for fun? Anybody down there speak English?

"Alligator. Hunt alligator. Eat it," Gorilla grunted.

"Hey, Isaiah, start serving alligator sandwiches at your diner," Mitch Klausner chimed in. "I'd drop in for that." The boys all laughed. Even Pops.

"That'd be good," Gorilla said.

Joey reached beneath his bed and removed his clarinet from its case. He raised the smooth black instrument to his lips, his fingers gliding over the keys with practiced ease. His mind drifted to a different place. The first note was soft, like the whisper of a breeze through tall grass, and then continued sweet and wistful, the lilting tones carrying a warm ache of homesickness and a fleeting sense of peace. All the boys stopped what they were doing and listened. The notes swirled gently, rising and falling, with a calmness in sharp contrast to the tempest raging outside, the thunder providing an eerie percussion to Joey's mini-concert while the rain beat the roof continuously like a maddening round of applause.

"That's nice, Joey," Stomp said. Pretty Boy Swanson nodded his approval.

Squirrel saw a figure outside moving in the storm like a grey ghost. "Lights out, nose pickers!" Sergeant Mealy hollered from outside the hut, banging on the door. Even in a thunderstorm, the maniacal drill sergeant haunted and taunted the boys.

Joey put his clarinet back beneath his bunk. "Fuck you," he whispered. The rain continued to pound the tin roof, a sweet lullaby. Joey closed his eyes and fell asleep.

When the recruits were not running and climbing, they attended classes in map reading, aerial photographic interpretation, and infantry tactics. Someday one of them might have to lead other men in battle, which was happening often with the casualties mounting among officers overseas.

They received ten-inch knives designed to attach to their rifles and serve as bayonets. Nearly all these boys, fresh from farm plows and city streets, grappled with a fear of taking another man's life. The Army's grim task was to forge them into cold-blooded killers. Joey saw how the men were hardening like steel, eager for combat, their thirst for violence growing, whether against Germans or their own comrades. Fights among them, especially between different squads, were becoming increasingly frequent.

For days, they practiced lunging and stabbing dummies with their bayonets. Each thrust aimed to drive into the enemy's body, twist to widen the wound, and then withdraw with a sickening tear.

Their training spanned a full range of weaponry: British, German, and American machine guns and rifles, sixty-millimeter mortars, bazookas. They also learned the use of the garrote wire for silent kills, slicing through neck arteries with chilling efficiency. Joey grimaced at the thought.

The days went by quickly. Letters from home brought both happiness and sadness to Joey. He wrote home every few days to his family and to Kathleen. The guys would razz him that he was wasting his time writing to his girl, who was probably in the arms of the first John she saw after his bus left Chicago. "You don't know my Kathleen," Joey would reply, but wondered if it was the truth. He masturbated out in the latrine nearly every day thinking of her. It helped him keep his sanity.

Joey didn't sneak into town for cheap whiskey and willing women when Pretty Boy Swanson and some of the others did. He preferred to play his clarinet, or to gamble, as there was always a card or dice game going on. He won more money than he lost and would send some of it home to his sister Dorothy, who controlled the dime store money.

Joey would reread his letters before he sent them to Kathleen and grimace as to what a bad letter writer he was.

> *Kathleen, my love, I can say that I do not like the Army and I miss you terribly. I am tired of guns and shooting. Firing my rifle over and over gave me a bad bruise on my cheek, but that has gotten better. There are dances here on weekends, which lifts the boy's spirits, but only makes me miss you more. I only want to dance with you. Wish I could say something like in a poem how I feel about you. Please don't worry about me. I will not be brave. I will be okay. I love you to the moon and back. Joey.*

Isaiah Stomp walked over to Joey's bunk. "Come on, Joey. The USO starts at seven."

"I don't know. There will be a card game later, and most of these guys are chumps."

"The sign in the mess hall says, *Good girls, Good food, Good fun*. Most of the girls are pretty," Isaiah said. "Come on, get your face out of your letters. It will do you good."

Isaiah hung his arms over the bunk above Joey's bed. Gone was the chubby Topeka cook. Isaiah had become something leaner and harder. His biceps rippled with muscle. His pudgy face was no longer pudgy, and his sharp cheekbones, no doubt from his Cherokee heritage, became more prominent on his sunbaked skin. The boy from Topeka was disappearing and turning into a man. A soldier.

Pretty Boy Swanson stared at himself in the mirror on his locker door smiling, winking at himself. "Babes, get ready," he said to his image.

"C'mon," Stitch said, tapping Pretty Boy on the back of the head.

"Hey! My Hair!"

You ain't got no hair, you dumbbell."

"All right," Joey finally said. He swung his long legs over the side of his bunk. "I guess I will bless the *babes* with my presence."

"Let's go, Swanson," Isaia hollered. "Quit staring at yourself, you ugly bastard."

"Bring the mirror with you and you can dance with yourself all night," farm boy Hezekiah Walker chimed in.

Pretty Boy spun on his heels and led the charge out of the barracks, a chorus of laughter trailing behind him. Even Pops put down his book and joined the parade.

Pretty Boy broke into song, his voice ringing through the night air: "One, two, three, four. Babes are knock'n on my door. Five, six, seven, eight. Babes are knock'n on my gate." The others joined in, marching along with playful shoves and easy laughter, their boyish excitement unshaken by the looming call to war. The warm Texas night buzzed with the hum of crickets, as if nature itself, at least for the moment, was singing along.

The United Services Organization (USO) was formed in 1941 to help lift soldier morale. Their object was wholesome recreational activities for the boys who were pulled away from their homes. Thousands of girls throughout the country enlisted. The concept was to have a place for the men in training to relax and unwind, to keep them from heading to town for hard drink and disreputable women. Hopefully, this would rub off when they went overseas, where drunkenness and venereal disease were weakening the fighting force.

The dance hall buzzed with nervous energy as the boys filed in. The girls were asked to be sweet and clean—no provocative or tight-fitting clothing. Brightly colored attire was encouraged, including whites and pinks to help change the scenery from the soldier's drab khaki greens. Skirts only. No pants. Any sexual talk was to be avoided. No young lady was allowed to leave without their chaperone. If they came in private cars, they were ordered to leave immediately after the dance.

All the dances were chaperoned by older women. No alcohol was served, but there were doughnuts, sandwiches, hot coffee, and soft drinks. The young women attending were carefully screened for high moral character, or so the USO boasted. Beside the dance hall, there was an adjacent hall for ping-pong and places for the men to sit and talk with older women, senior hostesses. Many of the boys found it easier to unload their homesickness with someone they could associate as a mother figure. There were five men for every young lady at the dance.

More rules. The soldiers were not allowed to ask the women to dance. Those wishing to dance lined up like marionettes against a long windowless wall, and a girl, if she wished, would approach them and ask them to dance. The girls were asked to dance with each willing partner, no matter how ugly the boy might be.

Isaiah Stomp stood against the wall hoping to get a dance. Joey Kowalski watched the dance floor from a make-shift bar at the other side of the room. A fetching young woman all peaches and cream walked up to Joey. "Can I buy you a drink, soldier?" she asked.

"Sure," Joey laughed. "If you allow me to buy you one, too."

"Barkeep, two Coca-Colas!" she called out.

Her name was Ellie. She was short with a round face and pretty blue eyes. They played ping-pong and Ellie won. She worked as a secretary in a law office but wanted to help the war effort just a little bit by providing company for the boys. She did not like her job. "You want to dance?" she asked.

They walked to the dance floor and some jazzy tune was playing from a brightly lit jukebox. A crowd was gathering around a couple of dancers near the middle of the dance floor flying about with reckless abandon. It was Isaiah Stomp and his partner, a slender Latina woman. And boy, were they dancing! Isaiah was lifting the girl in the air and swinging her between his legs and catching her from behind. Soldiers and girls alike were laughing and clapping. It was a new dance called the boogie-woogie and Joey had no idea Isaiah could dance like this. When the song finished, both the woman and Isaiah were sweating profusely and smiling. The woman left him. She went and asked another boy to dance.

Ellie and Joey tried to boogie-woogie, but their attempts were laughable. Ellie said it was a pleasure meeting Joey and maybe they would see each other again at another dance. She walked up to another boy and asked if she could buy him a drink.

"Where the hell did you learn to dance like that?" Joey asked Isaiah.

"Me and the wife could really cut a rug back in Topeka." As good a shape as Stomp was in, he was still panting. He gazed after the Latina woman. "You want to know what she said to me?"

"What?"

"She said, 'Dance with me like you are making love to me.' Jesus, I sure wouldn't mind meeting her somewhere outside this prison someday.'"

"What's her name?"

"I have no idea."

Isaiah and Joey leaned against the bar watching the dance floor. Squirrel was dancing with a girl much taller than him. It was a slow dance, and he buried his face in the girl's breasts, dreaming of home. The girl pushed him away twice, but after a while she did not care. A senior chaperone eventually walked up and separated the two. Squirrel looked bewildered, like he just woke up from a long sleep. Before the woman walked away, she whispered something into his ear and slid something into his pocket.

Squirrel walked to the men's latrine with his head in the clouds. He could not remember ever being happier. It only took one dance, and he was in love. There were two grunts from another squad standing near the door watching him go in. They pointed at him and followed him into the latrine. Their look was menacing. Joey and Isaiah watched from the bar.

"I don't like the looks of that," Joey said. Isaiah nodded. Gorilla had also noticed and headed towards the latrine. Army training was coming into play. The men from Barracks 32-B were already looking out for each other.

Squirrel stood at the urine trough peeing when he heard two men behind him.

"This little boy likes to dance with pigs. You like piggies, little boy?" one of the men sneered. The second GI laughed.

Squirrel finished, and turned and faced the men. They blocked his path as he tried to leave. "Look, guys, I don't want no trouble. And she ain't no pig neither."

The huskier of the two soldiers grabbed York and threw him against the sink. Squirrel swung at the man and missed. The GI punched Squirrel in the forehead, knocking him backward. One of the men stuck Squirrel' s head in the sink Land the other started pulling at Squirrel's pants.

"I've got something for you little girl," the GI said.

In walked Gorilla and Joey.

"Evening, gents," Joey said. Lightning struck. Joey grabbed the grunt who was watching the assault, spun him around, punched him in the stomach, then grabbed him by the neck and rammed the stunned man headfirst into the plywood wall. The wall buckled and the man dropped to the floor like a sack of potatoes. The husky grunt came at Joey, but the youngster from Chicago swiftly kicked the GI in the groin, making his face pucker. Joey threw a sharp left jab directly into his jaw, standing the man straight up. He followed with a right hook to the side of the head, causing the soldier's face to crunch as he toppled to the floor. His street fighting and boxing in the basement Saint Gerard's Church with Father Martin as his instructor had not gone to waste.

Gorilla watched, arms folded. Seeing he was not needed, he nodded approval. "Good," he said.

Squirrel stared in astonishment at what happened in only a few seconds.

"Come on," Joey said. "Let's get out of here before any officers come. They dashed from the latrine and disappeared on the dance floor. They decided to call it a night. The dance was ending shortly anyway.

Walking back from the dance Squirrel tugged at Joey's sleeve.

"What's up?" Joey asked. "You okay?"

"Yeah. I just wanna say thanks. Nobody has ever stuck up for me before."

Joey smiled. "Forget it, I don't like bullies."

All in all, Joey had a good time. Ellie was sweet, quick with a laugh, and surprisingly skilled at ping-pong, her competitive streak catching him off guard in the best way. By 10 PM, the boys shuffled back into the drafty chicken coop they called home with the thoughts of pretty girls still in their veins. They stayed up and chatted about the women they met.

"Hey, Squirrel, you almost got thrown out of the dance. Sergeant Mealy wouldn't like that. I think you were dancing with the ugliest girl at the party," Fatman Elliot said.

"She ain't ugly. Don't you be talking that way. Her name is Irene." Squirrel blushed. "Her breasts were like a pillow. I asked her to marry me."

"What did she say?"

"No."

The boys all laughed until there were tears in their eyes. Gorilla grabbed Squirrel around the neck and gave him noogies on top of his skull. Joey looked at his own knuckles. They were bloody from the fight. He shook his head. It didn't hurt. He went beneath his bunk and pulled out his clarinet and began playing a festive tune. Stitch Hansen produced a bra and a wig from his locker. Where he got it, no one seemed to care. He grabbed Fatman Elliot by the hand. "Come on, sailor." The two began dancing. The men made a circle around them and began clapping. There was a riot of laughter. Swanson tapped Fatman on the shoulder. "May I butt in?"

Squirrel was able to pull away from Gorilla. He went and sat on his bunk and reached into his pocket and pulled out a note. It read, *I think you're cute. Look me up when this damn war is over. Write me. Irene Plunk. 22 Redbud St., Justice, Georgia.* He had never felt such ecstasy. He put the note to his nose and took a deep breath.

Other soldiers started dancing with each other, although Stitch Hansen, in wig and bra was in demand.

Pops looked up from the book he was reading and watched the show. He smiled at these rare moments of mindless joy. These kids were not far removed from the high schoolers he taught. Squirrel edged over to Pops's bunk and sat on the edge of his mattress.

"Pops, could you write a letter for me?"

"You don't know how to write?" Pops sat up in his bunk.

"Not too good." He showed Pops the note.

Pops smiled and nodded. "Sure." He reached under his bunk and tore out a page from the journal he was keeping. "Irene?" he said. "That's the girl you were dancing with?"

Pops remembered her from the dance, and the comical slow dance Squirrel had with her. She was as plain as a burlap sack and had a head like a donkey. Pops chuckled to himself. Love was a mysterious thing.

"Okay. 'Dear Irene.' No, not good enough," Pops said. "'My Dearest Irene, I will never forget this evening and our first, but not our last dance together. You are a rose I will carry in my heart until the end of time. I will return to you, my angel. Love and kisses. Erskine York.'"

Squirrel's smile was so wide it hurt his face. Tears came to his eyes. "Thanks, Pops. Thanks. I'll put this in the mail tomorrow."

Sergeant Mealy was walking by the hut and heard men shouting and roaring with laughter. Someone was playing a musical instrument. He looked at his watch. It was late—past lights out. The boys should not be happy, he thought. They did not know it, but they were going off to war in two days. Training camp would be cut short.

Mealy did not holler, "Lights out!" Let them have a little fun. He had trained them best he could. Many would not be returning home. As he walked away, with the sound of a clarinet fading in the Texas night, Sergeant Mealy worried about his own son, who was a Marine fighting the Japanese in the Pacific. He had not heard a word from him in over a month.

Chapter 4

The men of Camp Wolters were shipped by train
northeast to New York City. There was no guarantee
that Joey's crew would be assigned to the same
companies once they reached their destination which
made Joey sad since he had grown fond of most of these
goofballs he had spent the last twelve weeks with. New
York, the Big Apple swallowed them whole, spitting
them out at Camp Shanks, also known as Last Stop
USA. All were given medical exams for signs of
contagious diseases, which could have caused an
epidemic onboard the transport ships.

The boys were going overseas on gigantic vessels
capable of carrying 10,000 soldiers or more on a single
ship. Joey had never even been in a rowboat. There was
training at Camp Shanks, and he paid attention. He
learned how to climb up the ship on a rope ladder,
everything to know about life jackets and lifeboats, what
to do if he was captured by the enemy. Name, rank, and
serial number. Joey was glad he knew how to swim.
Most boys didn't.

Joey was winning daily at cards and dice. He
sent two hundred dollars home and all his monthly pay
of fifty dollars, and still had sixty in his pocket. On
leave, he went and dined on a fancy meal in Manhattan,
bought tickets to a prizefight, and went to the top of the
Empire State Building, all the while trying to forget he

would soon be crossing an ocean to fight strangers who would be trying to kill him.

The day of embarkation came. The men were loaded on a ferry that would take them to the hulking ships waiting offshore. Joey, marching with most of his mates from Camp Wolters, noticed soldiers armed with machine guns watching the men as they moved along the wharf in single file. "What's the guys with the guns all about? Are they going to shoot us?"

"Maybe," Pops said. "They are watching for any of us who suddenly gets 'gang plank fever' and decides to make a run for it."

Joey and his squad were sailing on the USS *Henry T. Gibson*. It was part of a forty-ship escort. There would be three ships, each carrying nine thousand soldiers with their personal gear and weapons. The rest of the convoy were cargo ships, destroyers, minesweepers, and tankers. The US Navy finally figured out that the safest way to move shipping across the ocean was in a large convoy. So far, the Germans had been winning the war of the Atlantic, with their wolfpack submarine attacks sinking over 3,500 ships, killing over thirty-six thousand soldiers.

It was a Tuesday, and the formidable armada cast off into a gray sea, under gray skies, in gray ships. Joey and his comrades braced themselves for what could be a perilous journey across the sea. Stinging rain strafed the ocean, making it look like boiling water. The men were told to stay below deck, as heavy seas were predicted. Only three hours into their Atlantic Ocean voyage, the ship pitched and rolled violently from a

November storm. Nearly every man became plagued with seasickness, and the smell of vomit filled the ship's interior. Joey wished he could go up on deck, but getting washed off deck in the storm was a real possibility. He did not know if he envied or pitied the sailors standing at their jobs all night in this storm. It was the Navy's job to get the men overseas safely. He wished them luck.

The bunks stacked two high were hung with ropes. During the rough weather, they swung like swings at the park. The men had to hang on. Joey asked some of the boys where they were going. Nobody knew. Was it England, Italy, Africa? Most knew nothing of the world beyond their own homes. If you told them that France was on the Chinese border, most would believe it. The ships sailed on.

It was seventeen days of sheer monotony so Joey sought out card games. Finally, his luck ran dry, and he soon found himself penniless. He sat on the deck floor with a circle of GIs playing cards, but he could only watch.

The dealer, a runt of a boy with black eyes, kept glancing at Joey. Suddenly he said, "Hey, Joey. Here's that twenty dollars you loaned me. Keep playing." He gave Joey a mischievous smile and tossed Joey a twenty-dollar bill.

Joey blinked and hesitantly took the money. He never loaned this guy twenty dollars and had never even seen him before. Joey studied the boy. He had coarse black hair and bushy black eyebrows that connected over his nose like angry crows. The queerest thing was his ears, which were nearly translucent and stuck out like tiny wings.

Joey stayed in the game, riding a wave of luck that defied explanation. Every time the black-haired stranger dealt, the cards seemed to fall perfectly into Joey's hands. By the time the game wrapped up, Joey's pockets bulged with nearly two hundred dollars, the bills crumpled but real. The other players grudgingly congratulated him on his terrific luck. The game broke up for lunch, and when Joey turned to pay back the odd looking dealer, the black-haired stranger had vanished like smoke.

Before supper that evening, most of the GIs gathered topside to watch a hot dog eating contest. Jack "Fatman" Elliot, the unlikeliest contender from their company, stepped up to the challenge. The other grunts laughed at the wire thin soldier whose belt could barely keep his pants on. But when the contest began, Fatman proved them all wrong. He didn't bother chewing. Each hot dog disappeared down his throat like a greased bullet, one after the other, with astonishing speed. The crowd's laughter turned to cheers as Fatman shattered the Navy's hot dog eating record, devouring fifty-two in just five minutes.

From that day forward, he was a legend in the mess hall. Soldiers watched him with newfound awe, whispering about the feat as if it were some Olympian triumph. Fatman, however, wanted none of it. "What're ya lookin' at?" he growled at any gawkers, stabbing any who got too close with a fork.

Pops, Gorilla, Isaiah Stomp, and the rest of the squad stayed away from Joey's love of gambling. Isaiah's reasoning was simple: "I always lose." They formed a basketball team for a ship tournament. A basketball court was set up on a large open area at the bow of the upper deck. The boys fashioned T-shirts for themselves with their team's name, which Stitch Hansen came up with. They called themselves DOGS, which was an acronym for "Doze Other Guys Stink." Soon Gorilla was evicted from future games for mauling opponents, causing injury. Still, he was an intimidating cheerleader on the sideline and cheered the DOGS with ferocious intensity. They ended up taking fourth place in a twenty-team tournament. They would've done much better if Joey had played, as he would've been one of the tallest players out there, but Joey preferred the company of poker.

Twilight came and Joey went up on the deck for some fresh air. The evening had turned cold, and he threw on his jacket. Other soldiers were up top mulling about. Stars filled the sky like a million light bulbs, as Joey filled his lungs with the cool saltiness of the evening. All the ships were under "lights out," but a half-moon lit the deck with a spectral glow while the dark blue sea rolled gently. Joey could see the other boats in the distance. Trails of white foam followed each vessel. The USS *Gibson* was nestled in the middle of this flotilla, which was reassuring.

Joey looked along the railing towards the stern of the ship and saw the little soldier with the funny ears whom he had been playing cards with. He began to walk towards him but was passed by two grunts who were in a hurry. Joey saw the two men approaching the little man and sensed trouble was brewing.

The short kid with the funny ears was Rico Adduci from New York. He saw the two soldiers coming his way, and fingered the razor in his pocket, but this was not part of his plan. He needed to get to Europe, not the brig. He lifted one of his hands. "Whoa, boys. Why the nasty faces?"

"You been cheating us," one of the men snarled. "You give us our money back or you take a swim."

Rico smiled. He left one hand in his pocket. "You boys are wrong. Maybe you're just shitty card players." This did not amuse the two men, and one lunged at Rico.

Joey Kowalski suddenly shoved himself between the men and stood in front of Rico.

"You saw him cheating?"

The men did not answer immediately. "No, but we know he was."

"Maybe you guys are just shitty players like the man says. I'd walk away before this gets ugly."

"You know this little prick?"

"None of your fucking business, and I don't like to see two guys ganging up on anyone."

The GIs surveyed Joey. He was at least six inches taller than either of them. The men thought better and backed away. They mumbled profanities, turned, and left the deck.

A hand tapped Joey on the shoulder. He put out his hand. "The name is Rico. Rico Adduci. My friends call me Deuce."

"Joey Kowalski." He reluctantly shook Rico's hand. "What's this all about you loaning me twenty bucks?" It began to dawn on Joey that maybe this little fellow *was* cheating.

"You looked like a guy who likes to play cards and wanted to keep playing. Are you glad you kept playing? You pulled in over two hundred bucks. Am I right? I'll take half of that."

"You wish. What are you talking about?"

"You think that was all luck or great card playing when you started winning every hand? Don't be a sucker. I needed someone to team up with me. Me winning all the time attracts attention, and not the good kind."

It started to make sense to Joey. His luck was remarkable. He had a good eye for cards and always watched the dealer's hands. He never saw how Rico was cheating.

"Well, you fooled me, but you didn't fool those goons."

"I'll take half of what you made today. Drop me a hondo. I'm getting a game up tomorrow. You play with me."

"No, thanks. I don't like your game. You're nuts. Nobody has to see you cheating to beat the crap out of you and throw you overboard. If we got caught, I'd be thrown overboard, too. Your game is way too dangerous."

"Life is a fucking dangerous game, my friend. We're heading over to get our heads shot off by Krauts. Why? Uncle Sam has never done shit for me. Now we're heading over to Europe to defend those bastard British, and those French cheese-eating surrender monkeys. Not me, brother."

Joey shook his head. "Well, we don't have a choice."

"The hell I don't. I plan on disappearing the first chance I get."

"You mean deserting. Don't you worry about what your folks will say back home? When they find out you are a deserter? My mom and all my relatives would be ashamed of me. I'd never be able to show my face in the neighborhood again."

"What's your mama's name?" Deuce asked.

"None of your business."

"You know what my mom's name is? And I'm not lying. Cinderella."

Joey listened. This kid had a sincerity about him that Joey found both intense and disarming.

"No kidding," Rico said, smiling. "Cinderella Adduci. I'd be riding my bicycle down Prospect Avenue." Deuce looked out over the ocean, but his mind went back to his childhood days on the streets of New York. "And the neighbors would look out their windows, and they wouldn't say, 'There goes Rico,' or

'There goes Deuce.' They'd say, 'There goes Cinderella's boy.' Rico smiled and nodded his head.

"Sophia," Joey replied. "But everyone calls her Zosha."

Joey found himself drawn to Rico in a way he couldn't explain. There was something about the guy, a raw honesty mixed with a devil-may-care attitude that spoke to Joey. Rico had a straight-talking charm about him that made him alluring and dangerous. Joey had met crooks before. Some were good people, and Joey was no angel. The two strangers talked to each other over the railing. Rico told Joey he had been on his own since he was about ten years old. He left out the parts of his criminal background, which had now been put on hold by the war. Joey told Rico about the struggling Kowalski dime store, his girlfriend, and his plans to attend college now ruined by the war. He didn't mention his role in the Woolworth arson.

Joey reluctantly reached into his pocket to give Rico his hundred dollars. He had planned on sending all his winnings home when they hit England.

Rico raised his hand and stopped Joey. "Keep it. I like you, kid, and I think you kept me out of a little jam here. Listen. Don't be a sap. You want to send money home? Stick with me when we get to Europe. I got plans to make a ton of dough. And I always take care of my friends."

Rico had plans. He already had contacts in southern France who were making a killing in the black market. If he ever did get to France, he would disappear and start making some real money. The Army was filled with crooks. Rico did not plan on being a chump for generals who didn't know their ass from a hole in the ground. He planned on taking what the world owed him.

Joey kept the money even though it was dirty. He was going to send another one hundred dollars home as soon as they hit shore. He knew the dime store needed money badly. The next day, Joey went and watched a card game Deuce put together. He didn't join them. Some dogface in the game, sitting on the deck floor, was winning a lot of money. Joey knew Rico was cheating, but he still could not see how he was doing it. Deuce with lightning hands was amazingly good at dealing from the bottom of the deck.

Joey and Rico Adduci saw each other later in the voyage. Deuce had loaded dice and wanted Joey to get in a game with him. Joey didn't want any part of it. No, thanks.

The soldiers watched movies on the ship on how to behave when they reached England. *Be courteous. Don't show off how much money you have.* American soldiers were being paid five times the amount that the British soldier was making. *Never insult the Queen!* But they were not sailing to England. After three weeks at sea, the transport ships landed at an Irish port called Belfast. They arrived in the dark of night.

For the rest of the trip, Joey Kowalski kept his distance from the dangerous Rico 'Deuce' Adduci— neither boy suspecting that fate, with a cruel sense of irony, would soon be stitching their paths together in the blood-soaked fields of France."

December, 1944.

Joey and his squad debarked at Belfast, Ireland, which was a separate island west of England. They were just a few of the one and a half million American soldiers that would pass through the United Kingdom on their way to war.

Only on the last few days of their voyage they were given a pamphlet called *Pocket Guide to Northern Ireland*, which tried to educate the boys to the customs, and culture of their temporary home. The pamphlet remarked, *Argument for its own sake is a Scotch-Irish specialty and arguing politics might be called a national sport*, a prescient warning in this land riven by ancient divides. Another important tidbit of common sense: *It is always impolite to criticize your hosts; it is militarily stupid to criticize your allies.* Stupid was not in short supply during what was called "the American invasion" of the British Isles.

The population of Belfast had seen the incoming of American soldiers for over a year, and their disposition turned from joy to resentment and a lot in between. Many of the population grumbled that the Yanks were "overpaid, oversexed, and over here," but the Irish children loved the amount of candy the GIs tossed to them, and the merchants enjoyed the soldiers' pockets overflowing with money. Most women were more than happy to entertain the young men who also brought jazz music and partying at an unseen level even for the Irish.

Joey hit the local pubs with the rest of his mates and got drunk more often than he wanted. The splitting headaches and nausea from hangovers kept him staying in more and more often reading books and writing letters. Pretty Boy Swanson, the squad's over-sexed braggart, took shameless pride in his nearly nightly conquests, boasting that many of the local girls could be charmed into bed with only a bribe of chocolate and a few sweet words. His pleasure, however, came with an unfortunate price. Gonorrhea.

The burning sores and relentless agony sent him limping to the medics, earning him a stint in quarantine with an additional punishment of forfeiture of pay during his medical treatment. The other boys took note, ensuring they were well-stocked with Army-issued prophylactics whenever temptation led them to the plentiful brothels scattered through town.

Months stretched into a seeming eternity of training and boredom, punctuated by raucous nights in the local pubs. Fights erupted with monotonous regularity, fueled by Irish whiskey and pent-up bravado. The diminutive, Erskine "Squirrel" York became a frequent target at the taverns, his tiny stature an irresistible invitation to bullies. The CO, weary of the mounting injuries and drunken brawls, finally put his foot down. No more town for Joey's company. The locals and the MPs had had enough.

Chapter 5

Battle-tested, Sergeant Albert Krims was twenty-six years old going on fifty. The weight of the war had stolen his youth. Two years ago, on New Year's Day, Albert Krims was holding the tiny feet of his newborn daughter in the palm of one hand. The toes wiggled as he rubbed her feet with his thumb. The little girl giggled, and there was no one happier in the entire world at that moment than Albert Krims. His wife Amy tied a little red ribbon around the baby's ankle. Amy, fragile from a difficult birth but still radiant, named the baby Agnes, after her beloved grandmother.

Life was going well for Albert as he was prospering as a salesman at the Beverly Shoe Store in Akron, Ohio. Handsome, with an easy-going, non-pushy style that customers responded to, especially the ladies, he was top salesman month after month, and had dreams of opening his own store someday. Two weeks later, only a month after the bombing of Pearl Harbor, Albert Krims received a letter saying he had been drafted into the Army. He and his wife were shaken badly by the news. He was a shoe salesman, not a man sculpted for battle. After three weeks of shared tears, he was forced to leave home. His wife Amy gave him a red ribbon and told him to wear it around his ankle. It would bring him luck and remind him to hurry home to the woman and baby he loved.

A short six months later, Albert Krims was running to and from German artillery and bullets, trying to survive the dust and dirt of the North African war. He learned how easily men die. He saw men erupt in a spray of crimson mist, life brutally snatched in a numbing, indifferent moment. He watched three different commanding officers die in his first three months on the continent. His ability to follow orders and not get killed promoted Krims to sergeant and then staff sergeant. In only a few bloody months of fighting, he had gone from a blissful shoe salesman to a commanding officer in a murderous war. Returning home in one piece, let alone alive, became harder and more distant.

With North Africa firmly under Allied control, Sergeant Albert Krims found himself leading a squad of green GIs during the invasion of Anzio, Italy, dubbed "Operation Shingle." The landing, intended as a daring strike to outflank the Germans and push toward Rome, quickly devolved into a nightmare. Orders came down to hold the beachhead but not advance until reinforcements arrived, a decision so bafflingly shortsighted that even the most inexperienced private could see its folly.

The delay gave the Nazis ample time to regroup and mount a ferocious counterattack. Holding the high ground, the German forces unleashed a torrent of shelling and machine gun fire with ruthless precision, turning the rocky shoreline into a death trap, the air thick with smoke, screams, and the deafening roar of explosions.

In the chaos, a jagged stone, blown loose by an artillery blast, struck Sergeant Krims squarely on the

head, crumpling his helmet like a tin can. He dropped
instantly, his squad scrambling to drag him to cover as
blood seeped from beneath the twisted steel.
Unconscious, Krims was evacuated to a field hospital
and later shipped to Ireland to recover. He awoke three
days later, dazed and hollow-eyed. Anzio would haunt
him, a bitter reminder of inept orders that cost so many
lives for so little gain.

Belfast, Ireland. May, 1944.

Months had passed, and although he still had headaches
and waves of nausea, the Army decided Albert Krims
was fully recovered and ready for combat, again given
command of inexperienced recruits. But Albert had
changed. He was no longer the carefree shoe salesman
from Ohio. He was afraid of death, but it was dwarfed
by the crushing weight of the young lives entrusted to
him in a war that showed no mercy. Having faced the
harsh realities of battle, the comrades lost, he had
inherited a steely resolve to fight the Nazis in a war he
never asked for, and help these boys, fragile and
untested, somehow survive. He knew the long periods of
boredom, and then the short periods of sheer terror
where the death seemed certain and the minutes turned
into hours.
        Immediately leaving the hospital, Sergeant
Krims drove in a jeep to meet the new platoon of men
he would be commanding. He looked at the baby faces
of his rifle squad sitting on bunks, chatting and laughing

in a cramped corrugated steel hut that had been their home for months.

He shook his head skeptically. Somehow, he had to teach these mostly teenagers not only how to fight, but how not to die. Many would survive if they would only listen to him. He learned at Anzio to always keep moving in combat. *Stand still and you die.* Many of the generals in charge did not realize this, causing the needless death of hundreds of men. He knew how the Germans fought. The Nazi soldiers had been fighting for years and were sufficiently deadly on the attack or in retreat. He knew half of these boys might be dead a week after landing on the shores of France, whenever that day would come. And it *would* come.

"Attention!" Sergeant Krims hollered.

The boys jumped to attention; some were half-clothed. The salutes came with varying degrees of proficiency.

Krims glared at his squad. "Listen to me and you might stay alive. Listen to me and you might survive this war and go home to your loved ones. Pay attention to the drills. Don't blow them off. They may save your life."

All the GIs had heard this crap before. Isaiah Stomp snickered.

"And you will be the first killed, I wager." Krims went and stood in front of Isaiah but did not look at him. "I was like all of you a year and a half ago, but I'm nothing like you now. I want to live, and I want the war to end. What you do when we finally invade France will save your life and the soldier next to you. Know your assignments. I want everyone to be able to dismantle and clean your weapons blindfolded. We must kill and not be killed. Leave the corpses alone, because there will be many. I don't care if they are American or German. They are likely booby-trapped, especially if you see a shiny souvenir sticking from a dead man's pocket."

Sergeant Krims walked between the bunks, and the men started listening, all their faces turned to stone.

"When we are on the move, I want absolute quiet. No talking. Hand signals only. No clinking of canteens. Nobody lights a smoke unless I give the okay. The Krauts know how to kill, and you guys don't know shit. They know that listening is just as important as seeing. We make noise, we die." Now Krims stared directly into Isaiah's face. "We will be quiet killers and maybe this war will end soon."

A knot of dread tightened in Sergeant Krims's gut. None of these babies knew about the recent disaster at Slapton Sands. Over seven hundred soldiers and officers died practicing for the invasion because of inept preparations, and that was only a drill. Wait until the real thing, he thought.

Joey was watching the sergeant's feet. "Sir? Why the red ribbon around your ankle?"

"None of your business, and don't call me 'sir.' I am Krims, or Sarge. 'Sir' is for prissy officers, and right now, you're looking at the best damned noncommissioned officer you'll ever meet. Remember that, and you might make it out of this alive." Krims left the hut and the boys relaxed. Their new CO did not enlighten them at all as to the news they really wanted to hear. When would they be landing on European shore?

"Pops," Gorilla asked in his deep guttural Cajun voice, "When da we go on boat to kill Nazis?"

Pops who seemed to know the goings on better than anyone didn't know.

"Where does this Krims guy get off telling us we don't know nuthin?" Stich whined. "What makes him so great?"

"I heard he's seen a lot of combat. Been wounded in Italy," Joey answered.

Stitch was having none of it. In a nasally voice, he attempted to mimic Sergeant Krims, pitching his voice in a high mocking tone. "Listen to me, little children, and you'll stay alive."

No one laughed. The mood in the barracks had grown heavy, the war pressing closer and closer, and Zeke Walker, for one, was getting sick of Stitch's antics.

"Shut up, Stitch," Zeke muttered, his tone an explicit warning.

"Why don't you make me?" Stitch shot back with a cocky grin.

Zeke didn't hesitate. The oversized farm boy rose from his bunk, his boots hitting the floor with force. Stitch's smug expression crumbled, and his eyes widened in a panic as he back pedaled.

Before fists could fly, Pops jumped from his bunk and stood between the two. "Okay, okay. That's enough. We got to save the fighting for the real thing. Back off, Zeke."

Zeke stopped, and stared bullets at Stitch. The glare in his eyes spoke louder than words: *Pops just saved your skin, smart ass.* With a final look of disdain, Zeke Walker turned and dropped back onto his cot, the springs groaning beneath his weight. The barracks fell silent.

PART II

*"Beware the calm before the storm—it's only the silence
of the beast taking its breath."*
-Anonymous

Chapter 6

Flashback. 1943 – Chicago

Joey Kowalski, without his mother's permission, tried to
enlist in the Army when he had just turned seventeen.
Full of bravado and patriotic determination, he walked
into the recruitment office and lied about his age at a
time when the United States was not checking ages too
carefully. Fortunately, he was rejected 4-F along with
millions of other young men. The reasons could be
physical, mental, moral, or criminal. Joey had flat feet,
and a whopping size thirteen shoe. The Army did not
make boots that large. He was 4-F on account of foot
size.

Joey's mother Zosha knew nothing about it until
the rejection telegram arrived at their door. She was
furious with Joey as her life had already been tortured
with death. But for now, Mrs. Kowalski's boy was not
going to be killed by the Japanese or Germans. He was
heading to Illinois State University on a scholarship. He
was going to be the only Kowalski, or any of his
mother's relatives, to have a college degree. He would
be a success—a lawyer, a doctor, a senator.

The Kowalski Five and Dime Store stood on the corner of Throop and Hillock next to a vacant shoe and leather repair shop. The houses and storefronts in this Chicago south side neighborhood had no front yards or parkways of grass. If you walked out your front door a few steps, you were standing in the street. Rowhouses leaned, glued together to help each from tumbling over, block after block, all with the same tired gray and brown asphalt siding, mirroring each other across each street with the same weathered faces of hope—and too often, broken dreams. Here, surrounding the Kowalski store, the grit and grind of Chicago's working class pulsed.

If you lived in the neighborhood and needed any small items, or sundries, or soup, or a sandwich, or a place to duck into out of the rain, Zosha Kowalski's Five and Dime was the place to go. Zosha cooked breakfast or lunch at a stove in the kitchen at the back of the store where she and her children slept. The front of the store had large plate glass windows stretching from floor to the ceiling. Mr. Dempster, an old man who owned the building, lived above on the second floor.

Zosha's children helped with the store when they weren't in school. Joey washed the storefront windows every morning. He then met the trucks with any deliveries while his mother and sister swept the floors and straightened the merchandise on the shelves. Then Joey and his sister Dorothy would be off to school.

Inside the store, there were aisles of everything Mrs. Kowalski could think of to fill them with. Greeting cards, yarn, model airplanes, housewares, toy pistols, boxes of buttons. The store floor was a checkerboard of brown and yellow, cracked asbestos floor tiles. There was a small sit-down counter with five stools for eating. Next to the cash register were stacks of penny candies, chocolate bars, chewing gum, wax lips, straws filled with sugar. The vaulted, tin ceiling was stained from years of cigarette smoke and gaslit lamps. The owner of the building, Mr. Dempster, converted to electricity only a few years earlier.

Sophia Kowalski, better known as Zosha, ran the store from sunup to sundown. She was short and thick with arms like steel, and muscular legs. With the help of Joey and Dorothy, they were able to get by. Barely.

Zosha knew pain and heartbreak more than most. Like so many others, she and her husband Henry struggled horribly during the Depression trying to raise their young children. The family often did not have enough to eat. She was ashamed that she had to garbage- pick food while Henry waited in line to find work wherever it could be found.

When the Depression finally loosened its grip, she and Henry were both able to find work and started saving money. In 1937, they rented a small store. Henry got a job as a butcher at the Chicago stockyards and Zosha ran the small dime store. The labor in the stockyards was unionized, so pay was better than most occupations for the poor. Life was not so desperate now. The children were no longer hungry and didn't have to dress in rags. The store was profitable, and they had plans to knock down the wall to the vacant store next to it, doubling their size. The owner above, Mr. Dempster, had no problem with this. He would be happy with the extra rent. "Beat your brains out," he said to Zosha and Henry.

The scars of the Great Depression ran deep. Families throughout the United States became terrified of losing employment, which often led to real starvation. The past deprivations were on Henry's mind when he opened bank accounts for not only his son, but also his daughter. Girls, let alone women, were not allowed to open their own bank accounts, as the gender was considered financially irresponsible and incapable of managing their own money. The banking community thought that allowing women control over their own money would surely upend civilization, plunging the nation into financial chaos. But Henry Kowalski, an open-minded man who knew the sting of empty pockets, decided to open bank accounts for his kids, even his daughter, Dorothy. With steady work, he put five dollars in each account every month.

Henry Kowalski worked the night shift at the Chicago Union Stockyards which was a grim city in itself—one square mile to accommodate over 120,000 hogs, cattle, and sheep at any one time along with forty thousand employees. The poet Carl Sandburg aptly described Chicago in a poem as "Hog Butcher for the World." Stench from the animals stretched for miles over the impoverished neighborhoods. No one complained. The stench meant employment.

Slaughterhouse work was brutal for man and beast. Seventeen to twenty thousand cattle, hogs, and sheep were butchered daily. For three years, Henry Kowalski worked in a part of an assembly line called "the killing floor." Cows and pigs were herded through narrow chutes until they were stopped one by one at a gate. The gate stopped the animal in front and another gate closed from behind—a death sentence for the animal. A man standing on a bench in front of the corralled animal swung a sledgehammer down on the back of its neck, hopefully killing it with one blow. If not, the animals could be dangerous to the executioner.

Once the animal was motionless, other men dragged the carcass to a conveyor belt. Henry Kowalski was what was called "a finisher." He would then insert a razor-sharp knife into the beast's neck deep enough to expose the windpipe without piercing it. On one side of the windpipe the knife sliced the carotid arteries and jugular veins. For a moment, a crimson geyser of blood would spray like a firehose. Henry had to wait while the blood fully drained from the animal. Often, the floor drains were not cleaned properly, and men would stand ankle-deep in blood and animal fluids. Thirty-five minutes was all the time Henry was given to skin and dress each carcass as it moved along the assembly line. The skins of the animals were thrown into a scarlet heap on a large flat wheelbarrow. When the pile got big enough, others dragged the skins to the tanning rooms. Some days, Henry butchered hogs, sometimes cattle.

Henry would stuff his nose with cotton and cover his mouth with a handkerchief to filter the horrible smell. Most of the butchers, including Henry, drank whiskey to dull their olfactory senses. Ventilation on the kill floor was zero. While working the second of a twelve-hour shift, Henry chain-smoked cigarettes to help him keep from vomiting onto his work.

The Pure Food and Drug Act did little to improve the conditions in the Chicago stockyards. Supervisors were warned well in advance when government inspectors were scheduled to arrive. Otherwise, cleanliness was ignored. All the men wore aprons of heavy linen that were once white. They were supposed to be changed daily with new aprons. After several days, the aprons turned brown and hard as cardboard from blood and other animal secretions. The morning shift manager would take the aprons and cut them into strips and sell them as bullion at his butcher shop on 39th Street. The strips of apron, soaked in hot water, made a fine broth for soups.

Thirty-five minutes. That was Henry Kowalski's world. Legs were severed with the screech of saw against bone. For cattle, the prime cuts—T-bone, porterhouse, sirloin, chuck, brisket—were separated and sent to the refrigerators. Leftover meat went to the grinder to make ground beef. With a family at home sleeping, the minutes of Henry's night shift crawled along each hour with bloody certainty, and as the dawn painted the sky orange or crimson, he and the other workers hurried to Smitty's Tavern at 6 AM for a well-deserved shot and a beer.

Just when things were going well, hard times for the Kowalski's returned with a vengeance. Henry cut his hand badly one night at the slaughterhouse, and after it was stitched up, it became infected. The doctor had to cut off his arm below the elbow. That, too, became infected.

For nine agonizing days and nights, Henry lay groaning in their bed at the back of the store. Nine agonizing nights Zosha and the children prayed on their knees in front of a statue of the Virgin Mary propped on the kitchen table. The youngest, four-year-old Timmy did not know the words to the prayers, but clenched his hands together and bowed his head like the others. For the little boy, his mother's nightly tears told the gravity of the situation. As they prayed before the Virgin Mary, a small candle glowed. Dorothy put a towel beneath her knees. A rosary was said each night. Ten Our Fathers, ten Hail Mary's, five times each. Each child prayed a decade of the rosary, holding a string of small beads passed to each to help them keep count of each prayer. "Hail Mary full of grace . . ." Zosha prayed the first and last decade. "Please, God, help us," she cried weakly.

On the tenth day, Henry died in their bed behind the dime store, his body bloated and blackened, his face twisted in a pathetic mask of pain. The loss shattered the family, leaving a gaping hole that grief alone could not fill. But fate was not finished with them. Less than a year later, Zosha's youngest, Timmy—their bright-eyed, tireless little spark of joy—was struck by a car outside the store and killed.

Zosha crumbled under the weight of it all. The sturdy and determined matriarch, became a shadow of herself, feeble and consumed by despair. For weeks, she lay motionless in her bed, her abandoned gaze fixed on the dim, shifting light filtering through a drawn shade, as if the world outside had ceased to exist.

With no choice but to keep the store running, fourteen-year-old Joey and twelve-year-old Dorothy stepped into roles far beyond their years. Together, they managed the shop, balancing orders, customers, and grief. Aunt Sherry came by and helped when she could, her presence a small comfort in a storm of loss. But for over a month, it was Joey and Dorothy who kept the Kowalski Five and Dime alive, waiting and hoping for the day their mother would be well again.

Zosha believed it was because of her unyielding faith in Jesus, and the boundless compassion of Father Martin at Saint Gerard's Church, that she was finally able to get through the pain. Father Martin held her in his arms often as she cried uncontrollably in the church pew after mass. He assured her God's plans were mysterious but always good. She would survive this, he told her. God would look after her and her family. She would meet her beloved husband and baby boy in heaven. They were in a wonderful place now, and Zosha believed him.

Although Zosha continued to worry about money, she was determined to have her children finish high school. She saw from their earliest childhood that Joey and

Dorothy were extremely bright, and now her boy would be going off to college. Her husband Henry would have been proud.

At thirty-seven, she was not a wilting flower and, in time, her strength returned. She worked fourteen, sometimes sixteen hours a day, but still the Kowalski Five and Dime was in debt, and the opening of a new Woolworth store at Archer Avenue and Halsted was a bad omen. The Woolworth was larger, had more variety, and their volume allowed them to keep prices low. The Kowalski Five and Dime did not have the room or money to buy volume. Zosha and her husband had dreamed of leasing the vacant store next to theirs, but with Henry's death, the dream of expanding was just smoke. Their merchandise was already cramming the small shed and garage at the back alley that served as their warehouse. She knew her beloved dime store was a sinking ship with the new Woolworth competition. She prayed that God must help her find a way.

In her kitchen, Zosha cooked soup daily and sold it for twenty-five cents a bowl. The pungent odor of sauerkraut and sweet onion filled the storefront while she made corned beef sandwiches and frankfurters in their back kitchen. Zosha was compassionate to a fault, allowing struggling neighbors to eat for free. Old men hunched over cigarettes and the daily news, whiling away the day at a small table at the far back corner of the store. She did not mind if they were not too loud but there would be no cussing. Next to the front door was a stack of daily newspapers, and the news was always about the war.

It was Saturday morning, and a trickle of customers walked the aisles buying a few small items. Zosha's daughter Dorothy rang them up at the cash register.

A man walked through the front door, which jingled with a bell.

Zosha smiled. "Hi, Bert." He was a regular.

"Any news from Chester?"

"No," she sighed.

"Well, no news is good news these days."

"I guess." Chester was Zosha's brother, who joined the Navy a week after the Japanese attack at Pearl Harbor.

"That boy of yours is a heck of a card shark. Cleaned us out last night."

Zosha did not approve of Joey's card-playing with Henry's old friends, but she did not order him to stop. And apparently, he did very well. She paid him very little for working at the store, and if he could earn a little money elsewhere, she would not complain.

Young Dorothy already knew Bert's order. Two eggs scrambled dry, two sausages with toast. Ketchup for his eggs. Coffee, black. Eighty-five cents. She went through a swinging door to the back of the store to prepare it.

Bert came in every day. He had eyes for Zosha, although he could never get the nerve to ask her out on a date. He was a shy bachelor of forty. He saw in her a beautiful, tortured woman. Her dark hair still shone, and

when she smiled, which was not often these days, he
blushed and fell more in love with her.

A man in a gray suit with a navy-blue necktie
walked through the front door. He immediately removed
his black fedora and went and sat at the counter a few
stools from Bert. It was Mr. Simpson, a city of Chicago
health inspector. Zosha went behind the counter to meet
him. She shuddered.

"Good morning, Mr. Simpson."

"Morning, Mrs. Kowalski." He spoke quietly in
almost a whisper. "You know, Zosha, I will be retiring
this January, and I don't know if the next inspector is
going to be as lenient as I am."

The Kowalski Five and Dime had numerous
health code violations. Living quarters could not be in
the same area as food being cooked for the public as the
Kowalski's did at the back of the store. It was
impossible to keep the mice and rats out of the building,
especially with the garbage men on strike. Even with the
mouse scat swept up every night, it still became
noticeable the next day. The Kowalski's could hear the
rodents run across the floor as they slept at night. The
vermin were taking over.

Zosha brought Mr. Simpson a cup of coffee on a
paper napkin. As usual, she slipped a ten-dollar bill
under the napkin.

"I hope you have a nice retirement, Mr.
Simpson. I will remember you in my prayers." She had
no intention of remembering him in her prayers. Mr.
Simpson, with his crinkled face, seemed to enjoy
threatening her, even more so after Henry died. She

would need to confess in church that she had lied about remembering Mr. Simpson in her prayers. The health department inspector left. He did not finish his coffee. Zosha glared at the door that closed behind that hideous man. The war raged on for Zosha, not just on distant battle fields, but here, in the cramped confines of the Kowalski Five and Dime.

Zosha looked out the front window and could see her boy Joey across the street sitting on a neighbor's front porch talking with friends. It was a wonder how a woman so short with a husband of average height could produce a teenager already over six feet tall. Dorothy came out of the back of the store with a piece of cake for Bert, and then hurried out the back of the building to the garage to get more items to restock the aisles. Sewing supplies were low. The bolts of cotton and linen they bought in bulk sold quickly and they were all out of stock.

The war had caused nationwide rationing. Fabric was difficult to come by, so most families in the neighborhood had to mend or make their own clothing. The mannequins in the storefront window were clothed in cotton skirts and blouses, homemade by Zosha's sister Sherry. The sale of sewing supplies was brisk. Toy rifles and pistols also sold out fast. It seemed every little boy in the world wanted a toy gun so they could kill Nazis and Japs. What to buy with the store's limited funds vexed poor Zosha.

"Mom," Dorothy hollered. "We need ribbons! We're all out of ribbons." Zosha sighed as if she could pull ribbons out of her apron pocket, and she wished Dorothy wouldn't yell when there were customers in the store. It was unprofessional. But Dorothy couldn't help it. She was outspoken, and sharp tongued with an intelligence beyond her sixteen years. She had broached the subject of taking over the store inventory and management, but in a nice way. She felt she could do this a lot more efficiently, but to Zosha, this would take away from Dorothy's school work. So, no way.

Although Zosha would strictly forbid it, Dorothy longed to quit school. She hated it. Like her older brother, she excelled in her classes, but unlike him, her intellect was coupled with an air of superiority that made her an outcast among the other students and teachers alike. That was okay. She didn't like them either. With a tattered, homemade dress clinging to her slender frame, Dorothy walked the school halls as though draped in silk and velvet, her chin held high, her gaze distant, as if the school and classmates were somehow beneath her. In math class, she would blurt out answers to equations with unsettling speed—often before the teacher could finish writing the problem on the board. The other students exchanged resentful glances, while the teachers masked their irritation at her presumptuous gall. However, around family her devotion was unquestionable. She wanted the store to succeed as much, if not more, than Zosha.

With school still in session, Dorothy helped at the store on Saturdays. She and Joey were also corralled into work on Sundays. Zosha was troubled that her children had to work Sundays, the Lord's Day, but she did not have a choice. Money could not buy happiness, but not having it, as she knew, made life miserable.

Zosha harbored a constant fear for her children's safety and only felt at ease when she had them in sight. She trembled at her memories. It seemed like only yesterday that Timmy was hit by a car right in front of the store. Barely five feet tall, Zosha had the strength of five men that day. She and another man lifted the car off her boy so he could be pulled from beneath. Timmy lay there like he was asleep in his little blue coat. There was no blood. He looked like a little doll. She brushed back the black curls on the little boy's forehead and kissed his brow over and over and over.

Zosha walked to the storefront window. She could see Kathleen O'Brien traipsing down the street towards Joey and the other boys. Zosha shook her head disapprovingly. Proper girls do not swing their arms and walk with gaiety. Her skirt was hemmed provocatively above the knees. It was well-known that the young girls from the neighboring parish, Saint Mary of Perpetual Help, were far less virtuous than the girls from Saint Gerard's. Kathleen and her boy Joey now attended the same high school. Zosha worried that her Joey, was smitten with the pretty girl, that such a little tramp might steal her boy's innocence.

Zosha took off her apron and wiped her hands.

"Dorothy, take over the register. I need to go to Saint Gerard's for confession."

"Mom," Dorothy asked, "didn't you go to confession yesterday?"

Chapter 7

The grimy stained-glass windows of Saint Gerard's Church threw a dusty spectrum of colors across the marbled floor like splattered paint. Zosha looked up at the carved angels hanging from ornate columns, their arms outstretched as though pleading. It was noon and she knew Father Martin was in his confessional. The confessional line was mercifully short with only one bulky Ukrainian woman in a kerchief who reeked of kielbasa in front of Zosha. So Zosha waited, kneeling in front of a chipped statue of Saint Joseph and began to say acts of contrition. She feared for today's confession. Her true feelings loomed like a bad toothache. Each second she was losing courage. The woman in front of her left the confessional, and Zosha entered.

"Bless me, Father, for I have sinned," she began. Her voice was a whisper. Father Martin became attentive. He knew the shadow behind the screen was Zosha Kowalski. Since her little boy's death, he had discovered an unholy attraction to Zosha. It was shameful, and he did everything he could to squash those feelings, but every time he saw her at mass or she entered the confessional, the feelings were undeniable. He took a deep breath.

"Yes, Zosha," he said. Zosha went on to tell him the sins she had committed since yesterday. Father Martin told her that burning soup was not a sin. She told him she lied to the health inspector about praying for him in his retirement. A harmless fib, he answered. Then Zosha said she had improper thoughts.

"Yes," he said. "Go on."

"I . . . I wished ill will," she stammered. "On the new Woolworth. I wish it would be struck by lightning and burned to the ground."

Father Martin sighed. "That's not much of a sin but wishing ill will on others is not good. Say two Our Fathers and two Hail Mary's for your penance. And remember God loves you and is watching over you and your family."

Father Martin understood her hatred for the Woolworth, another glittering symbol of soulless corporatism sucking the lifeblood out of the small, local shops like a monstrous vacuum cleaner. He resented large corporations such as Woolworth and Marshall Field's, which were beginning to plague small businesses everywhere in the parish. There was a new Kroger supermarket that had already put several small family grocers out of business. The little stores could not compete with the low prices of the conglomerates. He felt pity, and now love, for this young woman who had a family and had seen so much personal hardship. The anger in his own heart swelled.

Father Martin had changed. He was torn with doubts about his faith. He was human, not some pious statue. God, he was certain, existed in a realm beyond human frailty. He hated the corporations whose profits broke the backs of the poor, but hatred was wrong. What would Jesus do? The question gnawed at him.

The day had made him exhausted. He served two funerals in the morning and had confessions until three. He was still a young man at thirty-nine, but the work of the church never stopped. He was tired and wanted to take a nap.

There was a long silence. "Is there anything else?" Father Martin asked.

Zosha hesitated and her stuttering words at first failed her, and then her words tumbled out in a rush. "I have had impure thoughts. For a man." Oh, God, she thought to herself. What am I about to say?"

The priest's ears perked up. "You are still a young woman, Zosha. God allows for feelings to manifest themselves in such ways. Is this man married?" He waited for a reply.

"It is *you*!" she blurted. A choked sob escaped her lips.. "I love you, Father, in a way that is . . . sinful."

Father Martin's heart hammered against his ribs. He blushed and felt a rush of blood travel through his entire body. *My God, this can't be happening?* "Zosha, I am married to the church," he stammered. "You must forget such thoughts." He stared down at his hands. They trembled. He found himself wanting to walk out his confessional door and open the door to Zosha's compartment and hold her in his arms.

He, too, had improper thoughts and had confessed them to the pastor, Father Pelford. Zosha was an attractive woman, tiny and stout, and very pretty. Beautiful eyes. A lovely smile. Sensuous lips. He had felt sexual desires he had not felt in a long time when he comforted Zosha in the back pews of the church.

Zosha hurriedly left the confessional booth and saw other parishioners in line for their confessions. She immediately dropped to her knees in front of a statue of Saint Joseph to say her penance, but she couldn't remember what that was. She clenched her hands together until her knuckles were white and decided to say an Act of Contrition. When she had finished, she slowed her steps to calm herself.

Pigeons scattered when Zosha opened the heavy church doors. She walked down the front stairs and looked back at the spires reaching towards the heavens. She felt a weight lift from her shoulders. She had confessed her deepest sin, but would God forgive her? Would Father Martin?

Father Martin was stunned. He stayed in the confessional booth, long after the church had emptied, afraid to come out. A dim light shone through a crack beneath the door. The darkness helped him think. He realized he loved her too. There was scratching on the floor near his shoe. He could barely see the shape of a tiny mouse. "Why, hello," he said. He smiled at the tiny rodent. "Can you help me little mouse? What should I do?" The mouse stood on the toe of his shoe, and then suddenly darted beneath the confessional wall. Father Martin closed his eyes. "I know. I'm afraid, too."

He decided he was going to do something to help Zosha, something dangerous, something extreme. The new Woolworth was going to destroy Zosha's little dime store. But what could he do? He became excited at the thoughts running through his head. He couldn't make the store get struck by lightning. Prayers were not going to protect her. Was God only beholden to the wealthy? He would need someone to be a lookout. He wondered who he could trust with such a thing. "Bless me, Father, for I *will* sin," Father Tom Martin murmured to himself.

Zosha decided to take a long walk home so she could think. She walked down Archer Avenue until she found herself in front of the new Woolworth. The store front gleamed. Like a moth to a flame, she found herself drawn through the front doors. Shiny chrome and impossibly bright colors assaulted her senses. On her right was a long bright blue counter with a dozen stools with bright red upholstery. The stools swiveled. The chrome posts beneath the stools shone like mirrors. Most of the seats were taken by patrons.

The store was immaculately lit, and workers with identical powder blue uniforms were helping customers. There were two cash registers and a line of buyers at each. The registers sang with revenue. The aisles and shelves were clean and neatly organized. Zosha leaned against a wall near the front door, next to a rack of postcards. A young girl with a smile full of Chiclet-white teeth asked if she could help her.

Zosha felt like crying. She thought the Kowalski Five and Dime was the store that should be burned. The pathetic stools in front of her counter all had torn upholstery mended with duct tape. She shook her head, left the store, turned into an alley, and wept next to the garbage cans. *God is punishing me*, she thought. *Please, Lord, help me. Forgive me.*

Chapter 8

Joey Kowalski and his friends, Jimmy and Clarence, lounged on the creaking, sun-faded porch of a neighbor's house, their eyes occasionally drifting across the street to the familiar sight of the Kowalski Five and Dime. Joey, just turned eighteen, had a round pleasant face, unruly sand-colored hair, and an innocent smile. His nose was broad and flat like a careless hand had pressed too hard on soft clay. He had a blond glaze of fuzz above his upper lip that he was hoping passed for a mustache. It didn't, and he was disappointed none of his friends noticed.

The boys could hear the rumble of the trolley car passing along Archer Avenue, and the distant cry of a factory whistle. Joey traced the chipped blue paint on the porch railing with his thumb. The patch his mom sewed over the hole at the knee of his blue jeans was coming loose, and he was better off keeping his leg straight to avoid tearing the stitching further. Their conversation, like every conversation these days, circled back to the same inescapable topic: the war, which had touched all the boys and mostly everyone in the neighborhood. Joey's uncle Chester was in the Pacific somewhere. Clarence's older brother was somewhere in Africa. Jimmy had two cousins in the Marines somewhere near the Coral Sea, wherever that was.

Joey changed the subject to their pathetically beloved Chicago White Sox.

"What the hell happened to Lee?"

"The Sox are screwed," Clarence said. Clarence was Joey's best friend, a skinny seventeen-year-old boy with a sad, narrow face and round wire-framed glasses. His father was the president of the union pipe fitter's union, so his family was better off than most of the kids in the neighborhood. He stood out because his clothes were always clean and free of holes. He wasn't sure why, but this embarrassed him. He was the rich kid, so he intentionally dirtied or ripped his clothing just to try to fit in.

Under a bright blue sky, the boys chatted and insulted each other playfully. Bruised patches beneath Clarence's eyes pronounced the shadow of his suffocating household, and his ears burned from his father's latest raging tirade. He could never live up to his father's standards of manhood, and the coldness between them deepened with the years. Why couldn't he be more like his older brother? He knew he was not like other boys, and he suspected his father knew it also.

"As soon as you turn eighteen, you are going straight into the Marines," his father started saying when Clarence was fourteen. He was seventeen now and just a year away from becoming a "real man". He winced at the thought. He stayed away from home as much as possible and often found sanctuary sleeping on the Kowalski's' floor next to Joey's cot.

The back of the Kowalski Five and Dime was one large room, so Zosha's brother Chester built partitions to create separate spaces for the family. Joey slept on a cot at the back corner of the room next to the space heater. There was a curtain hanging from the walls on a string so Joey could have some privacy. There was a small room with a toilet and a shower stall, but no sink. There was a sink and stove in the kitchen area where they prepared food for themselves and their customers at the front of the store. The only daylight came from two windows facing Hillock Avenue, which would freeze up with ice in winter. That was when sleeping near the space heater paid dividends for Joey.

"Lee's got a dead arm. He's useless. The Sox are screwed," Clarence said.

"What kind of name is Thornton anyway?" Joey asked.

Thornton Lee—a twenty-two-game winner two years ago, a beacon of light for the White Sox—was completely broken for unknown reasons, dooming the Sox to another dismal season.

Jimmy Wilson, with a perpetually runny nose, stared down at the broken shoelace of his right shoe. He tried to mend it together by tying a knot, but that wasn't going to work. He knew if he tried to run, his shoe would fall off. The guys would all be making fun of him. The boys planned on going over to an empty lot two blocks away to play ball. "At least we still have Appling," Jimmy said feebly.

"At least we still have your mother," Joey said to Jimmy knocking the cap off his head with the flick of his wrist.

"Hey." Jimmy's face turned red. "Yeah, and your mother wears combat boots."

"And your mother wears spurs," Clarence said. The boys laughed.

"Are you going to come play ball with us, Joe?" Clarence asked.

"Nah, I got to help with the store."

"Ha, you mean you've got to help with Kathleen O'Brien's brassiere."

Jimmy giggled.

Joey smiled. It was true. He was waiting for Kathleen. He had walked her home from school nearly every day for the last half year, and was spending more and more of his free time with her instead of his friends.

"What time is it, Clarence?"

"I wouldn't give you the time of day if Big Ben was strapped to my ass," Clarence said. Joey grabbed Clarence's wrist and looked at his watch. Kathleen would be along soon.

Joey had just graduated from Du Sable High School, a public school. His mother would have preferred him to attend a Catholic high school, but there was no money for that. Joey did well at Du Sable. He played clarinet in the school band and was class salutatorian. In the fall, he would be off to Illinois State University on a full scholarship.

All the boys turned their heads to watch Kathleen O'Brien walk down the sidewalk to where they were sitting. There was no doubt she was beautiful, and she knew it. Despite her perfect girl looks, she could be as determined and hard as the sidewalk she was walking on. She always got what she wanted, and right now, she wanted Joey. With practiced ease she greeted the boys.

"How's it going, guys?" she said, swinging her purse.

"Where you all going?" Clarence asked.

"We're just going to hang around the park for a while," Joey said. He and Kathleen walked away holding hands.

Clarence looked on jealously. He remembered the good old summer days when he and Joey would climb the outside walls at Comiskey Park, home of the Chicago White Sox, and sneak into the ballgame. The exterior left field wall had protruding bricks scattered every few feet as part of the architectural design. Like monkeys, Clarence and Joey would scale the wall thirty feet high. While the police and security screamed, the fans filing into the stadium cheered them on. Slipping and falling from that height was not an option, but they were young, nuts, and fearless. All those innocent feelings that Clarence and Joey felt as children were disappearing.

On the way to MacArthur Park, Kathleen and Joey cut through the White Sox stadium parking lot, which was filled with cars for a daytime doubleheader. Most of the cars were old Fords and Chevys, dull and shabby, until they walked past a bright red Lincoln Continental.

"Oh, God!" Joey exclaimed. "A Cabriolet! I've only seen these in magazines. How can anyone afford these things?" He ran his hand over the hood of the luxury automobile, which seemed a mile long.

"Do you know what these things cost? About three thousand dollars. Holy smokes." Joey shook his head. "Someday. Someday," he said mournfully. Three thousand dollars was triple what the average laborer was likely to make for an entire year of work.

Kathleen was mesmerized by the luxury. "It's not locked," she cried, and in a second, she was sitting in the plush red leather back seat.

"Kathleen! What are you doing?"

"Come on. Get in."

Joey looked over the tops of an ocean of cars and did not see anyone. The crowd in the ballpark roared. Joey jumped in the car next to Kathleen. They both sighed, breathing the new car smell of fresh leather.

"Please, Jeeves," Kathleen said with a stuffy, fake British accent to the imaginary chauffeur. "Do hurry along. You know how dreadful it is to arrive late to the opera."

Joey laughed. "Yes, Jeeves. Do hurry, my good chap. And cheerio, hip hip, and all that rot."

Kathleen suddenly grabbed Joey around the neck and began to kiss him violently on the lips. She pressed her tongue inside his mouth. Joey, stunned and terribly excited, feverishly answered her kiss. Kathleen took his hand and pulled it under her dress, where he felt the moistness between her legs.

As their lust became more frantic, Kathleen lifted herself up and pulled her underpants completely off. Joey's fumbling fingers felt the fur of her pubic hair and his erection became uncontrollable. He felt her hand open his fly, and she stroked him up and down. Joey became dizzy and felt as though he would faint as he ejaculated. He regained his senses and saw a shadow pass the steamed windows of the car. Whoever it was passed by.

"Oh, Jesus," he said. He zipped his fly and saw that his semen was all over the back of the driver's seat. He grabbed Kathleen's hand. "Come on." They both jumped from the car and ran towards MacArthur Park like a couple of terrified hens. They finally reached the park winded and laughing, equally shocked at what just happened. At the park, they climbed into a small playhouse that was built to look like a colonial cabin. They were still breathless.

Joey was suddenly uneasy about what just happened. "My God, we are both nuts."

"Oh, my God," Kathleen gasped. She had a look of horror on her face. "Joey!" she cried.

"What?" She did not answer. "What?" he repeated. His face became worried.

"I left my underpants in the car. You have to go back."

Joey shook his head. "No way, I'm not going back."

"You have to. You have to! My mother sewed my name on them."

"What? Why in the world would she do that? That's crazy."

"So my sister's laundry doesn't get mixed with mine."

"So what? There are a million Kathleens in the world."

"She stitched our last names, too."

"Your whole name?" The absurdity made Joey's head rattle. He put his hands over his face. Who in the world has the time to do something so ridiculous? Apparently, Mrs. O'Brien did.

He took a deep breath. "Okay."

Joey walked stealthily to where he thought the car had been. It was near the fourth row next to the viaduct. He finally found it. He looked over the parked cars and saw a man in a security uniform looking at him from a distance.

"Hey!" the man yelled. "What do you think you're doing?" The man started walking towards Joey.

Joey opened the back door of the car and grabbed Kathleen's underpants. The man chased after him as he raced back to MacArthur Park. Joey easily outran the portly security guard.

When he got to the park, he danced around the little playhouse holding Kathleen's underpants triumphantly in the air, hooting and hollering like a savage holding a scalp.

"Give me those, you idiot," Kathleen pleaded from inside the playhouse. Joey entered, and she pulled the underwear from his hand.

"Did your mom also stitch in your address and phone number?" Joey asked.

Again, they heard the crowd roar. The White Sox would go on to beat the Washington Senators in both games, giving them an unlikely three-game winning streak. Kathleen rested her head on Joey's shoulder.

"What's the time?" Joey asked. Kathleen looked at her watch. "Two-thirty."

"Crud. I got to get back to the store. We're supposed to get some supplies, and I have to unload the truck."

"Why can't Dorothy do that?"

"She's been on shift all day. Some of that stuff is heavy."

Kathleen grabbed Joey around the neck and kissed him. "I'm never going to let you go." Joey twisted away and crawled out of the little cabin. They walked together holding hands for a few blocks and then went separate ways. Kathleen decided to walk past the precinct station, where her dad was a police officer.

Joey was confused as he cut through alleys on his way home. Wasn't it the boy who was supposed to take the lead when it came to sex? Nothing like this had ever happened to him, and it all had happened too fast. He could not figure out what it was, but something seemed wrong. Kathleen was a year younger than him, and yet she seemed to know exactly what she was doing.

Joey Kowalski was a child growing into a man's body. He would not admit it to anyone, but even at eighteen years old, he still crawled into bed with his mother some evenings and hugged her as she sang softly to him. He wasn't ready for adulthood. Real men didn't cry, yet he still shed tears when he thought about his dad and his little brother gone forever. It was a hole in his heart that would never leave him. The whole family suffered together and alone. Joey suddenly had this sad, aching feeling that he just wanted to go home and hug his mom.

Old Mr. Dempster lived above the Kowalski Five and Dime. He owned the building and spent his days and evenings in a threadbare rocking chair in his front room glued to his radio for the latest news and entertainment. His windows, with yellowed shades dry and brittle as autumn leaves, brought in murky sunlight. He never went outdoors as far as anyone knew. He paid the Kowalski girl, Dorothy, one dollar a week to dust and clean. She also brought his groceries.

He was nearly deaf and kept his Philco Cathedral radio on a small table next to him with the volume turned as high as it would go. Zosha or Dorothy brought soup to him every day. They were not sure if he ever ate anything else. The Kowalskis were indebted to him. Not just for money, but for his kindness. He had not raised the rent on the store in the three years since Mr. Kowalski died. He did not complain when Zosha was two months late with the rent last winter. He had even reached into his pockets offering twenty dollars to help pay for Mr. Kowalski's funeral, and another twenty to help bury little Timmy.

Zosha was caught up with rent, but barely. She said prayers for Mr. Dempster every Sunday at Saint Gerard's. She also said daily prayers for her brother Chester, who was in the Navy, and begged God to keep him safe. She sent her daughter to Saint Gerard's Church every day to light a candle and put a penny in the charity basket. She instructed Dorothy to kneel in front of the Blessed Virgin and say a rosary. Dorothy would drop a penny in the basket but skipped the rosary. She felt a brief sign of the cross was good enough.

Mr. Dempster was the voice of current news for the Kowalskis. He had a tube hooked up in his front room that ran through the floor and into the ceiling of the dime store beneath. It was he who had shouted the news to Zosha, and the startled customers in the store, that Pearl Harbor had been bombed by the Japanese.

Mrs. Kowalski did not mind, because typically the music of the radio would drift down into the store and create a nice ambience. It was a novelty for music to be playing in the store, and her customers seemed to like it.

After the Japanese attack at Pearl Harbor, Zosha's brother Chester immediately enlisted in the Navy. He was a crackerjack carpenter at Wilson Cabinetry but felt compelled to serve his country. When Zosha's husband died, Chester took Joey under his wing and taught him basic carpentry, which Joey picked up easily. Uncle Chester left all his tools in their shed and told Joey he could use them any time he wanted. Little did Joey know that this simple skill would soon play a

role with unforeseen and fateful consequences in war-
torn France.

Chapter 9

The rain had stopped, and the emerging late afternoon sun cast a long shadow in the alley behind the Kowalski Five and Dime. Joey and his sister Dorothy wrestled crates of merchandise onto pallets from a delivery truck. Once on pallets, it was easy to drag into the garage with their hand truck. Joey had built a storage system of shelves and compartments to consolidate merchandise. Toys in one compartment, sewing supplies in another, paper goods in another. He and his sister would load one side of the shelf, pushing the older goods to the other side. That way they could always stock the store with the older goods first and get a good idea of inventory.

Only sixteen years old, soon to be seventeen, Dorothy was already keeping the books for the Kowalski Five and Dime. It was she that made the daily dime store bank deposits. Besides the clerks, every person in the bank was a man, including the customers waiting in line for the tellers. The stares were irksome, so one day she decided to light up a cigarette while waiting for a teller. This was scandalous, she knew. She could hear the murmurs and see the looks of disgust at her boldness. She liked it.

Dorothy blew smoke in the air with arrogance. She was thoughtful and kind like her mother, but also short-tempered. Her patience wore thin quickly when dealing with idiots, and most of the older men and women she had to deal with at the bank fit that description.

In the morning, Joey Kowalski would take the truck to the Fulton Street Market and buy fresh fruit and meat for the store. The new refrigerator they bought was expensive and the monthly payments were high. Business, once brisk, was slowing because of the new Woolworth, and Dorothy and Joey could see the writing on the wall that the store would not survive without a miracle.

In the alley as they moved items from the garage to the shed, Joey, who saw Dorothy every day, was suddenly shocked at how much older she looked. Her skinny, bony legs were gone, and the face of a child had disappeared. He realized with some sadness they were both growing up. Dorothy flashed a look around the garage to make sure her mother wasn't around. She took a pack of cigarettes from her purse. She handed one to Joey and they both lit up.

Joey remembered the hungry days during the Depression, but he didn't remember it being so hard for him or his sister. Dorothy would cause a scene at the market, crying uncontrollably for no reason. With the store employees distracted, Joey, nimble and swift, pilfered food from the shelves. Then they would run off to a nearby alley and gorge themselves on whatever they could take.

"Do you remember the Flash Gordon show?" Joey asked Dorothy.

Dorothy's eyes lit up. "Oh, gosh, yes. I wish that was still on."

The Kowalski kids loved listening to it on the radio and playing Flash Gordon. Little Timmy was too young to play their make-believe games. Joey was the handsome space adventurer, Flash Gordon. Dorothy was the brilliant scientific genius, Dr. Zarkov. They battled the evils of the universe in the backyards and alleys of the neighborhood.

Joey and Dorothy sat on crates and rested, watching the cigarette smoke drift away from their mouths. Joey could blow perfect smoke rings, but Dorothy couldn't.

"Here, take a drag and make an *O* with your mouth," Joey instructed. When Dorothy did this, Joey tapped her on the cheek and a beautiful smoke ring jumped from her lips. She coughed and howled with delight at this accomplishment.

"You're a genius."

In his best radio announcing voice, Joey deadpanned, "The Amazing Interplanetary Adventures of Flash Gordon. Brought to you by Chesterfield cigarettes." Then Dorothy chimed in, "The Taste That Satisfies." They both laughed, then became quiet, thinking of the old days when there wasn't a care in the world, or so it seemed. It was a blessing that as children they hadn't yet learned how to worry.

"Mom is acting strange again," Dorothy said.

"I know. It's the new Woolworth."

"I wish it would burn down."

"Yeah. That would be nice."

After they finished stocking shelves, Clarence arrived. Clarence told Joey he would help him take the garbage to the dump on the north side of the river. Neighbors were letting garbage pile up because of the strike, but Mrs. Kowalski would not allow that behind their store. The rats in the neighborhood were doubling with each passing day.

The steel garbage cans were almost as heavy as the garbage inside. With a grunt and a heave, Clarence and Joey hoisted them into the back of the Kowalskis' Chevy pickup truck. The truck was fifteen years old and constantly breaking down. Joey's Uncle Kevin, his dad's brother, worked at a filling station and was repairing the truck, it seemed almost weekly.

Joey built a fence around the back of the pickup so things would not fall out. It looked like a small corral.

"You believe in God?" Clarence asked Joey as the old truck rattled along.

Joey grinned. "You think too much, Clarence."

"I don't. If I told my parents I didn't believe, my mom would drop dead on the spot, and my dad would beat me over the head with a pipe."

"You think too much."

"I have to. I'm not heading off to college and have the prettiest girl in town. I don't know what I am."

But Clarence did know what he was, and he wasn't like other boys. He loved Joey like boys should not love boys. He loved how he smelled and how he looked and longed to hold him in his arms. It was an urge that he could never reveal, and it hurt and haunted him.

There were thousands of seagulls at the garbage dump shrieking and fighting, a swirling mass dropping and rising above the garbage in dizzying numbers. The sun was setting, and the sky dazzled with bizarre beauty behind Chicago's industrial sky. The thick plumes rising from the factory smokestacks shimmered pillars of pink against the fading orange sky.

After dumping the garbage, the boys sat on the truck's tailgate, cigarettes dangling from their mouths. They watched the sunset. Joey took a pint of whiskey from beneath the car seat and had a swallow. He passed it to Clarence, who took a swig and started coughing.

"Where'd you get this?" Clarence asked.

"Smitty's. He always leaves the back-alley door wide open. It's easy pickings." He took another drink from the bottle.

"Have you and Kathleen done the dirty deed yet?" Clarence quizzed.

"No. And I wouldn't tell you even if we did. I'm a gentleman."

"Ha." Clarence smirked and both boys laughed.

"Do you believe in God?" Clarence asked again.

"I don't know," Joey said thoughtfully. "I guess so. Yeah."

"You have to know. You either do or you don't. Has God ever answered your prayers? Do you remember all the nights you were on your knees with your mom and sister saying the rosary in front of that

Virgin Mary? Many nights I prayed with you. Did it help save your father?"

"I don't know. My mom believes, and if she believes, that's good enough for me. The church and Father Martin really helped her get through everything."

"Has it helped you?"

Joey did not know why Clarence was going down this path. He had felt so good earlier and now the mood had darkened.

"Thou shalt not kill," Clarence said. "Thou shall not steal. Don't lie. All these things that happen every day. God is all-powerful, but he's helpless." Clarence shook his head. "Thou shalt not covet thy neighbor's wife. Think about it. God impregnated Mary so she could have Jesus. She was married to Joseph. That's adultery."

"Oh, God!" Joey shrieked. "Shut up, Clarence. You think way too much. Come on, let's go home."

The sun had set, and the birds had stopped shrieking.

"Did you ever wonder where the seagulls go at night? Never seen a single nest . . ."

"Ahhhhh!" Joey screamed. "Shut your piehole!" He stretched his arm across the front seat and punched Clarence in the arm.

It was 8:30 PM by the time Joey finally walked in the back door of their home. There was a heavy silence. Kathleen wanted him to go to a dance that night at the Saint Mary of Perpetual Help gymnasium, but he told her he was too tired. Maybe he would get a second wind and join her. After all, it was Saturday night.

The only light on, circled by a solitary moth, shone dimly above the kitchen sink. Dorothy was not home. Joey could see the silhouette of his mother slumped over the kitchen table sobbing. *Oh, my God*, he thought, *something bad has happened to Uncle Chester.* The boys in the Navy were taking hard hits in the Pacific. He walked quietly behind her and put his hands on her shoulder. He could see it was a telegram from the United States government.

"Mom," he said quietly. "What is it? Is it Uncle Chester?"

"No." Zosha was having trouble breathing. "You have been . . ." Her voice cracked. "You have been drafted by the United States Army." She grabbed Joey around the waist and burst into tears.

That evening, Joey couldn't sleep. Dorothy would not stop crying or let go of him once she heard the news. He didn't want to call Kathleen and tell her over the phone and ruin her night at the dance. His sister and mom had finally dozed off, and he listened to their gentle breathing. He quietly took his clarinet from beneath his bed and played a soft, sad melody. A tabby cat outside the window near his bed nuzzled itself against the glass while Joey mulled his now uncertain future.

Chapter 10

Father Thomas Martin lay in his bed staring at the yellow ceiling of his room. The plaster was cracking and lifting away from the lath. He didn't have time to repair it, and the church lacked the funds to hire someone. A cigarette burning in the ashtray next to his nightstand fell to the floor. Forgetting he had one lit, he threw his legs to the floor and grabbed it. He rubbed the remaining ashes into the worn carpet with his bare foot.

He stood over his washstand and ran his fingers through his thinning hair. In the mirror he saw a helpless old man. He never wavered from his belief in God and Jesus. He was, after all, a priest. The Almighty just never came around to help. And it wasn't Father Martin's discovery of his love for Zosha that compelled his now determined desertion from the Catholic Church. For years, it seemed his faith in religion was being dismantled brick by brick. With the Great Depression, and now the war, his misery grew. His job was to give hope to the hopeless. "There is heaven after life," he would say, but he no longer believed his own words. "Why can't we have a little heaven right now?" It seemed God did not give a hoot about mankind or the agony and slaughter in this world. The divine had other plans, and Father Martin no longer cared what they were.

He heard confessions each day: adultery, lying, stealing, perversion, and even murder. They could not be forgiven by reciting prayers and rosaries. His parishioners thought that confessing gave them permission to sin and keep sinning. The hypocrisy ate away at him. He was no longer an instrument of God and Jesus. He was an impostor.

Humanity was good and humanity was evil, he reasoned, and nothing could ever change that. Not even God. The ghosts of the parishioner's sins, the church's sins, the war, the grief of so many, haunted him at every turn. How could he possibly comfort the shattered men returning from war? Men whose bodies and minds were irrevocably broken. Blinded, disfigured, haunted by the trauma of battle, they wandered aimlessly, lost in a fog of agony and blood. And then there were the wives and families, the loved ones with invisible wounds, left behind by this ghastly war. They poured out their anguish to Father Martin day after day. The love of God was comforting to many, but it no longer comforted Father Martin. He stared at his sad reflection. He could not continue this charade.

Even more troubling, his friend Donald Crane, also a priest, a Dominican like Father Martin, was stationed in Rome. Letters he sent were uncensored because they came through the Vatican. Donald told of the evil of the Italian Fascists and Nazis. And the Pope, leader of all Catholics, the champion of good throughout the world, was doing nothing to protest. Was God watching?

The Pope felt it was better to embrace the Nazis than take sides with Russia and the godless communists even though it was well-known that the Germans were eliminating Catholicism throughout their empire.

Nothing was making sense anymore. Like Father Martin, his friend Donald was shaken terribly by the shroud of wickedness that had descended over Europe and the world. Donald wrote in a disturbing letter that the murder of Jews was already well-known yet the Pope was doing little to help them. The Pope needed to speak out publicly condemning the Nazis, Father Crane wrote.

Another letter Father Tom Martin received from his friend told of a group of Jesuit priests who were ready to sneak Nazis out of Germany as the war was slowly turning against the Third Reich. Father Crane also added that he and others were willing to take matters into their own hands to stop this smuggling of Nazis and their riches. He did not say what this meant, but it did mean that his friend would be doing something, whereas, he, Father Tom Martin in Chicago, was doing nothing.

The bricks kept tumbling. One day, he heard a disturbing confession from a child only twelve years old. He wanted to know if it was a sin to let the pastor, Father Pelford, touch his privates. The boy also confessed to touching the pastor's penis. Stunned, Father Martin told the confused boy in so many words to stay away from Father Pelford.

Father Martin decided to write to the Archbishop of the Chicago diocese about Father Pelford's behavior. Later, another boy confessed to him that Father Pelford had touched his privates. He received no reply after the first letter he sent to the diocese. After he sent a second strongly worded condemnation of the priest, he received a reply from the archbishop's office that appropriate action would be taken.

The following day, with his church duties done, Father Martin hurried from the church through the back door. His cassock made irritating sounds as the black fabric rubbed against his legs with each step. He brushed the sins he had just heard in the conventional from his mind as he brushed the dandruff off his shoulders. His eyes thinned and he stared at the broken asphalt pavement of the parking area in front of him. Even if God had given up, he would not. A warm fire glowed inside him. It was hope. Had God given him hope? Did God want him to do ungodly things? He walked briskly to the rectory with a youthful vigor. He wanted desperately to see Zosha Kowalski, to kiss her passionately, to hold her tight.

The afternoon before Joey would be off to an army training facility, he unloaded a truck full of merchandise as though it was just another day at the Kowalski Five and Dime. He was somehow able to block out the enormity of change that his life would soon be taking. When he finished stacking goods in the garage, he walked in through the back of the store. He was sweating. As Zosha worked the cash register, she stopped and stared at her boy.

"Joey, you need to get over to the church now before confessions are over."

"Mom, I got nothing to confess. I'm going to be okay. Stop worrying. Plus, I'm going to help Dorothy finish restocking the shelves."

"You let her finish. You get over to Saint Gerard's now." Joey frowned.

"Now!" she barked.

The church was claustrophobically quiet. Foggy light strained through the stained glass windows. *Why do the saints always look so sad?* Joey wondered. He waited in a pew until it was his turn in line. In the confessional, he closed the door behind him. A small thin window from the priest's compartment slid open and through the fabric Joey could see the outline of a priest's head.

"Bless me, Father, for I have sinned." Joey had to think about it. He would have to make up some sins.

"Joey? Joey Kowalski?" the priest said. It was Father Martin.

Joey's eyes widened with surprise. "Yeah. Yeah, it is." He relaxed and smiled. He had never had a priest talk to him in a confessional booth like he was an actual person. He liked it. He had always liked Father Martin.

Father Martin let out a deep breath. "Listen. I know all about what you and your family are going through with that new Woolworth. It's not right what those big businesses are doing."

"I know," Joey answered.

"I'm on your side. I want to do something about it. Something besides praying. Could you meet me tonight behind your garage around 9 PM?"

Joey was puzzled. "What's this all about? You know I'm leaving tomorrow for boot camp?"

"Do you think you can get ahold of a gallon of gasoline? We're going to do something about that Woolworth."

Joey began to follow the priest's train of thought. The recklessness of it excited him. He nodded. "Yeah. I can get some gas. I'll meet you at nine."

Sixteen year-old Dorothy Kowalski called a family meeting at the wooden kitchen table at the back of the Kowalski Five and Dime. It was evening. The store had closed. She knew Joey was leaving for the Army the next day and she did not want to depress him, but everyone had to face facts. She had bad news, which Zosha already anticipated. Dorothy opened a black accounting book and laid it out in front of the family. Zosha was surprised when Dorothy pulled out a pack of cigarettes from her purse and lit one. She knew her children smoked but liked it better when they hid the fact. Dorothy felt she was too old to be hiding it any longer.

"Can I bum one?" Joey asked. Dorothy pushed the pack across the table to her brother. Joey took a cigarette and lit it. He stood up and pulled a string on the ceiling fan. He opened the window near the kitchen sink. The fan made an annoying grating sound, like fingernails scratching glass.

Dorothy put on her glasses. "The spreadsheet does not lie," she said. "Every month we are just getting by. Barely. Since the opening of the new Woolworth, our income has dropped twenty-eight percent. That is just from the beginning of summer. With Joey gone, we will be forced to hire someone to help, and we can't afford it."

"Your aunt Sherry told me Leo would help," Zosha said.

Dorothy sighed. Cousin Leo was dimwitted and could probably do only half the work Joey could do. He was the son of Zosha's sister and could do chores adequately only after being shown the right way multiple times. Dorothy knew he could not be trusted with driving the truck, so she would have to do it before school in the morning to pick up store supplies. Dorothy was not afraid of work. Despite what her mom insisted, she was not going back to high school for her senior year.

Zosha hated the idea of Dorothy quitting school. Maybe it was time for the Kowalski Five and Dime to close its doors. The thought, sharp and unwelcome, made Zosha's heart ache.

Dorothy looked up from her accounting book. "The summer months will help some, but I don't know if we will make it till Thanksgiving. I expect our gross income will continue to decline. We are a month behind on payments for the new refrigerator. We are a month behind in rent. Thank God for Mr. Dempster, but we can't rely on his patience forever."

Joey said nothing and was deep in thought. With him leaving, he felt he had let the family down. Maybe he could help change that tonight. Zosha just folded her arms and nodded. She also seemed to be somewhere else. "Can I have one of those?" she said, pointing at Dorothy's pack of cigarettes. The children looked at each other. They had never seen their mother smoke a cigarette. The smoke rose and swirled in the fan above the kitchen table.

Joey looked at the clock above the kitchen sink and jumped up from the table. Nine o'clock. "I gotta go." Dorothy looked at him quizzically. "I'm going to go for a short walk with Kathleen." His mother said nothing.

"You know, I hate to say this, but I think we are looking at bankruptcy," Dorothy said after Joey left the room. The light above the kitchen table flickered.

Instead of leaving through the back of the building, Joey walked through the front of the dime store, locking the door behind him. It was a warm and windy night, and the stink of garbage was gone. The garbage strike was over. As Joey walked away from the store, the trees were waving with the wind and speckled the street with a yellow glow. He walked down Hillock Avenue and turned down the alley and headed back to the garage behind their home. There was a man standing next to the garbage cans. Joey took out a key and unlocked the service door of the garage. He came out carrying a gallon of gas.

"Are you sure you want to do this?" Father Martin said. "I only need you to keep a lookout." The priest was carrying a hammer and crowbar. The two walked silently down the darkness of the alley toward Archer Avenue.

Chapter 11

Sergeant "Big Jim" O'Brien kicked his shoe through the charred remains of the Woolworth store. Some areas were still smoking. It was lucky there were no other buildings nearby, just a parking lot and an alley, or there would have been much more damage. The Woolworth was a wasteland. Every type of merchandise was blackened or burned. The store, five months old, had yet to put in an alarm system. A young man would lose his job for that.

The store manager said it did not look like anything was stolen. The steel safe was untouched. There had been no cash on the floor. It was clear that the back door to the alley had been broken into.

The fire chief, Lawrence Carmody, walked up to Big Jim.

"Definitely arson," Chief Carmody said. "An incendiary was ignited near the middle of the store. Probably gasoline."

This kind of fire did not make sense to Big Jim. This was something he would see owners do to collect insurance, or the Mob to make a statement. None of those scenarios fit.

The only witness was an elderly woman who was walking her dog and saw a man running by the store before the front windows exploded from the heat. It was terrifying, she said. She thought the man running was a Negro. Big Jim thanked the woman but shook his head. Nobody torching a building was going to run in front of it after they set the fire. The perpetrator entered and exited the back door at the alley.

He kicked his shoe through wet, charred muck at his feet, and saw small beads and the glint of a metal crucifix. He reached down and picked up a rosary. He cleaned away the wet ashes with his thumb. There were initials on the back of the crucifix: *T.M.* He showed it to the store manager.

"Do you sell rosaries?"

The store manager looked at the beads on a string. "No. We don't. Is that a clue?" Big Jim didn't answer.

Sergeant O'Brien walked down Hillock Avenue towards Throop Street. *Tap . . . tap . . . tap . . .* His wood nightstick rattled the metal streetlamps with his menacing approach. The Woolworth fire had been on his mind since it burned down a week ago. There were no leads. He had to think about motive, and what better motive would there be than for a small Five and Dime to put a large competitor out of business?

He looked through the front window of tiny Kowalski Five and Dime and observed bustling activity. He saw customers moving up and down the aisles. There was a pretty girl stocking items near the window.

A tiny bell rang when he walked through the front door. Zosha Kowalski looked up from behind the counter. O'Brien grimaced at the heavy smell of sausage and sauerkraut. So this was the family of the boy that his daughter had been seeing. He frowned. He never asked his daughter about the boy's family but now saw for himself. Immigrant gutter trash, pure and simple.

"Hello, officer. What can I do for you?" Zosha asked the tall police officer in blue. Sergeant O'Brien sat down at the food counter. "A cup of coffee?"

"No, thanks, ma'am. I'd like to ask you some questions, if you don't mind. Do you have a moment?"

Zosha's face became serious. She wiped her hands on her apron.

"Are you aware of the fire at the Woolworth last week?"

"Oh, yes. Horrible."

"Yes," Sergeant O'Brien repeated "Terrible. Can you tell me where you were last Wednesday night?"

Zosha smiled. She was not afraid of the policeman. "I know you, Mr. O'Brien. You have a lovely daughter, whom I believe my boy is smitten with."

Big Jim's jaw clenched. "Yes. I'm also aware of that which makes this somewhat difficult."

Zosha did not respond. Big Jim tapped his fingers on the countertop.

"Again. Do you remember where you were that evening?"

"Are you insinuating I had something to do with that fire?"

"Did you?"

Zosha folded her arms and stared at the police officer.

"Do you sell rosaries here, Mrs. Kowalski?"

"Are you in need of a rosary, sergeant?"

Sergeant O'Brien reached into his pocket and removed the rosary he found in the rubble of the burned-down Woolworth. "Perhaps you lost this?"

Zosha looked down at the rosary in Big Jim's hand. He turned over the crucifix to show her the back. "Do you know anyone with the initials T.M.? Perhaps you recognize this?"

"What does a rosary have to do with all of this?"

"It was found at the crime scene."

"Crime scene? The fire wasn't an accident?"

Big Jim became impatient. "Listen. I know times are hard. But it will be a lot easier if you confess to anything you know about this. I know this is awkward because of the relationship between your son and my little girl. But I am a police officer and bound to do my duty."

"Does your duty include bashing the head of a little high school student who was doing nothing wrong? Yeah, I heard about that." Zosha's anger began to peak. "Maybe you should get one of your detectives to look into that. If that is all, I have work to do and customers waiting."

Big Jim's ruddy skin turned redder. "Suit yourself. But I will get to the bottom of this." He stood up and turned and looked around the store. "I can think of a half-dozen code violations that could shut this dump down. You have a nice afternoon, Mrs. Kowalski."

"Sergeant." Big Jim turned and looked at Zosha. "Maybe you need a rosary. They are in the second aisle."

T.M? T.M? Zosha's head began to spin. Father Martin's first name was Tom. "Oh, my God," she whispered.

Zosha Kowalski kneeled in the first-row pew of the church and whispered prayers. She was about to go into the confessional where she knew Father Martin was. She looked up at the giant crucifixion above the altar. An emaciated Jesus was on a wooden cross bleeding and dying slowly. She took a deep breath and entered the confessional booth.

"Bless me, Father, for I have sinned." Zosha did not know how Father Martin would act. This was her first visit since she confessed her love for him.

"You do not have to do that, Zosha," Father Martin said quietly. "We have both sinned. I should be confessing to you. And I am."

Zosha was confused. "Confessing to me?" There was silence. She waited.

"I am confessing my love to you." Zosha's entire body was jolted with an electric current of joy. She wanted to jump through the thin partition wall of the confessional and hug this handsome man.

"I've known it for a long time but thought it sinful. I was wrong. What I feel is not a sin." Father Martin felt a wave of relief wash over him. *Here I am,* he thought, *giving my confession to a parishioner.* But there was more.

"Zosha, I am going to enlist in the Army."

"What?" Zosha gasped.

"Shush! Quiet. Please. Whisper. I am not fit for priesthood. I've changed. I must do something to help our country. I can't sit here and do that. I've done research. I called the recruitment office. With my college degree I can enter the Army immediately as a chaplain and an officer."

"This is all my fault. I am going to burn for eternity."

"Nonsense. If anything, you have saved me, and you are wrong. God only looks kindly on love. A just God does not punish love. If he does, then there is no just God. And it's not just you. There is so much more that I can't talk about right now."

"I love you," Zosha said through the thin veil of the partition. "I will pray for you every day. To me, you are a saint." Her hands trembled. She decided not to mention the visit from Sergeant O'Brien.

Zosha was startled by a soft knock on her confessional door. The door opened, and she found Father Martin standing in front of her. She glanced around the dim church, its pews silent and empty, the faint scent of incense still lingering in the air. For a moment, time seemed to suspend itself, but before either could summon reason or restraint, an invisible force pulled them together like magnets defying all logic and law. Their embrace was urgent and desperate, a collision of forbidden love. Their lips met with searing passion as the saints and angels gazed down from the vaulted ceilings to bear witness.

PART III

*"The nursing child will play by the hole of the cobra,
and the weaned child will put his hand
on the viper's den."*
—Isaiah 11:6-9

Chapter 12

Rico Adduci was born Enrico Salvatori Adduci, in the year 1917, to a teenage mother in Lentini, Sicily. He did not know his father. His mother, Cinderella (Cenerentola) Adduci, an Italian Jew, was a slender, dark-skinned woman with raven hair and black, fiery eyes. She had ignored, as best she could, the hateful and malicious stigma that came with having a child out of wedlock. Even her cousins, aunts, and uncles had shunned her. Her violent temper was well-known, so she suffered only the scornful looks of her neighbors. She walked with her head held brazenly high down the sunbaked streets of Lentini, breast-feeding the infant Enrico in full daylight, a knife hidden beneath her blouse.

Cinderella was named by her father, a peasant dreamer who had hoped the name would bring his daughter luck like in the old folktale of the young peasant girl who eventually married a prince. Her mother died while giving her life. But folktales were folktales. Real life was far more vicious. Her father was murdered by robbers when Cinderella was fifteen years old. He had nothing of value to steal, only his life. She inherited her father's tiny home, a mule, and a coop of scrawny chickens.

Within Cinderella burned a passion for sculpting, and she named her boy after the famous Italian sculptor Enrico Salvatori. Before the economic Depression cast its long shadow across all of Sicily, Cinderella became well-known for her ceramics and pottery, earning her a grudging respect from the locals. Curses from her neighbors became whispers. Walking with his mother from the market through the orange dust of the village streets, little Enrico became known as Cinderella's boy, the bastard.

When the Depression came, as in all of Sicily, the times were hard in Lentini, a tiny village just a few miles west of the Mediterranean Sea. Drought had choked the life out of the once lucrative crops of oranges, and the desolate landscape mirrored the empty pockets and stomachs of nearly everyone. But nothing stopped the local mafiosi from extorting money from the large landowners and even the desperately poor. There was no market for artwork or sculpture. The safety of a young woman with a young boy was precarious, and there was no one to protect her. Young men were not interested in courting the little whore with the bastard son. She rarely let tiny Enrico out of her sight. Life was dangerous.

Cinderella would gaze with wonder and trepidation upon the beauty of her little boy, and his wide chestnut eyes. His tiny ears were delicate and nearly translucent, like butterfly wings. Like most of her neighbors, the young mother was desperate for money, so she sighed when she looked at her kiln and pottery wheel for the last time. The round wooden disk she used to move the pottery wheel with her bare feet was worn away from years of spinning. She sold her mule, the chickens, and the house—all she owned—and was able to save enough money to book passage for her and Enrico to America. By 1920, Cinderella and three-year-old Rico would become just two of the four million Italians to emigrate to the United States.

There were no tearful goodbyes with loved ones. Cinderella was on her own, she and little Rico. The departure point from Italy was at Naples. They joined hundreds of others on a crowded ferry to mainland Italy. It was little comfort that so many Italians were as destitute as her. An old woman who walked with a limp held Rico while Cinderella experienced the humiliation of fumigation, her naked body sprayed with some chemical that made her skin burn and break out in rashes. All passengers were fumigated.

One hundred fifty dollars—a fortune—was required to ride steerage in an old coal ship converted to a passenger liner. Third class was in the bowels of the ship, a Dantean underworld of crammed humanity lit by flickering gas lamps. Cinderella and Rico shared a single metal bunk. The beds were stacked two high with straw mattresses. The pillows were life preservers filled with deteriorated cork that had no chance of floating if there were a catastrophe. With little ventilation, the steerage class was filled with the cries of children and the putrid stench of buckets of human waste, which spilled across the floor during the violent ocean voyage.

These immigration ships were christened "coffin ships," for good reason. Tight quarters and lack of ventilation spread disease quickly. The food was rancid. Cinderella and others onboard soon developed dysentery from the fetid, brackish drinking water. The latrines were on the main deck and were closed off during harsh weather, which could last for days. The buckets put out for human waste were often knocked over, so the passengers walked in urine and feces. After a three-day stretch of violent weather, it became less stormy, and the seven hundred people in steerage rushed to the deck for fresh air. It was raining, and their clothing became soaked. For many, it was the only clothing they had brought for the trip.

Cinderella, her dress soiled with bloody diarrhea, was too sick to join them. The old woman who held Rico during her fumigation took him up deck so he could breathe fresh air. She did not fill her jug with the water from the ships casks but instead filled it with rainwater from the tarps on top of the lifeboats. She returned with Rico and freshwater, and from her bag she removed a lemon and squeezed it into the jug.

Little Rico smiled. He loved the taste. "Not so much," the old woman gently told Rico. "Your mama needs this more." She also fed Cinderella stale bread from her bag, which was better than the moldy offerings the ship provided. She wrapped Cinderella in a blanket, took her soiled clothing up ship top, and washed them in tubs of seawater.

"You are an angel," Cinderella said weakly. The old woman's name was Gabriella, and she was going to a place called Cleveland, Ohio, to live with her son and his family. She likely saved Cinderella's life.

"Why do you limp?" Cinderella asked.

"Oh, it is nothing." Gabriella had been run over by a vegetable cart in Naples a week earlier. The pain was getting worse every day.

Gabriella played games with Rico and kept him hydrated with lemon water. She whispered songs into his ear, which lulled him to sleep. After a few days, Cinderella was able to smile and go ship top for fresh air. Gabriella warned her not to drink the water that the ship provided. The old woman was always alert to fill her jug with rainwater wherever she could find it.

After twelve miserable days and nights, the East Coast of the United States of America came into view. Seagulls wheeled and cried overhead at their arrival. The cries of anguish heard throughout the journey were now universal cries of joy when the Statue of Liberty came into view. Twenty-two passengers died on the trip. It was a US law that the captain of the ship would be fined ten dollars for every passenger who died in transit, so it was in the captain's best interest to take care of the passengers. Despite the fine, it was a very profitable trip. It was small consolation to the passengers that their lives were worth ten dollars each.

Before the ship could release its passengers, medical examiners descended upon its decks to make sure there were no outbreaks of contagious diseases such as typhus. With the ship finally docked, the ecstatic and frightened passengers entered the dark halls of Ellis Island, where a cacophony of every language imaginable could be heard. All the newly arrived immigrants were subject to a six-second medical exam. The medical staff used chalk to mark the clothing of those with obvious medical problems. *P* for pulmonary problems, *L* for lameness, *CT* for trachoma, and a dozen other initials that could keep the immigrants from entering the supposed paradise of America.

The women were separated from the men during the medical examination. Children were allowed to stay with their mothers. Cinderella stayed close to Gabriella and held her hand tightly. Gabriella was having trouble walking. Cinderella passed the medical exam and was told to move along. She waited for Gabriella. Then her heart sank when she saw the large damning letter *L* in white chalk on Gabriella's blouse. She was being ushered away by a man in a heavy blue uniform.

Cinderella screamed at the man in Italian. "Stop! Where are you taking her?"

The guard did not understand but gathered that the two were related. "She will be taken care of," he said with a sneer. He pushed Cinderella and Rico away violently. "Keep moving!" he shouted. Other immigrants behind Cinderella began pushing for her to move out of the way, and she was swept up in the current. They traveled down a long, dark corridor through large steel doors and were blinded by the sunshine of the promised land. Cinderella and Rico waited outside the Ellis Island immigration doors for hours. They never saw their guardian angel, Gabriella, again.

With what little money they had, Cinderella and Rico settled in New York City on the Lower East Side in the squalid Five Points neighborhood of southern Manhattan. Overcrowded, with stacked apartment buildings falling on top of each other, she made her home along with thousands of other immigrants. Disease was rampant. Petty theft and violent robbery were a scourge.

For a while, Cinderella and Rico shared an apartment with a family of seven Ashkenazi Jews who were escaping the pogroms of Russia. They spoke Yiddish. Cinderella spoke Italian. The Russian Jews were kind and shared food even though they had little.

Years passed as they moved from one tenement to another. Young Rico developed a brow-raising knack for bringing fresh vegetables and fish home, which they shared with the other tenants. Cinderella dared not ask how he procured these victuals. Even the adults began looking upon the youth with respectful admiration. The tenements became an organism of cooperation. Families helped each other watching the children of strangers while parents were out trying to find work.

Cinderella found a job in the dim, suffocating confines of the Waltz cigar factory rolling cigars twelve hours a day. Time passed slowly. The work was tedious and repetitive, stretching time with its monotony. The assembly tables were segregated by gender and race. The black workers had their own section of the building.

Cinderella's station was next to a young Irish woman who seemed forever cheerful. Cinderella suspected she was crazy, but they became friends, and the Irish girl, named Mary, taught Cinderella passable English. Cinderella had heard of another tobacco factory that was unionized. At that factory, they worked eight-hour days, and the pay was better, but there were never any openings. Any talk of unions overheard at the Waltz cigar factory was grounds for immediate dismissal. Cinderella was able to gab quietly with Mary to pass the time, and the smell of fresh tobacco was pleasant. In a matter of weeks, her fingers turned chocolate brown.

Years slipped by in a blur of hardship. Cinderella's once strong and nimble fingers became brittle with arthritis. Management noticed when her cigar rolling production fell off. The foreman, a large, lecherous man with thinning hair, offered her a sinister bargain—to keep her job if she would please him sexually at the end of each day. Cinderella was not stupid and understood economics. If she was going to please a man with sex, she was going to get paid to do it, and not the pittance she earned at the cigar company. Thus, her jagged path in the promised land, the land of milk and honey, led to prostitution, by which she could at least pay her share of rent, save money, and keep her little boy fed.

She worked nights at local bars and slept during the day. Little Rico wandered the mean streets of the

Five Points alone. He became adept at pickpocketing money and watches with his quick hands. With the money, he bought food and shared it with the other children wandering the streets. His generosity forged bonds of loyalty and Rico soon became the leader of a wild gang of twelve-year-olds. He was soon helping his mother pay rent. Cinderella did not want to know where he got it or how, just like she did not want him to know where she got the money she brought home. Each day Rico's mother slept, exhausted, making herself ready for another night of smoke-filled taverns, blackened rooms, verminous alleys, and disgusting men.

If she turned tricks in the room behind Blackie's tavern, she had to split her earnings with the owner. On a good night, she could make ten dollars, which was twice as much as she could make in a twelve-hour day rolling cigars. The fee was two dollars for twenty minutes, which she split fifty-fifty with Blackie. She kept one hundred percent of any sex she could sell in the alleys behind the tavern. It was more money, but the risk was higher, the clientele was always repulsive.

After one night of work, before the gritty light of dawn, Cinderella trudged up the four flights of stairs toward her flat. The building was asleep as she sat on the stairs of the third-floor landing and rested. She kicked at a skinny stray kitten rubbing its muzzle against her ankle.

"Shoo," she whispered. She finally gave up, lifted the little creature, and carried it up the remaining flight to her apartment.

Cinderella counted each step just like she counted the days left in this grimy tenement before she was able to leave it for a better place. She had left the building she had shared with the Russian Jews and now shared a flat with a family of four Italians. There was one bedroom, a small front room that was also used as a bedroom, and a kitchen. There was a common bathroom in the hallway. She quietly lifted a corner of the mattress she shared with Rico, and beneath was a loose floorboard. It had been a good night, and she deposited seven dollars and sixty cents beneath the board and quietly moved the mattress over it. She was able to save a small fortune, now over one hundred dollars. She had found a two-bedroom apartment above a hardware store on the Lower East Side where she could have her own room with Enrico, and a separate room for her artwork. The apartment had its own bathroom.

Cinderella removed her shoes and sat on the mattress. She stared at her hands lit by the dull light of dawn peeking through the yellowed window above her bed. Sparrows outside in the gutter announced a new day. Her arthritis had mostly cleared up, and she dreamed of going back to her artwork and sculptures. There were rich people in New York City, and she would make a life for herself where her artistic talent could flourish. It was now only a few short weeks before she and little Rico could leave this hellhole.

As usual, Blackie's Tavern reeked of burnt-out cigarettes and stale beer. Two men, one short, one tall, both drunk and slimy, agreed to meet Cinderella in the alley. Cinderella had seen them before—they wanted sex on the cheap, so they went out into the rain to the alley behind Blackie's. They waited under an awning next to the back door. She would give each man a hand job for only a dollar, but now they wanted more. One of the men punched her hard in the back of the head, knocking her nearly unconscious to the pavement. The other man lifted her skirt and mounted her from behind. He grunted like an animal until he was finished. Cinderella gained consciousness and began to fight but was only kicked again and again in the side of the head. The other man also raped her. Scarlet ribbons of blood mixed with rainwater flowed into the alley sewer.

"Come on, Patrick, let's get out of here. She don't look too good. We could get into some real dice here. I already got a problem with the law."

"She can't ID us if she can't see us." Patrick rolled Cinderella onto her back and pressed his thumbs into both of her eyes until both eyeballs popped.

Cinderella Adduci never recovered from her head injuries and died a day later, leaving her only boy an orphan. There was no murder investigation, just another dead immigrant whore. Rico was sent to the city orphanage, which was a vile asylum of filth and violence filled to twice its intended capacity. Twelve-year-old Rico Adduci ran away from the Angel Guardian Orphanage after only one week. He was better off on his own, he thought. The Five Points, a festering wound on the city's underbelly, became his home. He slept in doorways and haunted the streets with the multitude of homeless and lost children of the neighborhood.

Being alone and unloved as many of these orphans were left a crippling scar. At least Rico had a mother once, and he loved her. And he knew she loved him, too. This somehow made him stronger than the others. He was brought to tears when he remembered the bicycle Cinderella bought him years ago when she was working at the cigar factory. It was old and put together with the parts from other bicycles, with a tiny front wheel and an enormous back wheel, the seat made from an old catcher's mitt, and handlebars so high Rico could barely reach them. Cinderella bought it for him for one dollar. It was a gift he would never forget. He had ridden it with pride that no other destitute boy in the neighborhood could match.

Young Rico was small, but the other kids around the Five Points soon began to respect his fearlessness and the razor he kept in his pocket. Word spread quickly after Rico nearly killed another boy who had been bullying him and his friends. Nothing in the Five Points district made a more lasting impression than violence.

Violence and sin became the classroom for the hundreds of homeless children living off the streets. They bathed when it rained. They slept in doorways and abandoned buildings. Lice was a daily companion in their hair and clothing. Under horrific conditions, Rico showed an instinct for survival and self-preservation. His success at thievery without ever getting caught awed the other children.

He shared his food and money, and loyalty followed. His friends became family. An oversized boy whose only name was Hogan, and Mad Anthony, a thin boy with a scarred cottage cheese face, became his closest friends. Hogan was a rough quiet character and prone to violence even when it wasn't warranted. He and Mad Anthony became the feared muscle of the teenage Adduci Gang.

Rico was soon making money playing cards with the older men in the saloons. He had a natural aptitude for numbers and odds and was soon winning regularly. He was also adept at dealing off the bottom of the deck. His hands were a blur, and he was never caught cheating. He found he could count cards easily, increasing his odds of winning.

The rampant crime and debauchery on the Lower East Side was the only education the boys needed. Hogan and Mad Anthony started an extortion business breaking the windows of storefronts and charging the owners a small fee to make it stop. It was free money. The police were never eager to help the immigrant trash or their small stores.

At seventeen years old, Rico's criminal ambitions bloomed through the cracks of the urban pavement. He and his gang pooled their money together and bought a rundown tavern on Baxter Street where they could run whores on the second floor and gambling in a back room behind the bar. All the local beat cops, easily swayed by well-placed bribes, turned a blind eye to his enterprise. And Rico decided they did not have to cheat at gambling. It was bad for business, and he found that the house always won in the end.

Rico knew to pay tribute to the big boys who ran most of the city of New York: Meyer Lansky and Lucky Luciano. There was nothing that these gangster kingpins did not know about when it came to illegal revenue. They sent a man to Rico's tavern once a week to collect tribute. The big-time gangsters would leave his little business alone. At least for a little while.

And Enrico vowed that the men who murdered Cinderella Adduci would meet her son one day.

Chapter 13

By the 1940s, the Lower East Side of New York had changed much from the slums that dominated the neighborhood in the 1920s. Enrico "Deuce" Adduci also had changed. Through brains and brass balls, Deuce was able to carve a small section of his old neighborhood into a profitable business—gambling, prostitution, and extortion. Alcohol was now legal, and Rico and the gang moved their operation to a much larger building. Local police were once again well paid to leave him alone. Blackie's Tavern, where his mother had been raped and beaten, had been torn down. Most of the framed multi-story slums had either been demolished or burned to the ground.

On the first floor of the property was a rowdy tavern that he named *Cinderella's*. There was a long mahogany bar with a mirror just as long behind it. It made the place look bigger than it was. Red velvet curtains hung over the walls. On weekend nights, Rico always had a band playing the latest ragtime. He had his own office on the third floor. The entry door was carefully watched by two bodyguards.

Rico's brand of crime was new and rarely violent. He kept his gambling honest. The neighborhood pimps paid him tribute so they could operate safely. Rico had his own brothel on the second floor of the three-story building. He had handrails installed at both sides of the stairway to help keep the drunks from falling down the steep flight of stairs. It didn't help much.

In a special room in the basement that no one ever wanted to enter was his torture chamber to persuade rivals that they were better off working with him rather than having their fingers cut off with pruning shears. The room was soundproof. There were two heavy oak chairs with steel armrests. The chairs were bolted to the floor.

Rico walked slowly down the dark back stairway to the basement. The time had come for revenge. He had learned years ago through the street grapevine who was responsible for his mother's death, Patrick Egan and Josh Kelly. Kelly was lucky. He died of consumption months earlier but not so Pat Egan. He was tied to one of the basement's oak chairs. Narrow chains around his neck and waist held him tightly. Leather straps held his wrists firmly over the armrests. The prisoner wept pathetically.

Deuce's toughs, Hogan and Mad Anthony, stood behind the chair. They wore butcher's aprons. The fronts were covered with blood. Hogan pulled out a heavy pair of pliers. With a sickening crunch, he broke Patrick Egan's teeth with a swing of the tool. Then with practiced ease, he reached into his mouth with the pliers and ripped out the man's tongue. The gurgling noises from Egan's throat bothered Mad Anthony, so he stuffed a rag into Egan's mouth. Small bubbles of blood grew from Patrick Egan's nostrils. The ends of his hands were a bloody mess. Hogan had snipped off all his fingers with pruning shears.

Egan's terrified eyes followed Rico, who paced in front of him with an ice pick in his hand. Mad Anthony and Hogan stepped back and leaned against the wall. Hogan smoked a cigarette. Mad Anthony chewed a large wad of bubblegum. He blew bubbles that burst with a violent pop.

"I'm not going to kill you, Egan. Although you will wish that I did." Rico walked in circles around the chair. "You blinded my mother so she could not identify you. And the police never did anything about it. Why should they? Just another Italian whore left for dead in the gutter. You and that piece of shit, Kelly. May he rot in hell."

Rico stood in front of Patrick Egan with the ice pick. "You won't be able to see me in a lineup either. Or mention my name." Rico grabbed the top of Egan's hair and drove an ice pick into one eye and then the other. Not deep enough to go into the brain, but just enough to make jelly of the eyeballs. Egan gagged and groaned.

"Take him to the river. But don't throw him in. I want the police to find him. Justice is served." The two men nodded.

Hogan removed a blackjack from his pocket and hit Egan hard across the back of the head. They untied him from the chair, and he fell heavily to the floor like a bloody marionette with its strings cut. There was a tarp waiting for him, and they rolled the body up in it. Unfortunately, Egan was a big man, and Mad Anthony and Hogan grunted and strained from the weight as they lifted him.

Halfway up the basement stairway, Mad Anthony wheezed. "I'm hungry. Let's get Chinese."

Hogan nodded. "Let's go to Chan's. They got good eggrolls." They carried the body out through a back door to a waiting car in the alley.

In the shadowed recesses of Midnight Rose's candy store, nestled deep within the streets in the Brownsville neighborhood of Brooklyn, two titans of the underworld discussed business over billowing clouds of cigarette smoke. The men were Meyer Lansky and Albert Anastasia, Mafia crime bosses. Although criminals, the US government and FBI had struck a Faustian bargain with these kings of vice. The war effort needed their help in quelling the rampant theft and sabotage of war goods from the shipping docks in New York and New Jersey. The federal government knew all too well that the Mafia had an iron grip on the longshoremen's union and all the activity in and around the shipping docks. Through a rare feeling of patriotism and an under-the-table deal, the hoodlums ordered the thievery on the wharves to stop. And it did.

The gangsters were also asked by the US government to control any communist troublemakers trying to get the longshoremen to strike. Soon, any pro-union agitators were beaten or disappeared altogether. The mafiosi also provided maps and information from their connections in Italy for a future landing of Allied forces in Sicily. It was all for the benefit of the US war effort. The US government aptly christened the unholy alliance with the organized crime syndicates, "Operation Underworld."

The quid pro quo? The US government would lighten the sentence of their criminal friend and boss, Lucky Luciano, who was in prison on prostitution and racketeering charges. For cooperation from the gangsters, Lucky Luciano's prison sentence would be commuted, and he was to be deported after the war to Italy with an agreement never to return.

However, the meeting between Lansky and Anastasia was about another matter that concerned the men: what to do with Rico "Deuce" Adduci. Once a petty hoodlum, Rico had created a very lucrative niche of illegal revenue in the south Chinatown and Lower East Side neighborhoods. Rico paid tribute to the bosses, but it soon became known that he was pulling in thousands more than he admitted. The Mob bosses knew Rico Adduci was a stubborn beast, and dangerous. Rather than ask for additional weekly payouts, they felt his elimination was the best option.

Albert Anastasia, crime boss of Murder Inc., allegedly responsible for over one thousand murders, wanted Rico and his associates Hogan and Mad Anthony killed. Anastasia had a horrible temper and just plain liked to kill people. Lansky, on the other hand, always wanted to avoid bloodshed if possible, and had a more subtle approach in mind. Although Adduci had a small gang, Lansky knew they were devoted to Rico. And another gang war, even a small one, would be bad for business, which was already hurting because of the war. Through back channels, and a discreet conversation with his FBI contacts, it was arranged for Rico to be drafted into the Army. He would not be stationed statewide but sent overseas—far, far away. With Rico Adduci conveniently absent, the Mob could slowly take over his piece of the action.

Rico Adduci always had a sixth sense for trouble. He knew the New York crime bosses were itching to take over his territory, which probably meant his murder. He became extra cautious, knowing that now the shadows may hold more than just darkness. Changing his routine became a daily ritual. He showed up at his tavern at different times. He stopped eating at the same restaurant he always did and ate more meals at home. His girlfriend Annette was a good cook. He switched automobiles every few days. He added extra bodyguards. He also was doing surveillance on Albert Anastasia, whom he knew was the most dangerous of his enemies. Eliminating him might ease some of his concerns or add to them. Meyer Lansky and his people would likely be mad as hornets if Rico assassinated Anastasia. Regardless, Rico was not giving up what he had worked so hard to achieve.

Rico's girlfriend Annette Constantino was a former prostitute with curves that could stop a trolley car in its tracks. She was a head taller than Rico and could throw most men out a door or through a window if needed. She was completely devoted to Rico, loyal as a guard dog, and he trusted her. She managed his lucrative brothel business, counted the money, got a doctor when the girls were sick or needed abortions.

Annette, like Rico, was an Italian immigrant forged from the same steel of New York's mean streets. She hailed from the town Aosta in northern Italy, just across the border from southern France. She came from a long line of criminals who cooperated with the 'Ndrangheta, whose criminal arm reached the entire length of the country. The 'Ndrangheta was an organized crime group whose reputation for murders, thefts, and kidnappings went back centuries. Annette's father had a disagreement with the 'Ndrangheta and was murdered, so she and her mother left Italy for the United States. Her mother died on the journey. Her brothers, however, stayed in Aosta, and somehow made amends with the northern dons of the 'Ndrangheta.

With criminality in her blood, Annette Constantino started her own prostitution ring and was doing well until Rico took over the Lower East Side. She decided she needed his protection and fell in love with the little man with the black eyes, unibrow, and ears like butterfly wings. Despite his temper, he never hit her.

No doubt because of what happened to his mother, Rico would not allow any man to rough up his girls. When one of his whores was beaten badly, Hogan and Mad Anthony broke the man's arms, took him into the basement, and tied him to a chair. He was then blinded with an ice pick. They only blinded one eye per Rico's instructions, but that was enough to send a message. Word got around quickly that physical violence with any of Rico's ladies would be punished severely. After that, there were no future problems.

Against Mad Anthony's advice, Deuce entered his tavern through the front door. Mad Anthony went in first, his acne cratered, chalk-white face twitched back and forth like a sparrow looking out for a hawk. He, too, knew danger was in the air. The jukebox blared through clouds of cigarette and cigar smoke. Rico nodded to the bartenders. The patrons parted as though he were Moses as he walked to the back of the tavern. He climbed the narrow stairway behind the bar to his office. Annette was waiting for him with a letter in her hand. She was trembling.

"What is it?"

"You've been drafted. You gotta go into the Army."

Adduci nodded his head and smiled. So, *this* was how the Mob was going to get rid of him. Rico didn't have many options, but the wheels in his brain turned quickly. There was money to be made in Europe. He had heard of Vichy collaborators who controlled the south of France and were plundering the Nazis, lining their pockets with black market gold. It was a delicious prospect, rife with danger, the kind that thrilled young Rico. If he could get to France without being killed, things could turn out beautifully. He pulled Annette close to him.

"It's going to be okay."

Rico had a plan, a web spun with cunning threads. He already knew of a lieutenant in the Army shipping back boxes of stolen treasure. A Navy man in ordnance then took the crates to Rico's lawyer, Alan Waxman, who in turn fenced them for enormous amounts of cash. The money was then divvied up among the Army lieutenant's partners. Rico arranged for attorney Waxman to do the same for him. Rico planned on ditching the Army as soon as he hit the lawless playground of European soil. Then he would set up his own gang.

Rico made good use of the three weeks he had before being sent to boot camp in Virginia. He went and saw his banker, who had been helping Rico launder money for years. He opened a special account into which the proceeds of his European adventure would be deposited. That was, if his plans worked out.

Annette was told to get messages to her brothers in the Calabrian Mafia that Enrico "Deuce" Adduci was on his way. The gang was very active in Vichy France. He called a meeting with Annette, Hogan, and Mad Anthony.

"As you know, I have been drafted. I can't run away from this, and I know it's the work of Lucky Luciano and Meyer Lansky. They want to get rid of me so they can take over everything we have here. Once I'm gone, don't get cute. Sell everything over to the Outfit. Don't make no trouble. They're too powerful."

"But Luciano is in prison," Hogan said.

"Don't be fooled. He is still calling the shots. I don't know how long we could hold out against them anyway." Rico looked at all the faces of his partners.

The jittery Mad Anthony chewed gum wildly. He looked scared. Hogan had no expression.

"Maybe we kill those fuckers first," Hogan said.

"I thought of that. But they have too many connections. All the hoods in Jersey and up and down the shore would be after us." Rico looked at Hogan. "They got judges and senators in their pockets." Hogan was afraid of nothing and always knew he was going to die violently. He really didn't care.

"Don't worry. I got plans," Rico continued. "Give the Outfit what they want. Stay alive. Go work for them. I'll be back with more money than Rockefeller, and we'll settle things with these big shots."

PART IV

*"In peace, sons bury their fathers.
In war, fathers bury their sons."*
-*Herodotus*

Chapter 14

June, 1944. Portsmouth, England.

The Normandy invasion, "Operation Overlord," depended entirely on good weather with a clear sky, a full moon for air support, and relatively calm seas. Bad weather would be a disaster. A defeat on the shores of France could set the war effort back years. Months of training in England and Ireland left the young GIs going crazy from boredom and anticipation. There was only so much drinking, mingling with the opposite sex, and brawling the soldiers could take.

The invasion was set for June 5, but the ever-cautious General Eisenhower felt the conditions were wrong for that day. One hundred thirty-three thousand troops, twelve thousand aircraft, and seven thousand ships, the largest sea invasion force in the history of the world, waited like a tightly wound spring.

The Bravo rifle platoon, led by Sergeant Krims, along with thousands of other men, boarded massive transport ships at 3 AM, January 6. Once the mighty ships were into the iron-grey English Channel, the men climbed down cargo nets like bugs onto their landing crafts (LCVPs), which bobbed like corks in a bathtub. It was the same thing they had done the day before only to be called back. The boys from the boot camp in Texas, Joey, Squirrel, Fatman Elliot, Gorilla, Isaiah Stomp, Pops, Hansen, Pretty Boy Swanson, Zeke Walker, and thirty others jumped into their LCVP. In the blackness before dawn, they were finally going to war.

The LCVP landing craft was a shallow barge-like boat constructed of plywood. Sergeant Krims knew that German bullets would easily pierce the flimsy boat walls. Despite the seasickness pills the men took, it only took halfway across the English Channel for the men to start vomiting.

The coxswain, a nervous British soldier named Enright whose face was far too young for war, steered the 225-horsepower engine of the LCVP with a white-knuckled grip and surprising dexterity. As they splashed through the waves, the landing craft in front of them stalled. As all the men crouched low behind the landing craft walls waiting for the dreadful impact, Sergeant Krims saw the oncoming collision and yelled, "Left, left," but the young coxswain had already seen the problem and maneuvered around the stalled vehicle. The sides of the two boats scraped each other. A collision would have sent dozens of soldiers carrying forty-pound packs to the bottom of the English Channel. Two soldiers burst into tears. Isaiah Stomp looked at Joey and shook his head with relief. Joey thought he had wet himself, and didn't care if he did.

Thousands of bombers passed overhead like enormous silver-and-black birds. The beach, finally visible in a distant smear of ochre, erupted in a sudden storm of fire and smoke. Sergeant Krim's gut clenched. He could see men in the first wave running up the bloody beachhead, cut down by enemy fire as they advanced.

"Five minutes!" the coxswain hollered. "We'll be in five feet of water!"

"Get ready!" screamed Sergeant Krims.

A monstrous orange blossom erupted in front of them, a landing craft disintegrating in a shower of wood and flesh.

"Bloody minesweepers!" Enright cursed. "We were given the all clear!"

The young coxswain yelled at Krims. "Sergeant!" he commanded. "Get one of your men in the water. Now! Someone who is tall and can swim."

Krims shouldered through the crowded men. "Kowalski!" Krims shouted. "Get your pack off and get in the water!"

Joey whispered a curse at Krims and then at his own height. Isaiah Stomp, a ghost of a smile on his face took Joey's pack. "Good luck, buddy."

The air screamed with German bullets as Joey dove over the side of the landing craft. The water was icy cold, but he was too scared to feel it. He was sweating in frigid water.

"Keep swimming. Yell if you hit a mine," Krims ordered. Joey could barely hear what Krims was saying but soon realized that he was being asked to be a human minesweeper. He wouldn't have to yell if he hit a mine, he thought. Low-flying planes roared above, and exploding mortars were landing everywhere in the water. With the landing craft creeping behind, Joey swam a clumsy dog paddle, each stroke a desperate prayer to reach the beach alive. The slow-moving craft was an easy target for the German machine guns. Bullets splintered the plywood walls. Joey could hear the cries of wounded soldiers.

The minutes seemed like hours before Joey could feel sand beneath his boots. The sea was bright red with dead soldiers and shattered LCVPs. Machine gun fire made the water around Joey's head a poisonous dance of death.

Krims words from training kept ringing in Joey's ears. "When you hit the beach, keep moving forward or you will be dead." *Keep moving! Keep moving!* The beach was a horrific picture of carnage. Crimson water lapped at the shore. Broken bodies littered the sand like grotesque driftwood. Bullets whined overhead, a constant, maddening drone.

Joey sprinted as he never had in his life and dove behind a smoldering jeep. The heat of the fire made him back away. A soldier lay crumpled beside him. The dead soldier's eyes stared sightlessly at the sky. Joey snatched the man's rifle and backpack. Soon, Sergeant Krims, Gorilla, and Squirrel appeared through the smoke and chaos and were hiding with Joey behind the jeep. It was a good fifty yards to a concrete pillbox that was pouring machine gun fire across the beach.

A mortar exploded to the left of the jeep, showering them with sand and rocks.

"Kowalski!" Krims yelled at Joey, "put that man's helmet on. Now!" Joey grabbed the dead man's helmet.

"Squirrel, you see that pillbox at eleven o'clock?"

"Sure do, Sarge." Squirrel giggled. Inexplicably, there was a large grin on his face. Was this Tennessee boy really having fun?

"Can you put a bullet through that slit? Fill it up."

Behind them a man was screaming, "Medic!" The man yelling was their platoon mate, Stitch Hansen. He had Pops by the back of the neck and dragged him behind an anti-tank barrier. Pops was holding both bloody hands over a wound in his stomach. Joey wanted to crawl towards them and help, but Krims's firm hand clamped on his shoulder.

"We have to move forward and knock out that pillbox. We can't stay here. We are all dead if we stay. Everybody, grenades. York! Are you ready?

Squirrel rolled from his back to his stomach. He crouched up on one knee and fired off three rapid shots from his M1 rifle. One, two, three. Every shot went through the slit in the concrete. The machine gun fire stopped.

"Let's go!" Krims hollered.

They charged the bunker and hurled grenades through the firing slot. The explosion blew smoke and human parts through the slit. A lone German emerged coughing and blinded through the back door. Gorilla shot him dead. Planes sliced overhead, dropping bombs somewhere behind the beachfront. Soldiers on the beach were still diving from their landing crafts. Many ripped to shreds before they hit the water.

Krims surveyed the German defenses. He, Joey, Squirrel, Fatman, and Gorilla crowded behind the protection of the pillbox. Soon, Stitch Hansen was next to them breathing heavily. They turned and looked back at the beach and saw a medic with the red cross emblazoned on his helmet kneeling over Pops behind the shield of a steel anti-tank cross.

"Stitch, how bad is Pops?" Fatman asked Hansen.

"Gut shot. Not good. His stomach is a mess."

There was another pillbox fifty yards from where the men were hiding. Fire was pouring from the barrel of a German machine gun riddling the beach. All the men stared. Joey wanted to stay right where they were. Suddenly, Joey realized Isaiah Stomp was nowhere to be seen. "Jesus, anybody seen Stomp?

"We can't worry about him now. Grenades ready," Krims commanded. "Spread out, stay behind the line of fire. Run in a zigzag. Squirrel, there are snipers in the dune. Give us cover." Krims led the way and Joey found himself running behind, firing his weapon, screaming like a devil possessed.

Once the German pillboxes were cleaned out and the beach secure, the men rested briefly. But Joey couldn't rest. He ran along the beach, which appeared literally covered with corpses. The smell of cordite and death lingered, acrid on Joey's tongue. He went to a triage tent for the wounded that had hastily been thrown up. "Stomp! Stomp!" he bellowed over and over. He ran past a pile of sandbags and nearly tripped over a soldier removing his boots.

"Isaiah!" Joey cried joyfully.

"Hey. Kowalski. Got a rock in my boot. Don't know how it got in there."

"How the hell did you get way over here?"

"I have no idea. Just trying to stay alive."

Stomp seemed to be in a daze. Joey helped him to his feet. "C'mon. Let's find the rest of the guys. Keep your head down. There's snipers taking potshots."

After receiving orders from Krims's CO, the platoon began to move inland and found most of the land flooded. It was part of the Nazi defense for this particular landing area. The Germans opened the locks from the Douve River, which flooded all the low-lying areas, making it difficult for the enemy to move heavy military equipment. Only narrow causeways—arteries choked with men—could be used. They were death traps in disguise, easy targets for strafing enemy aircraft, land mines, and snipers. A carefully planned Kraut defense.

Joey's platoon had landed at a part of the Normandy coast code-named "Utah." The Nazis biggest defense against the invasion was concentrated at Omaha beach a few miles to the east. While over 250 soldiers were killed during their landing at Utah, ten times that many would die at Omaha Beach.

Krims immediately saw the trap the Nazis had set by flooding the fields. "Stay off the road," Krims warned. Joey's height was finally an advantage as the men waded through the flooded fields with the diminutive Squirrel clinging to Joey's back, the water sometimes five feet deep. A single German plane strafed the infantry on the causeway, the only dry place to move. The Germans also laid over fifteen thousand mines, which made land travel slow and dangerous. Casualties mounted. Sergeant Krims and his men waded slowly through the water to avoid the mines and enemy planes.

Stitch Hansen was sick of wading through the flooded fields. His feet were itching like hell, and he was dying to take his boots off. He moved closer to the dry road. A mine detonated. His body disappeared below his waist in an explosion of mud and flesh. Only half of his body could be seen on the dry land of the causeway.

All the men froze. Fatman stopped and began to cry. "Stitch," he screamed helplessly.

"Stay off the road! Keep moving!" Krims ordered. *Listen to me and you might stay alive.*

Krims knew the worst thing for a soldier was to be fighting alongside friends, and most of these guys knew each other since boot camp. Joey, Fatman, Zeke Walker, Gorilla, Pretty Boy Swanson, Squirrel, Mitch Klausner, and Stomp were now all having fleeting visions of the clownish Stitch Hansen from Camp Wolters, and his hilarious imitations of the weaselly Sergeant Mealy, or stuffing rags under his shirt to make large breasts while imitating blonde movie star bombshell Mae West. *"Is that a banana in your pocket or are you just glad to see me?"* The happier the memories, the more broken the men felt inside. School teacher Pops had been shot up on the beach; now Hansen was gone. Who from their company would be next?

The American Army knew that the German defense of this beach included flooding the area. They also knew that there would be mines everywhere. While the squad was equipped with mine detectors, the batteries were all shorted out from the flooded landscape, making them useless. No provisions were made to keep the detectors dry. Men would die because of this failure.

Once the squad finally reached higher ground, they were confronted with a different enemy—hedgerows. These ancient earthworks, thick and gnarled with impenetrable shrubs, made the landscape into a labyrinthian nightmare. Plots of French farmland were divided with these menacing walls, some up to sixteen feet high. A square mile of battlefield contained hundreds of these mazed barriers, perfect for hidden German snipers and machine gunners. Krims and his platoon tried blowing holes in the hedgerows with grenades, but it did no good. They just had to go around them until they found an opening. Even tanks could not penetrate this natural defense.

Eventually, the steel anti-tank crosses used cn the beaches by the Germans were cut up and welded to the front of American tanks, which finally allowed a tank to cut through these massive walls of dirt and vegetation. The men called them Rhino tanks, but those would come later. Right now, Krims and his platoon marched on. The fighting and killing continued with the Nazi soldiers in lethal retreat.

Chapter 15

Rico Adduci crouched low at the back belly of his landing craft, one of thousands ready to attack the beach code-named "Omaha." The Nazis were ready. German machine gun fire was making Swiss cheese at the front of every LCVP. The drawbridge front of the landing craft opened its jaws, and the commanding officer was shot dead before he could holler, "Let's go!" They were fish in a barrel as the enemy filled the landing craft with a fusillade of lead, creating carnage ripped from a nightmare. Rico crawled over the dead and wounded bodies and dove into the water, which was thankfully not over his head, because he could not swim. He pushed around the floating corpses until he finally hit the blood-red sand of the beach. He crawled as quickly as he could to safety behind the steel of an anti-tank cross that the GIs called "Hedgehogs."

The Germans had already spent years zeroing in on the designated killing zones in the event of an Allied landing. Omaha Beach was the most heavily defended, and storming American GIs were mowed down before most could get their feet to the beach. But the Yanks kept coming.

Next to Rico lay a freshly fallen soldier who was missing his head, a crimson fountain erupting from his neck, the feet of the man still twitching. The head was nowhere to be seen. Another soldier running by fell dead, his chest tattered with bullets. Rico reached into the gore around the decapitated man's head searching for his dog tags. From a clump of scarlet flesh, he snatched the man's tags. Rico immediately tore off his own dog tags and stuck them in the neck of the headless soldier.

Rico had lost his gun and took the M1 rifle from the fallen soldier. A steady stream of machine gun fire continued to knock soldiers to the sand. Rico's hand hurt. He looked and saw the top of his baby finger had been shot off. "Bastards!" he screamed. In a rage, Rico began firing at the pillbox, which was alive with machine gun fire. He emptied the clip of the rifle into the slit of the pillbox. The firing stopped. Other GIs rushed the pillbox and threw grenades through the slit for good measure. Germans ran through the back of the concrete fort with their hands up. They were shot dead.

Through the deafening cacophony of manmade hell, commanding officers were screaming, "Move forward, move forward," so Rico did. Breathless, he rested with his back against the cool concrete of a German machine gun nest. American GIs ran wildly past him. He pulled out a rag and wrapped it around his half-finger. It hurt like hell, but he didn't call for a medic. He reached into his pocket and found the dead man's dog tags. He wiped the blood from the metal. "Amos Prichard." He held the tags tightly in his fist and smiled. Enrico Salvatore Adduci was dead. Long live "Amos Pritchard." He put the new tags around his neck and laughed uncontrollably.

A passing medic looked at this little soldier laughing maniacally. He'd obviously gone mad. He wouldn't be the first. The medic asked if he was okay.

He looked at Rico's bloody hand. "Let me have a look at that."

"No, thanks. I've never felt better, doc," Amos Pritchard said. "Never felt better."

Chapter 16

July, 1944

Sergeant Krims arm raised up into the air, a silent command for complete silence as they entered an opening in one of the hedgerows. The continuous chittering of birds in the shrubs suddenly stopped. Joey, the point man, inched through the opening, his heart hammering. He was suddenly face-to-face with a German soldier. They both pointed their guns at each other, but Joey pulled the trigger of his weapon first. Nothing. The next moment a bullet pierced the face of the Nazi, who staggered back two steps and fell. Isaiah Stomp had been immediately behind Joey and killed the man. Swanson and Gorilla followed through and sprayed the area blindly with their weapons. They began throwing grenades over the next hedgerow.

Joey's face was white from fear. His hands trembled. Sergeant Krims came up behind him and put his hand on his shoulder. This settled Joey a little.

"M-m-my gun jammed," Joey stuttered.

Krims looked at the weapon. "You have to take the safety off your rifle, son. It works better."

Joey stared at his rifle, his expression blank, as the realization hit him: the safety was still on. Around him, the rest of the squad fired wildly into the dense hedgerows, their shots cracking through the air without direction or purpose. The chaotic barrage kicked up dirt and leaves, but the enemy remained unseen. It was a waste of precious ammunition, but panic had gripped them.

"Hold your fire!" Krims bellowed, his voice cutting through the madness. The gunfire faltered and stopped, leaving an uneasy silence.

Krims let out a frustrated sigh, shaking his head at the young, inexperienced soldiers under his command. They were green, too green, and it showed in every jittery movement and poor decision. God help us, he thought grimly.

Joey finally caught up with Stomp and walked beside him.

"You okay?" Isaiah asked.

"I guess. Thanks for what happened back there. You, you…" the words came slowly. "You saved my life."

Isaiah shook his head side to side. "I know we're at war, but I never thought I'd actually kill someone. I hate this." Joey also shook his head, his heart still pounding when it sunk in that he was very nearly a dead soldier.

It took over a month for the Allied soldiers to finally work their way through the hedgerow hell. Krims met the battalion commanding officer and discovered they were about three miles off course from their target area. The soldiers continued to slog east, fighting the retreating enemy the entire way. They were grateful to see no German planes.

Without air support, the retreating Germans were slaughtered by American and British bombers. Dead

Germans, burned-out Kübelwagens, the German version of the jeep, and other armored vehicles littered the roads leading east. It was a graveyard of twisted metal and smoldering flesh, a nauseating smell that Joey would never forget.

The charred and bullet riddled remains of dead German soldiers were everywhere. One corpse, his face frozen in a silent scream, sat behind the steering wheel of a blackened vehicle. Other dead soldiers lay on the ground nearby with skin gray as ash. One soldier's chest was torn open, his ribs already bleaching in the sun. Ravens inside picked away at the dead man's guts like birds in a grisly cage. The retreating Germans had a macabre joke about their lack of air support. *If there are silver planes, they are American. If there are green planes, they are British. If there are no planes, they're German.*

The men in Krims's squad marched and fought for twelve straight days eating only the horrific, tasteless C and K rations. There was no time for bathing. The casualties were light so far for their company: one wounded, one killed, one missing. Moving slowly through a wooded forest, Fatman, who was walking point, raised his fist high in the air and then dropped to the ground.

Krims crawled towards Fatman. "What'd you see?"

"Not sure. I saw movement atop that knoll. Eleven o'clock."

The woods became silent. Not even the chirp of birds.

"Swanson, Kowalski," Krims said softly. "Check out that hill. Eleven o'clock. Keep your heads down."

With dread, the two boys crawled slowly. When they reached the top of the hill, to their relief, they found it vacant. But the imprints of scattered leaves and the still smoking butt of a cigarette meant Fatman did see something.

"Stay spread out," Sergeant Krims warned. "At least ten yards apart." He didn't want his group to be ripped apart by a hidden machine gun. After a long day's march, Krims did a head count and found the platoon was one man short. Private Hezekiah "Zeke" Walker had disappeared.

"Anybody seen Walker? Damn it," Krims cursed the man. Not because he had apparently deserted, but he took the platoon's only bazooka. Desertion was plaguing large numbers of the American soldiers who had been in long periods of combat.

Tired of marching and the daily face of death, there were others who had a secret yearning, a shameful envy of those who walked away from this man-made hell. Of all the guys in their platoon, Joey thought Zeke, the husky farm boy from Nebraska, was the least likely to do such a thing. He had always seemed the most steady and fearless of the group. But with the strain of kill or be killed mounting every day, Joey couldn't guess who might be the next to fade away from this madness given the chance.

"Stomp. Back track and see if you can find Walker, and more importantly, the damn bazooka." The rest of the men waited smoking cigarettes and talked quietly until Isaia returned forty minutes later. No signs of Zeke Walker or the bazooka.

Out of the woods, the troop came upon a town recently cleared of the enemy by British soldiers. Despite repeated warnings, Wilbur "Gorilla" Lafayette could not help but pilfer from the dead Germans. He eagerly chopped off fingers to get at wedding rings and dug gold teeth from their mouths with a knife. He observed a British soldier stomping on the head of a corpse until, with a sickening crunch, the dead man's jaw popped from its mouth like a jack-in-the-box. Gorilla's own jaw dropped in admiration. The British Tommy even gave Gorilla a tutorial on his method for extracting gold teeth.

"Do it like this, mate—twist the 'ed just so and make sure ya stomp jus' below his bloomin' ear. Right? Otherwise, the bloody brains pop out, makin' an awful mess." *These Brits are damn smart*, Gorilla thought.

After another week and a half of marching and fighting, the platoon saw another death from Joey's boot camp days: Mitch Klausner from Elephant Butte, New Mexico. Walking point through what looked to be a deserted village, they heard the single crack of a rifle, and the quiet boy who thought that jack rabbit was a delicacy, caught a sniper's bullet in the throat. Diving for cover, no one saw where the shot came from. Joey crawled to the fallen boy and dragged Mitch against the side of a building. He hopelessly pressed a rag against the man's neck to staunch the bleeding only to watch helplessly as Mitch drowned in his blood.

Chapter 17

Portions of France were slowly liberated, village by village, as the Allies pushed east towards Germany. After four years of German occupation, the ecstasy of the French people was hard to describe. The hidden, haggard population poured into the streets like rats from a drain. They danced, waved flags, and cheered. The soldiers were hugged and kissed by men and women alike. The GIs rained candy upon the children, but their stays in these shattered liberated towns were always brief.

As the war raged on, continuous combat was exacting a heavy toll on the fighting men. Desertion was spreading through the ranks like a poison. An alarming ten percent of the soldiers experiencing combat were going AWOL. The brutality of war had turned many of the GIs into something less than human. Besides desertion, soldiers began to be arrested for rape and pilfering in alarming numbers.

The spontaneous celebrations of the French were in stark contrast to the destruction and destitution that the country had faced. France was in ruins. There was widespread hunger and poverty. Over a million children lost their parents and homes to the war.

Over forty thousand Jews had been rounded up by the traitorous Vichy French police and deported to their death at Auschwitz. Thousands of Jewish children whose parents had hidden them from deportation roamed the streets. The homeless were everywhere, sickly and weak as if death had crawled out of the ground. Tuberculosis cases climbed. Malnutrition was rampant. The German rationing of food, a cruel joke, had condemned the French to near starvation while the occupiers feasted.

With the Nazis in retreat, General Eisenhower gave no importance to the liberation of Paris which was still under Nazi control. It provided no logistical advantage and would be a distraction for the Allies in their pursuit of the main enemy army. However, it had immense psychological importance to France. To the French leader, Charles de Gaulle, not liberating Paris was unthinkable. An unenthusiastic Eisenhower grudgingly diverted part of the Allied advance south toward Paris. For the general morale of France, it was agreed the primary role in the liberation of Paris would be French troops.

The US military command was explicit that all soldiers liberating Paris should be white. Europe was just beginning to learn the intense racism that American whites had for Negroes, regardless of their valor or service to their country. US generals were concerned that newsreel footage might show black troops being hugged and kissed by euphoric white women. This would outrage much of the United States population.

While a small, lucky contingency of US soldiers were able to enjoy the "City of Light," Joey and his battalion continued the murderous pursuit of the elusive enemy across the scarred landscape of northern France.

August, 1944.

The exhausted men of Krims platoon were finally ordered to stop and rest. Their orders had changed and were now ordered to move east towards Belgium and the area surrounding the Hürtgen Forest.

Joey swatted at bugs. The air was thick and humid. Mud and sweat stuck to Joey and the platoon like a second skin. It had been five days since Mitch had been killed. Death was becoming the new normal. The men took refuge in an abandoned barn, and all fell immediately asleep in the hay. Joey awoke to shouting and laughing. He could not remember the last time he had heard laughter. There was a pond behind the barn. A dozen boys were naked, swimming and bathing, splashing each other like children.

Joey's mouth stretched into a wide grin. "What the hell?" He jumped up, stripped off his uniform, and dove in with a comical belly flop. The boys passed around a bar of soap.

Krims sat on the shore of this little lake, his back against a tree. He reached into his pack and took out a roll of red ribbon. He cut a fresh piece and tied it around his ankle. There was a photo of his wife and baby girl in his breast pocket, but he rarely looked at it anymore. It only made him depressed.

Only a few years older than these laughing jamokes, Krims looked on with envy at their oblivious gaiety. They could somehow—at least momentarily—forget the blackness they had been through, but he couldn't. He was once just like them, but no more. He'd seen too much. Memories were too painful.

Krims had become close with his own CO when he was just a green pup like these guys. Sergeant Butler cared for the boys in his command like a father, and Krims had grown to love the man who had a palpable care for his unit. He didn't lead from the rear like so many of these pathetic commanding officers. And right before Krims's admiring eyes, his life was snuffed out with the casual flick of a cigarette lighter and a bullet from the well-aimed barrel of a sniper.

The boys were coming out of the pond one by one, their skinny pale bodies white as milk. Pretty Boy Swanson was the first to put his uniform back on. He shook his head. His black hair glistened wet with cold water.

"Swanson, get your weapon and walk the perimeter. I know this is supposed to be a secure area, but do it anyway."

"Sure thing, Sarge."

Krims didn't want his squad's goddamned affection, just respect enough to follow orders, even if those orders meant walking into hell. *Just listen to me. I want you to live.* The boys might rest or find escape in these small moments of mindless splashing about, but for Krims, there was no escape. It was like a never-ending weight upon his chest. Each death, each casualty caused a small part of Sergeant Krims to die. The pressure was inescapable.

Krims reluctantly took the photo of his wife and child from his breast pocket. Their black-and-white images were beginning to fade. He sighed When this damn war was over, would there be anything left inside him for his family? Would he be able to return home and be a good husband, a good father? He didn't know anymore, and it scared him.

Once clean, Joey went back to the barn and was again swept up in a delightful sleep. He dreamed of his home in Chicago. He smelled sausage, onion, and sauerkraut. He was sitting at the kitchen table with a fork and knife, anxious to be served by his mom when Isaiah Stomp's sharp kick awakened him. Isaiah had two chickens, one in each hand flailing and squawking.

"Holy smokes. Where did you find those?"

"Just a little scrounging," A mischievous grin played on Isaiah's lips. "Help me pluck these suckers."

"Pluck?" Joey rubbed his eyes.

"You never plucked a chicken before?" Isaiah said in disbelief.

Squirrel came up next to Isaiah, grabbed one of the chickens from him, and quickly snapped its neck. Isaiah did the same to the other.

"Come on, city boy," Isaiah said. "We gonna cook us some chicken, and I'm gonna show you how to pluck some cluck." The men gorged on a makeshift banquet of roasted chicken and carrots foraged from an abandoned garden. They all agreed it was the best meal they had ever had in their entire lives. And they each, for the umpteenth time, shared their favorite foods, recipes, and what they would do when this cursed war was over. Most of the men fell back asleep until Sergeant Krims hollered, "Move out!"

On the march, the men moved slowly and quietly, spread out ten yards apart as Krims ordered. Planes swooped overhead in a sky of bruised blue. American and British planes were on bombing runs spreading a nightmare of carnage over Germany itself. Krims lifted his fist high in the air for silence and then dropped to his knee. The men all followed suit. There was a stone wall a short distance in front of them, and about a hundred yards behind that a two-story farmhouse. The men approached the wall, keeping low.

"Looks abandoned," Joey whispered.

The illusion of tranquility erupted with the staccato howl of machine gun fire from a second-floor window. The men dived for cover, crawling furiously to safety behind the stone wall. Krims could see German soldiers running to the protection of the farmhouse. He saw at least a dozen Krauts, and immediately recognized a German MG-42 machine gun firing from the upper window. The murderous weapon was capable of firing twenty-five rounds per second. Krims had seen a man cut in half at the waist by this death machine, which the GIs had nicknamed "Hitler's Buzz Saw." Sergeant Krims used a mirror to look above the wall and saw that there was also sniper fire from two other windows. Suddenly, his tiny mirror was shot from his hand.

"Jesus," he gasped. "Keep your heads down," Krims warned the men.

There was a small gap in the stone wall, and whenever Joey saw a gray uniform, he would fire through the gap. He didn't know if he hit anyone. Gorilla soon learned the accuracy of the German snipers when the top of his helmet was shot off his head. The hot, smoking slug of lead embedded into the steel of his helmet. He never raised his head above the wall again.

"Put that helmet back on!" Krims shouted. There was no way they were going to take this farmhouse without help. Swanson radioed for tanks. Isaiah Stomp and Gorilla were trained with bazookas, but Walker had walked off with the only one they had, so for now, they could only sit behind this wall and take potshots at the Krauts when they could. Joey leaned against the cool, white stone and lit a cigarette. Krims thought that maybe it would be best to back up and go around. The rifle fire coming from the second floor of the farmhouse was particularly troubling, as it gave them a good angle to shoot the heads off anyone stupid enough to lift theirs. "Stay down!" Krims screamed again.

"Squirrel, do you think you can take out those snipers shooting from the second floor?"

"I'll give it a go, but them boys is shooters. I'd kinda like to keep my own head, if that's all right."

They were pinned down. Retreating would likely get someone killed, so the men just sat and waited behind their wall and were grateful the enemy did not have mortars. They smoked cigarettes and chatted quietly.

It was autumn, and Joey could see apples in the small orchard next to the farmhouse barn. He felt ashamed that he wanted to kill just so he could taste their sweetness. He could not remember the last time he ate an apple, his favorite fruit. The chicken dinner they foraged seemed like years ago. Besides one day of rest, it had been a solid month of marching and fighting.

Krims took off his helmet and put it on a stick. He lifted it slowly above the top of the stone wall. Nothing. Maybe the Krauts had gone. "Fatman, flank left, see if you can see what's going on at the back of that house." Fatman left his weapon in the dirt and crawled away slowly. "Why the fuck is it always me," he muttered. It wasn't long before he returned. "They're gone. I seen at least ten Jerrys haulin' ass out the back. They headed for those woods. They were running fast."

Krims knew that the Germans would often leave behind a sniper to pick off someone before they completely vacated. He ordered each of the men to slowly lift their helmets above the wall. Still there was no enemy fire, only the rustling of the wind. Squirrel had removed some stones from the wall to make a peep hole. "I don't see nothin' moving," he said.

"Okay!" Krims called out. "Squirrel, Gorilla, Swanson. Give us cover. Stomp, Kowalski, Fatman, let's go. We got to clear that place out." The men slowly climbed over the wall.

"Spread out," Krims ordered.

At first, they crawled. Then Krims and the others jumped to their feet and ran at the farmhouse. Nobody fired at them. Fatman Elliott burst through the front door and dropped to his knee, training his rifle around the room, which was apparently a kitchen.

"Clear!" he hollered.

Joey and Krims followed behind. Stomp had gone around back and soon emerged from the back door. Krims motioned with his weapon for Joey to check the upstairs. Joey was all nerves as he slowly and quietly climbed the stairway. When he reached the upper hallway, he heard a noise from one of the rooms. He fired his BAR, spraying the plaster wall with a tornado of bullet holes. He heard a small whimper.

Joey edged towards the half opened doorway, a knot of fear twisted in his gut. He kicked the door open and jumped into the room. Sitting on the floor leaning against the wall was a small child. It was a girl. She stared at Joey. Her eyes were a deep-set brown that seemed to implore Joey for help, but he couldn't help her. She lifted her arm and slowly pointed her finger at Joey. A brown spot on her chest bloomed larger and larger. Her eyes blackened and her arm dropped.

Joey stood frozen, his hands trembling as he stared in disbelief at the dead child before him. His breath came in shallow, panicked gasps, and then, as though his legs had lost all strength, he sank to his knees. "I didn't know. I didn't know," he choked out, his voice barely audible.

Krims came up behind him. "God," he whispered. He too was shaken. "Come on, Joey. It's not your fault. It's war."

Fatman Elliott also came up the stairs and walked into the room. He shook his head and went back down the stairway. The other men had also arrived and began scrounging for food.

Joey walked numbly down the stairs cradling the lifeless child whom he had wrapped in a discarded blanket. He walked out the front door of the farmhouse. A short walk from the house was a small cemetery with several stone grave markers. Isaiah Stomp came from behind with a spade and began digging. Swanson and Gorilla also retrieved their spades and began doing the same, and soon there was a shallow grave in which they set the girl. The men gathered around.

"We should say somethin'. A prayer," Squirrel said softly.

"Jesus, York," Swanson said angrily. "God ain't nowhere near here. When you gonna figure that out?"

Squirrel ignored Pretty Boy Swanson and knelt next to the grave. Most of the men walked away but some stayed with their hands folded and their heads down. "The Lord's my shepherd," Squirrel prayed. "I ain't want nothin' even tho I walk through a valley of shadows. I ain't afraid." Squirrel nodded his head. "Amen."

Dazed, Joey walked away from the tombstones. Sergeant Krims was waiting in the doorway of the farmhouse and handed him his weapon. Gorilla had found a sack and filled it with apples. He passed one to each soldier. He held one in front of Joey, but Joey shook his head.

"Let's move out." Krims ordered. "Spread out. Keep your eyes open. They may have left a sniper in that tree line." Krims slowed his walk and sidled up next to Isaiah Stomp.

"Stomp, Kowalski is walking blind right now. It might take him a while to get over this."

"Or never."

Krims nodded gravely. "I know. Just help me keep an eye on him."

"No problem, Sarge."

Chapter 18

September, 1944.

West of the Meuse River, in the shadow of the Belgium Highlands, Sergeant Krims and the other staff sergeants met with their new virginal commanding officer, Lieutenant McCarthy, pristine in an immaculate uniform fresh from the USA. He saluted the sergeants smartly. One of the sergeants warned the lieutenant that saluting each other was dangerous because German snipers were always looking to kill an officer. Lieutenant McCarthy put his arm down. His trembling hands betrayed his nerves as he addressed the men. He was obviously scared to death. Krims looked at the other sergeants. This was not a good sign.

Lieutenant McCarthy spread a map on the front hood of a jeep. He rested his hands over the warm green steel of the vehicle, which helped with his shaking hands. "The Krauts are regrouping here." He pointed to a wooded area on the map. "They are in retreat. We will march at darkness along this road two clicks tonight at 0-1900 and get ready for a dawn attack. Extra artillery is being brought up as we speak. Once the artillery is through pounding the German position, we attack at 0-600."

"Lieutenant, we have been on the march for ten straight days. The men are exhausted. They need more than one day of rest," Sergeant Baxter said.

"We are here to follow orders. There's nothing we can do about it."

"What kind of heavy guns do the Krauts have? Any tanks?" Krims asked.

"Recon says no heavy guns and no tanks." McCarthy said. "This should be a cakewalk." The lieutenant seemed like he was on the edge of tears.

Not once had Krims run into a cakewalk fighting the Germans. This did not sound right. If the Nazis were in retreat, why were they stopping to regroup? Aerial reconnaissance? What could an airplane see beneath the canopy of this dense forest?

"Sounds like they are getting ready for a counterattack," Krims said. The sergeants walked away shaking their heads. "A cakewalk, my ass," one of the sergeants scoffed.

Without needing any official announcement, the infantry grunts sensed the weight of something grim hanging in the cool air, and it wasn't long before their instincts were proven correct; stone faced, Krims informed his squad that they would move out under cover of darkness, preparing for a major offensive at dawn.

Joey's platoon gathered as the supply trucks rolled in. Crates of ammunition were unloaded, and each man received his share: magazines for rifles, clips for Joey's BAR, and extra shells for the bazookas assigned to Isaiah and Gorilla. The dull gleam of the ammo seemed to reflect the gloomy countenance etched on every face. The weight of the rounds in their packs felt heavier with the knowledge of what lay ahead.

That evening at dusk, with macabre irony, a chaplain set up a makeshift altar amongst the M7 artillery vehicles that would be used for infantry support in the morning attack. The M7 was nicknamed, "The Priest," because the machine gun mounted at the top looked like a pulpit. Under the eerie glow of lanterns and the red streaks of a fading sunset, dozens of soldiers gathered around the little man with a white collar. Some knelt, others stood with heads bowed, their faces lit with dread and apprehension. Above the clamoring of war machinery and shouted orders, the chaplain's voice was strong and clear as he recited parts of Psalm 91, known as the soldier's prayer.

"I will say of the Lord, He is my refuge and my fortress, My God, in whom I trust. You shall not be afraid of the terror by night, nor of the arrow that flies by day. No evil shall befall you, for He shall give His angels charge over you to keep you in all your ways. You shall tread upon the lion and cobra. The young lion and the dragon you shall trample underfoot because God has set His love upon you. Know that He blesses all of you and will protect you. Amen."

Joey knelt at the back of the group, his hands clenched tightly together. Lost in himself, he heard not a word of the chaplain's prayer. Instead, he whispered into the void of his thoughts, "Please, Lord. Help me. Forgive me. I can't go on anymore. I just can't. Please give me strength."

The men marched two miles and stopped near the edge of a dense wooded area. Somewhere in that forest, less than a half mile in front of them, was the German Army. Sergeant Krims knelt and tied a fresh red ribbon around his ankle. Despite orders to prepare for an imminent charge, he insisted his men dig in, a premonition of danger overriding the official orders. The night was cold, the air crackling with a strange, almost electric tension. As dawn broke, a thick fog curled across the open field. Commotion erupted along the American front line as sergeants roused their men. Krims checked his watch. Any moment now, the American artillery would unleash hell.

At precisely 0600 hours, the quiet of the morning was shattered as American howitzers shook the earth. The trees above the forest where the enemy was hidden became a churning inferno. But there were also flashes of light coming from the enemy tree line that weren't from American bombs. The Krauts were firing 88s! This couldn't be. Absolutely nothing could have prepared Joey or most of these soldiers for the sheer, soul-crushing devastation of this enemy bombardment. Joey had endured mortar fire, machine gun fire, even the terrifying strafing of enemy aircraft. But the heavy cannon fire, the earth-shattering explosions raining down upon them, was a level of destruction Joey and the others could barely comprehend.

"Incoming. Take cover!" The soldiers could hear commanding officers yelling.

The Allied lines exploded like thunder. The screaming of the wounded was drowned by the roar of canon. The American artillery kept shelling the woods.

The enemy's 88s wreaked destruction along the Allied lines. The earth was being torn apart.

Joey curled into a tight ball, pressing his hands beneath his helmet and over his ears, desperate to stop this nightmare. Bombs roared. Men shouted. Suddenly, a soldier leaped over Joey's foxhole, his face pale with terror, fleeing in a frantic retreat. Dirt and debris rained down as Joey tightened his hold, trembling, willing himself to disappear into the ground until he heard the dreaded yelling of Krims. "Tanks! Tanks!"

The Germans were supposed to be in retreat. They were not supposed to have heavy artillery or tanks. Intelligence and reconnaissance were dead wrong. The bombardment from both sides stopped. Joey realized he had been whimpering. The now eerie silence was broken by the cries of the wounded and the hollering of "Medics! Medics!"

Out of the smoke and mist, like deadly phantoms, a half dozen tanks, massive and menacing, appeared through the haze with an escort of hundreds of German infantry firing their weapons, bayonets gleaming. It was the Americans who were being attacked.

"Bazookas! Bazookas!" Sergeant Krims hollered. Krims knew that without tank backup they would be slaughtered. They were not prepared for a tank attack. They were not prepared for any kind of attack. Sergeant Krims was on his field phone yelling, "Mortars, now! A hundred meters in front. Enemy infantry and armor advancing. Where are the goddamned M7's?"

Mortars from both sides were exploding on the battlefield. Isaiah Stomp aimed carefully at the oncoming tanks and had a direct hit on his first shot, which was able to take the turret off the lead tank. A swarm of Germans kept running forward. Joey, finally overcoming his horror, placed his BAR over the top of his foxhole and began firing, sweeping the field side to side. German soldiers fell, but more kept coming.

Their position was overrun. The enemy was in front of Joey and behind him. Through the smoke it was impossible to tell who was who. And then Joey heard the sickening moan of Isaiah Stomp, who had been in a foxhole just ten yards away. He lay in the dirt, his leg in shreds. "Medic!" he cried feebly.

Joey jumped from his foxhole and saw Isaiah trying to crawl away from the fighting. Two German soldiers were upon him with bayonets. Joey pulled his sidearm and fired two shots, and both Germans fell. He grabbed Isaiah by the arm and began dragging him away but was knocked over. A searing pain lanced through his neck, and he found himself rolling on the ground locked in a desperate struggle with a Nazi soldier who was stabbing Joey with a trench knife. Joey was able to pull his own knife and stabbed wildly. He felt warm, sticky blood gushing over his face and neck. He had run his knife through the German's throat.

The ground rumbled from the sound of an approaching tank. Joey saw Isaiah's bazooka lying on the ground. He could see it was loaded and remembered from training how to fire this lightweight weapon. He turned and fired, knocking the track off one side of the charging tank. The blast killed several German soldiers running next to it. With only one track, the tank drove in circles. Joey grabbed Isaiah by the collar and began dragging him. His eyes blinded by smoke, the last thing he remembered were the cries of the wounded and the smell of cordite.

Chapter 19

Chicago.

Catholic Archbishop Clarence William Perkins sat heavily in his office chair, the weight of his seventy-two years pressing down on him. A portrait of the Pope hung above, framed in dark oak, the pontiff's stern and unyielding gaze seeming to scrutinize his every move. The archbishop was weary, his sharp intellect dulled by decades of church politics and endless administrative burdens.

He sighed, shuffling through the stack of correspondence on his desk until his fingers landed on yet another letter from Father Thomas Martin. This one was no different from the others—brimming with grievances about the behavior of the pastor at Saint Gerard's parish. The archbishop's lined face twitched with irritation as he skimmed the letter filled with a familiar litany of complaints. He leaned back, rubbing his temples. The Pope's image stared down.

Continuing to open his mail, he came across another letter from this same priest. This one was actually welcome. Father Martin was requesting permission to enlist in the United States Army. Permission would be granted. With this troublemaking priest gone off to war, it would silence his condemnation of the pastor, Father Pembrook, and hopefully the letters would cease. He had already decided to transfer Pembrook to a diocese elsewhere.

At the rectory of Saint Gerard's parish, Father Martin sat alone at the worn wooden desk in his modest office, the faint smell of candle wax and cigarette smoke lingered in the air. His fingers trembled slightly as he tore open an envelope from his friend in Italy, Father Crane. Again, the scrawled handwriting painted a dire picture. In full view of the Vatican, over twelve hundred Jews had been rounded up in the Roman Ghetto. Mothers clutching children were forced into the cold streets, herded like cattle onto waiting trains. They were shipped to a work camp in Poland called Auschwitz.

Martin slumped back in his chair, the letter dangling from his hand. He stared blankly at the small crucifix on the wall opposite him, the serene face of Christ seemingly blind to the horrors unfolding around the world. Tom's helplessness cut deep. He closed his eyes, gripping the edges of his desk as if steadying himself. The room was silent, save for the faint creak of the wooden chair as he shifted uncomfortably.

His jaw tightened as he thought of the atrocities he had just received from his friend. Martin had done research. He would enlist in the army as a priest even though he had already decided to leave the Catholic Church. Being a chaplain, a man of the cloth, would be the fastest way for him to get overseas and he would not have to endure the required boot camp of regular recruits. This was his chance to contribute to the war effort, to finally make a difference, even if it meant leaving behind everything he had once believed to be sacred and unshakable. As the thought settled in, he let out a deep sigh, and with it, a tremendous weight seemed to lift from his shoulders, leaving him with a surprising sense of clarity and resolve.

Tom Martin pulled the collars of his coat above his ears. Winter had come early to Chicago, and the wind blowing down Dearborn Street was unbelievably frigid. He entered the large brass doors of the sterile limestone US Selective Service office and walked to the second floor. Two soldiers stood at attention outside an office, rifles by their sides.

One of the soldiers with a quizzical look nodded at the priest. "How's it going, Padre?" Father Martin nodded back. He entered the office and handed his enlistment papers to a soldier behind a desk along with ecclesiastical permission from the Catholic diocese. He also had documents saying he had already passed the health requirements.

"Glad you are enlisting, reverend," the colonel behind the desk said. "We could use a little of God's help over there."

"I would like to make a request, if possible," Martin said. "I would like to be stationed in Italy."

The colonel lifted his head from the paperwork in front of him. "Hate to tell you this, Father, but the US Army will send you wherever they think you're most needed. However, I don't make those decisions. The fighting in Italy is almost over, so I'm guessing you will go to France. I will make a notation for this special request."

In the hushed interior of St. Gerard's church, Zosha Kowalski prayed daily for her son and her brother Chester, and now for Father Tom Martin. Zosha's heart ached when he told her he was enlisting in the Army, but she decided to steel herself. She would be strong for all these young men in her life whom she loved so much and had gone into harm's way to fight the evils of Germany, Italy, and Japan.

When it was her turn in line, Zosha sat in the confessional booth opposite Father Martin, but she was not there to confess. "I will see you again before you leave?" Zosha asked. "I mean, not here in the confessional?"

"Of course," he sighed. "You know I love you, but it's best we keep this to ourselves. I know how cruel people can be. I don't want any harm thrown at you because of me. Unfortunately, I have learned that hate is a part of human nature and can never be fully extinguished. All we can do is fight against it with love and understanding."

"And with guns and bombs?" Zosha asked.

Father Martin sighed. "Yes, sometimes with guns and bombs." He paused for a moment. "I am going to borrow the parish car this evening. Can I pick you up at MacArthur Park at eight?" He almost let out a laugh at the absurdity of feeling like a nervous teenager asking for his parents' car.

Zosha beamed, a gentle heat rising in her cheeks. "I'll get Dorothy to close the shop early," she said excitedly. "And of course, I'll meet you."

Her mind began to race the moment she left the church. Oh, my God, she thought. My hair is a wreck. I don't have anything to wear. Her hands and nails looked horrific. Dorothy was right. They needed new rubber gloves for dishwashing.

When she stepped from the church into the sunlight, an irrepressible happiness surged within her. Zosha's pace quickened, her feet almost bouncing off the ground. Soon, she was skipping like a schoolgirl, her heart light and brimming with joy. A wide smile stretched across her face, and for the first time in what felt like forever, she was alive with hope. The shadows of war and hardship, if only for a moment, seemed distant.

It is said, "If God closes one door, he opens another." A miracle had occurred. Kindly Mr. Dempster who lived upstairs and owned the building had died in his soiled armchair. Dorothy found him when she brought up his daily sandwich. It was bittersweet for the Kowalskis. He had shown them so much kindness and patience with their perpetually late rent. He was a soft-spoken and gentle man who, besides the Kowalskis, had no family or friends. Zosha had always felt sorry for him. The miracle was he left the building and his considerable assets all to Zosha Kowalski. Suddenly, the weight of financial worry was not a daily migraine that caused Zosha so many sleepless nights. And another worry had disappeared to her relief. The police had stopped pestering her about the Woolworth fire. The initials on

that rosary were merely a coincidence. Father Martin
would never have been involved in such a thing.

Zosha's dreams of knocking a wall down and extending
Kowalski Five and Dime to nearly twice its size was
going to come true. She found herself dancing and
singing around the store as if she were in a cinema
musical. But her daughter had other plans for the dime
store, a golden opportunity.

"Mama," Dorothy said excitedly with dollar
signs in her eyes, "I am going back to the bank. I have
checked the real estate listings, and the Woolworth
property is for sale. We are going to buy it." Dorothy's
face gleamed.

"The Woolworth building is a burnt mess,"
Zosha said in disbelief. "And now we can double the
size of our store right here by knocking down that wall
with no money worries."

Dorothy was undeterred. "I know, but I already
went by the Woolworth lot with an architect. The
foundation of the property is concrete and wasn't
damaged. The city is already making Woolworth clear
out all the burnt framing. We will build on top of the
foundation. The location is ideal. If we keep the
property here, there will never be enough parking for us
to be truly successful. We will make Kowalski Five and
Dime a sensation. They only want one thousand dollars
for the lot. We have that and much more. I can get
favorable loan rates from the bank, and we will build a
wonderful new store. We can also purchase the
architect's drawings, which will already match the

existing foundation size. I have it all figured out to the last penny. We will rent this place here and the apartments upstairs. We will buy a house!" Tears began to well in Dorothy's eyes.

"Women can't get loans," Zosha protested.

"No, but the Kowalski Five and Dime can. Besides, money is the only thing the bank is interested in, and we have plenty now."

Dorothy was getting more and more excited as she spoke. She did not realize that she was jumping up and down, and soon her mother was, too. They fell into each other's arms and danced the polka around the kitchen table.

Cousin Leo walked in from the front of the store perplexed at the mad scene in front of him. He smiled at the merriment unfolding. "Um. Hate to break up the party, but I need help in front. You know, customers and all."

PART V

*"Behold, I am sending you out as sheep in the midst of
wolves, so be wise as serpents and innocent as doves."*
—*Matthew 10:16*

Chapter 20

After Normandy, it didn't take the deserter, Rico
Adduci, long to get a ragtag gang of misfits together.
With the beach secured and the Nazis in retreat, there
was nothing but chaos with thousands of soldiers, tanks,
and trucks landing on the shores around the clock.
Keeping track of everything was an impossible
nightmare. With Rico's quick wit, charm, and silver
tongue, it was laughably easy to convince soldiers to
disappear quietly with their trucks. Soon he had a gang
of twenty men, twelve trucks, and eight jeeps. He told
the men who had deserted along with him to keep their
uniforms. Men in uniforms were everywhere and not
likely to be questioned about what outfit they were with
or where they were going.

With the help of eager French collaborators,
Adduci's gang was able to find an old, abandoned barn
a few miles from the front. Stolen trucks filled with C
rations, chocolate candy, and cigarettes filled the barn.
All this booty was sold in a matter of days to the hungry
French population.

Small-town banks filled with French and
German booty that had somehow stayed in business
were more than surprised when Rico's motley crew of

military gangsters descended on them like a storm, armed to the teeth with bazookas and machine guns, ready to make an unscheduled withdrawal. The money from their thievery was making Rico and his gang rich.

October, 1944

From the depths of his morphine-induced sleep, Joey found himself back in his childhood bed, staring at the ceiling, which suddenly came alive with black bats and moths, their wings folding and unfolding in a maddening cyclone. And in the middle of this madness a face appeared—the pleading, tear-streaked image of the child he had killed. Her drowning voice whispered, "Help me. Please help me." The black mass descended, devouring the girl's face, spiraling down and down, closer and closer until Joey screamed for his mother. A hand, and the soothing coolness of a wet rag brushed over his fevered forehead. Nurse Helen was beside him, trying to calm him down.

"You are safe. You are safe here. You are recovering from wounds." Nurse Helen rubbed Joey's forehead in a circular motion with the tips of her soothing fingers. This seemed to calm him. It was his first week in a mobile hospital tent two miles behind enemy lines.

Nurse Helen held Joey's hand. "You need to take deep breaths. Breathe in deeply." Joey did. "Now exhale. Again. Inhale as deep as you can. Exhale."

It was nighttime. A generator coughed outside the canvas walls and the overhead light flickered casting skeletal shadows on the wounded like a physician's X-rays.

Joey began to relax. He felt better. "Thank you," he said hoarsely. "I'll be okay. I'm okay." He took deeper breaths. This simple bit of advice helped settle his mind. Another shot of morphine clouded his brain quickly and dragged him back to sleep.

The field hospital was a hodgepodge assembly of twenty dirty brown tents that could house up to four hundred patients. Inside, the air was thick with the mingled scents of fetid wounds, sweat, antiseptic, and blood. The beds were crowded with the injured—some writhing in agony, others motionless with bandaged stumps or broken limbs.

Besides the physical injuries were the invisible scars of battle. Shell-shocked boys sat silently, their eyes vacant, grappling with horrors only they could see. For these unfortunates, the Army preferred the term "battle fatigue," which made it sound like the mentally wounded were just tired and in need of a little rest.

The doctors and nurses were supposed to be working twelve hours on and twelve hours off, but the number of wounded arriving was causing sixteen- and sometimes twenty shifts. Dr. Clark, one of the physicians, had lost thirty pounds since the Normandy invasion, and the cavernous black bags under his bloodshot eyes were testimony to his exhaustion. As the battle moved, so did the mobile hospitals.

Besides dealing with the wounded, doctors and nurses helped set up the hospital tents as they leapfrogged over one another to get close to the fighting. Nurse Helen had no fingernails, which were worn down from digging in dirt and pounding tent spikes with a sledgehammer. She was a strong young woman with a serious face, and large, gentle eyes. When dealing with the wounded, she tried hard not to mirror their agony or helplessness. The soldiers called her "Mother Helen," even though she was only nineteen years old. She was one of fifty-nine thousand American nurses serving in the Army Nurse Corps. Joey's mobile hospital had only a dozen nurses and two doctors. Not nearly enough.

There were no cots for soldiers over six feet tall, so Joey's feet hung over the end of the bed. He needed thirty-two stitches in his neck from the knife wound, and a bullet had passed through the fleshy skin of his side. Dr. Clark thought he was healing fine and could be sent back to the front line in two or three weeks. Nurse Helen disagreed. Joey was one of many who cried in his sleep and was ambushed by nightmares nearly every night, leaving him drenched in sweat and gasping for air. She felt he needed to be moved to a fixed hospital in England to recuperate physically and emotionally. But the Army didn't see it this way and neither did Dr. Clark.

"Kowalski? Kowalski?" an orderly called out, walking down the aisles of wounded.

It was a name Joey barely recognized as his own. He lifted his hand. "Here."

"You've got mail." The orderly, a pimply kid hardly out of high school, carelessly tossed several envelopes tied together with a frayed string into Joey's bedpan on the small table next to his cot. The bedpan was thankfully empty. Joey had not received or sent mail in over two months. There were letters from his sister, from his mom, his best friend Clarence, and from Kathleen O'Brien. He decided to open Kathleen's last. Planes roared overhead. There was distant thunder, or was it bombs exploding?

Clarence wrote:

Hey Joey,

I hope this letter finds you alive. Ha ha. I turned 18 last week and no birthday card from you? Ha ha. True to my father's words, he brought me to the enlisting station and I am going into the Marines. I guess I'm going to fight the Japs. The White Sox actually had a winning record but finished in fourth place. Nothing new there. Nobody can stop the damn Yankees.

Joey, I'm scared. Not just for me but for you too. I wish everything could be like it used to. Playing ball at the lot. Sledding down Fulton's hill. But I guess we're not kids anymore. Right? I hope this war ends soon and we can see each other again. We'll go to the dump and get drunk and watch the sun set. Take care. See you when I see you.

Clarence

Joey never liked Clarence's father. He was a gung-ho former artillery man in the First World War and never treated Clarence with even a shred of kindness. Clarence was different and Joey knew it. But he and Joey had so many great times as children, and he never knew Clarence to tell a lie in his entire life. Joey hoped to hell that Clarence would never have to see what he had been forced to see. He thought back about the boy in his boot camp who couldn't take it and went AWOL. He secretly hoped Clarence would do the same.

Joey finally opened his letter from Kathleen O'Brien.

Dear Joey,

It breaks my heart to tell you, but I thought you needed to know. This damn war. Nothing turns out the way you plan. You deserve to have it straight. I have fallen in love with another. I didn't plan it. It just happened. I know you would like him. I hope you will find it in your heart to forgive me. Please be safe. Don't be brave.

Love always,
Kathleen

The groans of the wounded filled the tent. A chaplain was mumbling prayers over the bed of a dead soldier, the boy's face covered with a white sheet. Joey dropped his arms to the side of the bed and slowly crumpled the letter in his hand. The letter fell to the floor. He closed his eyes. *Nothing turns out the way you plan.* The words burned the wound in his neck.

Finally, he sat up in his bed and looked around the tent. One soldier, two cots from Joey, continued to moan until nurse Helen shot him up with morphine. Another cot had a wounded man wrapped in bandages from head to toe. He did not move or make a sound.

Nothing turns out the way you plan, echoed in Joey's head.

On Joey's tenth day of consciousness, another field hospital had leapfrogged theirs to get closer to the front. The Allies were making progress but at great cost. Joey heard the loud strutting of feet on the floorboards of his tent. A spit-shined colonel in polished boots marched through the center aisle and stopped at Joey's bed. He saluted.

"Private Kowalski, I am honored to present you with medals for your exceptional valor and bravery," the colonel announced. "A Purple Heart, and a Silver Star. Sir, you are a hero. The Allies and the United States of America are proud of you. Get well, son. We need men like you back in the fight. God bless." The colonel spun on his heels and marched away.

Joey couldn't believe it. Back in the fight? Hadn't they all, every soul in this wretched tent, done enough? He wasn't brave. He wasn't a hero, just a cog in a monstrous machine. The medals were pinned to the side of his pillow like a sadistic joke. He did not want to look at them.

Dr. Clark was at the front of the tent going over Joey's chart. Nurse Helen was at his side. She saw on the chart that Private Kowalski was ready to go back to the front. "Doctor," she whispered. "I don't think Kowalski is anywhere near ready to be sent back. He should go to England for more recuperation."

Dr. Clark sighed. He removed his glasses, which were making black dents above his nose. He rubbed his eyes. "Nurse, there's a war going on and every able man needs to be at the front killing Germans so this can someday end. I don't like sending these boys back, but without them the war will never end, and we can be here for years. He's going back. God help us."

Joey could walk freely now. His headaches had diminished. Once he was steady on his feet, he walked from tent to tent asking nurses if they had a Private Stomp in one of their beds. The rot of amputated arms and legs left in a pile beside the surgery tent left a nauseating stench in the air.

Isaiah Stomp was in tent six. Joey walked up slowly to his friend. Isaiah was pale. His left foot was gone, leaving only a bloody stump of bandages. Joey stood next to the bed and did not speak. Isaiah lifted his arm and shook Joey's hand.

"I don't remember much, but I'm told you saved my life," Isaiah said. "Thanks."

"I don't remember much either and don't want to remember. But you are welcome."

"I've been keeping tabs on you through the nurses," Isaia said. Heard you were healing pretty good. I must admit, even covered with blood and filth, these girls are damn good looking."

Joey looked at the medals pinned on Isaiah's pillow. A Bronze Star and a Purple Heart. "Looks like you are a hero, and the United States is very proud of you," Joey said sarcastically.

"Yeah. A couple pieces of tin and some ribbon. A fair trade for a foot. You sound like that colonel, who dropped this junk off."

Joey looked at Isaiah's leg. His dancing days were over.

"You hear from any of the other guys? Joey asked.

"Yeah. Krims came by about a week ago. He checked on you and said you were still unconscious. Squirrel, Fatman and Gorilla made it out alive. I guess the Krauts gave it to us good. Pretty Boy is dead. He was in the foxhole next to me."

Joey nodded, and thought about Pretty Boy and his self-proclaimed boast that he was, "God's gift to the women of the world."

"Krims still wearing that red ribbon around his boot?"

Isaia laughed. "Yeah, I guess the guy's bullet proof."

"You heard I'm going back to the front?"

"Yeah. Bunch of shit. They're gonna make sure they kill all of us. Well, I'll be heading back to the States. I guess I'm the lucky one." Isaiah winced. "Nurse," he called out. He wanted more morphine. "They're getting pretty stingy with the dope," he confided to Joey.

Joey shook Isaia's hand again. "Well, good luck."

"Even a peg leg can flip burgers." Isaia said.

"And make the best damned grilled cheeses in all of Kansas," Joey answered.

Chapter 21

Discharged from the hospital, Joey Kowalski waited
with the other soldiers to be transported to the fighting
near Reipertswiller. Most of the young boys were glum.
A few were cocky. "Let's go kill some Krauts!" one
young dogface yelled. The boy had wild, darting eyes
and Joey could see that he was scared.

As they marched along to the departing trucks,
any bravado cockiness evaporated in the morning mist
as they passed a row of dead bodies covered with
blankets. Only the dull black, muddied boots of the dead
showed beneath their olive-green shrouds. One corpse
lay alone, stiffened with rigor mortis, its arms
outstretched in a grotesque crucifixion. When Joey saw
the red ribbon around the man's ankle he crumpled to
his knees and put his hands over his face.

A wave of smothering grief swept over him. *It's
war*, Sergeant Krims's voice echoed in his head. A
lieutenant walked up and kneeled next to him. He knew
Joey had been wounded and seen combat. He put his
hand on his shoulder. The CO himself had never seen
combat, but the gravity of the dead men lying in a row
shook him along with everyone else.

Joey closed his eyes. He remembered the best
medical advice he had ever received was from Nurse
Helen: *Deep breaths. Deep breaths.*

"Come on, soldier. We need to move along."
Joey got to his feet and followed the others as if in a
dream. The row of dead men they passed covered in
wool blankets never seemed to end. Joey looked around

at the others marching with him. These kids had no idea what they were getting into. There was a sad joke from soldiers fighting at the front. *Please. Don't send any more replacements. We don't have time to bury them.*

The trucks pointed east because that was where the fighting was. There were only three trucks in the convoy where typically there would be at least a dozen. Two of the trucks were loaded with supplies and one with the soldiers. The engines idled and the air was full of diesel. With the increased risk of hijacking from black market bandits, it was odd for the convoy to have only three trucks and no armed escort.

The soldiers loaded into the last truck of the caravan. The first two trucks carried cigarettes, chewing gum, and K rations. In the Army's ineptness, there were also seven crates of beach towels and three crates of typewriters. The men loading the trucks followed orders, not common sense. If the manifest said ship typewriters and beach towels to the front, so be it.

The last truck in the convoy carried Joey and fifteen fresh-faced GIs ready to take the place of the dead and wounded. The truck rattled and swayed along an uneven dirt road as the countryside rolled by in muted tones, the landscape as bleak and colorless as their dull green uniforms. Sparse trees dotted the terrain, the skeletal branches shedding autumn leaves reached imploringly skyward. Dust kicked up by the convoy coated the trucks with a gritty film.

The truck's straining axles finally left the unpaved road and rattled along cobblestone and crossed a bridge. Joey sat at the back of the truck and peered out the opening in the canvas. A sign announced the village of Marle, a small borough, one of thousands torn by war. The main artery through town was narrow, paved with brick and stone, barely wide enough for the trucks. The three transport vehicles wound like a snake between small, whitewashed cottages, a tavern, a garage with old rusted vehicles that would never again spin their wheels.

The people of the village did not pour out of their homes with flowers and champagne as they had done a month earlier when the American Army first started passing through. These were just three more of the hundreds of armored vehicles chasing after the German Army. The faces of the villagers who watched them pass were now expressionless with stoic indifference.

A young woman framed in a second-floor window of a colorless building looked down menacingly as Joey's company of soldiers drove through Marle. The wild green eyes belonged to Monique Laurent, whose hatred of the war had been honed to a razor's edge. When the Germans first entered the small town of Marle at the beginning of the war, Monique's twelve-year-old brother fired their father's shotgun from a window. Although the shot hit no one, the boy was captured and hanged from the church steeple. Another twenty-two men, including Monique's aging father, were rounded up like cattle and marched to the gallows of a weeping willow tree at the end of town. Their rotting corpses were left swinging from its branches, a gruesome reminder that resistance would be dealt with swiftly and ruthlessly by the Nazis. Memories of her father, and Peter, her little brother with his mop of unruly hair and gap-toothed grin, never stopped haunting her.

She, too, had been euphoric when the first American soldiers liberated their town ending the oppressive grip of occupation. She threw flowers, and drunkenly kissed soldiers until she found herself dragged into an alley and violated by three bearded Americans. They smelled like pigs. Other soldiers watched as she was being ravaged and did nothing as she cried for help. Monique's mind and heart, once long ago filled with love and hope, were now barbed wire and broken glass. She spat at the passing trucks, who were no longer liberators, but just another wave of Satan in this bloody nightmare of war.

Four years ago, when the horrors of Marle began, a Nazi regiment had bivouacked in the town and were held there as reserves behind the advancing German Army. Some officers took command of the only hotel. Other soldiers moved into the town's homes and nearby farmhouses. Three officers stayed at the Fauxbourg farmhouse less than a kilometer away. The farm had become almost deserted, a barren shell of what it used to be. The men of the family had vanished, and only the daughter Yvette remained.

But many in Marle kept a quiet vigilant watch. Secret meetings were held by several of the villagers, including their ring leader, Monique Laurent. A list was being made of German collaborators whose deeds would not go unpunished. There was Francois, the garage mechanic in town who seemed more than eager to help the Germans repair their war vehicles. There was the mayor, Jean Claude Dubois, who had given the location of three French resistance soldiers who were soon found by the Nazis and shot. There were others who would face justice when the time was right. Besides these, rumors, thick and fetid, swirled around the Fauxbourg farm. Monique and others suspected Yvette had become the German officer's whore. When Yvette ventured into town, Monique noticed that Yvette had nicer and cleaner clothing than the rest. She seemed untouched by the hunger that was gnawing at everyone. To Monique, she was no better than the filthy Nazis who murdered her own family.

However, it was more than that. Hatred, a black and venomous snake, coiled inside Monique. She had always despised Yvette for as long as she could remember, dating back to their young schoolhouse days when Yvette was considered the prettiest girl around Marle. Monique, plain and overlooked, thought Yvette stuck her nose in the air like she was better than everyone. The Fauxbourg farm had once been the biggest and most prosperous farm in the area, and Yvette was the pretty girl who had everything. Monique's mind seethed whenever she thought of Yvette Fauxbourg. Judgment Day could not come soon enough for Monique. The harlot's crimes would not escape the punishment she deserved.

As the last truck clattered through the stone streets of Marle, Joey locked eyes with the angry women staring from the second-floor window. She shook her fist. Fury contorted her face. She screamed words, a torrent of French Joey could not understand.

The truck rattled on, and Joey's head began to ache. The bouncing truck shook his senses taking him back to a place that still gave him nightmares. The passing terrain became a sickly yellow. He saw the ghost of the little girl he murdered, and her pleading brown eyes. A finger pointed, piercing his soul. She whispered, "Help me." Joey's vision blurred, and his face twitched. A soldier bouncing on the seat across from him stared at him.

"Are you okay, bud?" he shouted at Joey, but Joey did not respond. The young grunt nudged the soldier next to him. "Check this guy out. I think he's somewhere on Jupiter."

Less than a mile after leaving Marle, the truck driver slammed on the brakes and several soldiers fell to the floor. There was shouting and shooting outside. It was the sound of a .50-machine gun, an American gun.

"Out of the trucks! Out of the trucks!" a man was hollering.

The driver of the transport truck suddenly appeared at the back and said calmly, "Nobody panic. We're being robbed. Nobody do anything stupid. Just do what they say, all right? Weapons and back packs on the floor. Get out slow."

The men squinted in the glare of the sun as they jumped from the back of the truck. They were on a dirt road with nothing around but fields of brown grass and stubbles of shrubs. A half-dozen men materialized from the tall grass, machine guns held nonchalantly, faces obscured by crude bandanas. Their menacing eyes, however, burned with cold purpose.

One of the men who wore a bright red bandana across his nose and mouth took charge. "We're Americans. We are not here to hurt or kill you, but we will if you fuck with us. We're taking these trucks and everything in them, and I want to see all of you walking back from where you came. Consider yourself lucky that you probably won't be slaughtered by the Huns today."

The drivers of the trucks seemed to take all this in stride, like they were expecting to be hijacked. One of the drivers, a corporal, spoke up. "Come on, men. Do as they say. We got a good hike back to camp." On both sides of the road and in front of the caravan were jeeps armed with heavy caliber machine guns. The bewildered GIs did as they were ordered and walked away in a loose line.

The sun bore down relentlessly, broiling the soldiers, prompting most to remove their helmets. One of the grunts muttered, "This takes the goddamned cake. It's 1944 and we've just been robbed by the Jesse James Gang." The bandit's guns stayed trained on the men until they were out of sight. Another jeep followed down the road to make sure all the soldiers were leaving.

However, Rico Adduci couldn't tear his gaze from the one tall soldier in the group. The soldier had a glazed look in his eye as though he were in a trance. Rico finally recognized him as the tall kid on their transport ship from the US. A cold dread snaked its way through Rico. What if this guy knew who he was? It would be best to shoot him now. As far as the Army and world were concerned, Enrico Adduci was dead. But he trusted Joey when he was at the rigged poker game on the transport ship, and he decided to trust him now. Rico watched Joey carefully as he walked away, and the boy seemed oblivious to what was happening. Still, Rico couldn't shake the unease. Even so, he let Joey walk away, unharmed.

Rico and his cohorts roared off in the stolen trucks while the unarmed soldiers straggled back down the dusty road. This was certainly a story to tell their loved ones back home when the war was over. Their commanding officer led the way, occasionally looking back to make sure everyone was following. Joey didn't know where he was going. He lagged behind and stumbled off the road into a field of knee-high grass.

He kept walking. He touched the top of the high grass with his fingers. There was the mild scent of rosemary in the cool air. The dry autumn leaves on nearby trees looked down at Joey and cackled in the wind. The world around him dissolved into a milky fog until a skinny boy in a ragged shirt and a rope tied around his waist to hold up his pants emerged from the trees. They both stopped and stared at each other. The boy beckoned Joey with his hands to follow. Joey, as if hypnotized, followed the child into the thickening darkness of the woods.

Chapter 22

Rico Adduci chewed his fingernails, except for the one shot off on D-day, which was still bandaged. He cursed. His mole at the Army supplies had said this caravan of trucks would be filled with weapons. *Typewriters? Beach towels? What the hell?* He got about twenty M1 rifles out of the heist, which would have to do. Rico had orders to fill. There were Caledonians from northern Spain looking to buy weapons for their insurgency. This pathetic caravan was supposed to be carrying bazookas and automatic weapons.

Rico had just filled an order of weapons for Mafia gangsters from northern Italy. They had traveled north into France to buy weapons. Besides two cases of Thompson submachine guns, Adduci and his crew had stolen and dismantled a tank. The mafiosi bought that as well and hauled it away in three large trucks.

The money was flowing in a subterranean torrent as Rico was now operating the largest black market ring in France. His biggest competition was the Beaumont Gang just south of Paris. He hated them not just because of the competition, but because they had a deserted Nazi colonel working with them. It burned Rico that Frenchmen would have a Nazi son-of-a-bitch whose armies invaded and raped France for years, teaming up with them. The only name the Nazi went by was Otto. He sported a patch over one eye and was rarely seen. Before Rico would leave France with his fortune, he was going to kill this one-eyed Nazi bastard.

Besides stealing contraband from the US Army, Rico had sculpted his own private death squad. He tried to go out at least once a week under the cloak of night with two French Resistance fighters and kill a German officer or two behind enemy lines. Rico just loved the danger. All this thievery was too easy, and he loved the hunt. This was Rico Adduci's own private war. The danger was intoxicating and gave him a perverse high that simple robbery lacked.

The US Army was aware of these American deserters turned thieves. They called them the Chicago Gang for no other reason than their extreme violence. But the gang was slippery, and the military had no idea where their hideouts were.

Ten miles west of Paris was an abandoned farmhouse. Its cavernous barn was crammed with pilfered goods, compliments of the US Army: K rations, cigarettes, candy, flour, sugar, clothing, cured sausages. The gang even boasted a large walk-in refrigerator, a marvel of modern engineering powered by a humming generator, all to keep meat from spoiling. Meat and petroleum were in the greatest demand from the French population.

Security was paramount. The hideout was carefully guarded. The narrow road to the barn and the farm perimeter were guarded twenty-four hours a day by machine-gun posts meticulously camouflaged in haystacks. Rico had officers in the US military police on his payroll, so being raided was not likely to happen. And most importantly, a Colonel Conway in Army logistics and ordnance was also on Rico's payroll. Conway sent crates of cash to Rico's connection in New York on a weekly basis. Bank accounts had been set up for Rico and his men. The money could be dispersed easily when they got home. If they got home.

Henri, Rico's second-in-command, asked, "What the hell do we do with these typewriters? This barn is already filled up."

"I don't know, throw them in there somewhere. Put out some feelers to see if anyone has any interest." Henri walked away, shaking his head and muttering to himself in French.

Rico continued to chew his fingernails, barely noticing the blood oozing from his fingertips. He was thinking about Joey Kowalski. The good looking kid he took a liking to on the Atlantic Ocean had transformed into something distant and haunted. It was the look of someone traumatized by combat. Rico had seen it before. *What a waste*, Rico thought. On the ship, he had offered for Joey to join his gang if they ever reached the shores of France. He should have accepted.

Rico spit a bit of blood onto the dusty ground. "Henri!" he called out. "Call in the sentries. We have to take care of Bruno."

It was a beautiful crisp autumn day, and the sun warmed everything it touched. A blindfolded man kneeled next to a hole in the ground at the back of the barn was sobbing.

"Please don't. Please don't."

"Gag him," Rico ordered. Henri took a filthy rag and stuffed it roughly into the man's mouth.

Rico's men gathered around staring at Bruno solemnly.

"Listen. We are thieves. But we don't steal from each other. Our success is based on trust. When this war finally ends, we are all gonna be rich as kings, but Bruno here thought he should get more than his fair share. He stole from us. A man who cannot be trusted may also decide to squeal on us."

One of the men, another deserter named Fricke, watched in horror. He and Bruno were best friends. Fricke's only friend. They had gone through basic training together. They had survived D-Day together. He was the one who talked Bruno into deserting and stealing their supply truck. Rico, who noticed everything, saw the grimace on Fricke's face. He didn't like it.

"Fricke, you got something to say?" Fricke stayed silent.

Rico pulled his revolver from his holster, walked behind the man, and shot him in the back of the head. He kicked the lifeless body until Bruno fell into the hole. "Cover him up," he ordered. Rico's mind went back to business. They needed to load up trucks to meet buyers early tomorrow morning. This was a part of his thievery that he hated. He did not have a good sense of his inventory, which made things easier for people like Bruno to steal. He kicked the dirt and walked towards a back door to the barn. He missed Annette, his gal from home. She had taken care of all the mundane, boring chores that made for a well-oiled organization.

"Those on sentry, get back to your haystacks," Rico ordered.

Chapter 23

Joey mindlessly followed the boy, his mind in a sluggish haze. The cool, damp air began to make his aching head feel better. The boy could have been leading him to his death, but he didn't care. Joey's senses slowly returned. He looked around the heavy wooded forest. Where was he? Where was he going? For all he knew, he could have been in a fairy tale heading to a witch's gingerbread house.

The woods rose around the two travelers, a cathedral of pine, oak, and maple—old-growth giants draped in blackened beech. Autumn had set the canopy of foliage ablaze, a collage of gold and blood-red. Joey stared at the back of the little boy's grey vest as he followed with increasing unease.

They followed a worn path, a ribbon of soft earth and rotting moss, winding through in hushed concealment. The air was thick with the sweet dank of decay. Crooked limbs arched overhead like gnarled fingers, blotting out the sun. Joey looked up and around him. Light filtered through in flickers, dappling the forest floor with trembling specks.

They kept walking until the path abruptly ended. The boy dodged trees and bushes while Joey trailed behind. The wooded area opened into a large empty field. In the distance was an old, weathered limestone farmhouse. Next to the house was a barn with a round turret. At one time this may have been a productive, busy farm. Now, the fields lay fallow, choked with weeds. The farmhouse bore the scars of neglect with holes in the roof, a patchwork of missing shingles.

As they neared the house a goat appeared from nowhere and began to walk beside them. It began chewing on Joey's jacket.

"Va-t'en, Agathe!" The boy swatted the goat on top of its head and shooed the skinny animal away. There were chickens clucking in the barn. A single brown cow with white spots, ribs protruding, stood in the middle of a field chewing on weeds.

The boy wrestled a large steel latch that opened the heavy front door of the house. They entered a surprisingly bright and clean room. Fabric, meticulously stretched across missing windowpanes, diffused the sunlight. The floor was a tapestry of red terra-cotta punctuated by orange patches worn smooth by countless footsteps. The walls may have once been painted a vibrant red, but had faded into a forlorn pink of different hues. Some parts of the wall were wallpapered with a pattern long ago faded. The boy led Joey into a room next to the kitchen with a fireplace. One of the walls boasted a small library covered with books.

Joey wondered about his predicament. Why was he being treated kindly? Who was this boy? He tried to focus on the boy's face. His skin was drawn tight over high cheek bones, a sign of malnutrition. The stunning aspect of the boy was his eyes, chestnut brown, young and old at the same time. A strange contradiction. Joey was led to a narrow wood staircase.

"You are tired. Come. You must sleep."

Joey followed the boy to a steep stairway which was more like a ladder that led to an upper hallway with three rooms. He was ushered to the first room, sparsely furnished with a bed, a small desk, and a chair.

"You speak English," Joey said.

"Oui."

The boy removed a large woolen cap, the kind Chicago newsboys wear while hawking papers on the street. When he removed his ragged jacket, Joey saw small breasts. The boy was not a boy. She shook her tangled head and a cascade of auburn hair fell to her shoulders. Joey said what was now obvious. "You're a girl!"

"Yes. My name is Yvette Fauxbourg. This is my farm. You are welcome here. Come now. You must sleep."

Joey had slept for he did not know how long. He rose slowly. The faint sunlight of dusk bled through the window. Looking out the window, he saw broken fields and a crimson sun beginning to drop beneath a distant tree line. There was a rotted wooden fence next to the barn which was once a pen for pigs, but pigs no more. Another broken fence stretched for several acres. All was overgrown and choked with goosegrass and prickly shrub.

There was a small area under his window which was apparently the family's vegetable garden. There were still some vegetables hanging from the dying plants. Winter would be casting its long shadows soon. The fence around the garden was a hodgepodge of posts, chains, and barbed wire designed to keep out deer. The farm had not seen a deer in years.

Joey went back and sat on the edge of the bed which was a large white cloth filled with straw. He recognized the cloth as silk from a parachute. He laid back down and again fell into a deep sleep. When he awoke, the moon was full and from the window the land glowed a soupy white. It was windy and scattered clouds blocked the moon now and again turning the land into a strobe of pearl white and then darkness as though operated by a switch. The wind grew stronger and wailed angrily through the trees. A storm was coming. Joey had learned since D-Day that a storm was always coming. He sighed the sigh of a tired old man.

Down below in the fractured moonlight, the girl who had led him to this place was preparing a bath in a large steel tub near a well. She was thin and her shoulders were bony. He could see her ribs which were like the emaciated cow Joey had seen earlier chewing on weeds.

Joey fell back into his bed and stared at the barely illuminated wood timbers of the ceiling. It was finally dawning on him that he was a deserter, a fugitive. He had deserted the US Army and could be shot if caught. What did it matter? He felt half-dead already. Sleep again overwhelmed him, and he did not awaken until the following morning.

The fog from the previous day had gradually disappeared from Joey's head. He smelled bread baking in the kitchen below. He walked carefully down the stairway grasping a skinny handrail.

"Good morning," the girl said.

"Good morning," Joey replied feebly. He looked around the kitchen. The smell of bread was intoxicating.

"You live here alone?" Joey asked. She didn't answer.

"Where did you learn English?"

"When I was 14, I served as a tutor in England for a year. My mother was a teacher before she died and taught me and my brothers English." She wiped flour from her hands on an apron that had little yellow flowers, and studied the tall boy sitting at her table. There was vulnerability in his eyes, a haunted quality that resonated with a loneliness she knew all too well.

"When my father died, my brothers took over the farm and I took a job in England. I taught French to three young girls in London who were the daughters of a wealthy aristocrat. I stayed on the third floor of their house with the other servants. When war started, I came back home. I worried for my family."

At one side of the kitchen was a short China cabinet with a red plaid cloth thrown over it. On it were photos of a man and woman which Joey assumed were her parents. And another of three young boys and a girl. One of the boys had an enormous smile on his face.

"And where are they now?" Joey asked.

"When the Germans invaded Belgium all three of my brothers went off to war. The French Army and my brothers fought the Germans as long as the Army could hold, but we were annihilated. My oldest brother,"

Yvette paused, "was killed in the fighting. My other brothers passed through quickly as the Army retreated. I have not seen or heard from them since. I don't know where they are." She had cried about this often but there were no more tears left.

"The way you dress like a boy? Did the Germans hurt you?"

"When the Nazis came through, three officers used our home for a full week. They never touched me. They were perfect gentlemen. I slept in the barn that whole time. And then they were gone. I'm sorry but it is the American soldiers that I fear. Many are disgusting and there are many stories of rape and worse. Many of your soldiers passed by. Two men tried to . . ." Her face reddened. She pointed out the window. "I was in the barn. But they were stopped by an officer. That is when I became a boy."

Joey understood. "I won't hurt you."

"I know."

Yvette Fauxbourg was 17 years old. She had the face of a young girl but there was a heavy shadow of pain beneath her dark eyes. When she told the story of her family, her gaze became fierce. Her dark eyes became darker. She had spent three years alone and foraged what she could. She survived on vegetables and potatoes from her garden. She bartered milk from her cow and goat with the neighboring farmers who were just as bad off as she, but the cow could no longer give milk. The corn feed they used to give to their cows and pigs in such copious amounts disappeared when the war came. The few chickens the Germans left were producing half the eggs they used to.

"Why did you lead me here?" Joey asked.

"Why did you follow me?" She smiled, and for the first time Joey saw beauty in her smile and eyes. He briefly felt a sexual longing for this girl, and then immediately was ashamed.

"You saw those men with the guns that stole the trucks I was in?"

"Oui. Americans. Black marketeers. They are part of the black market."

"You know where they are? Do you know where they hide out?"

"You do not want to know. They are very dangerous. They have stolen much and have much to sell but I cannot afford. Many people buy or trade with them. The rationing cards that the Americans have given us are not much better than the German rationing. Barely enough to survive. My people are forced to go to the black market."

Yvette continued to eye the American that sat at her table. He took a slice of bread and smeared jam on it. Joey noticed there was very little jam left in the jar, so he spread it sparingly. The bread was still warm.

"God. You don't know how good this tastes. My mom used to bake bread."

Yvette put dishes away in the cupboard pushing aside the pistol, a German luger, she kept behind the cups. "You have a family back home?"

Joey nodded, his family now a distant image. "Mom and a sister. Dad's gone. I also had a little brother." Joey' voice trailed off. "A long time ago."

"A handsome boy like you must have a girl back home?" Yvette immediately blushed from such a personal question to a perfect stranger. "I am sorry," she apologized.

Joey stopped chewing. "No. No girlfriend."

Maybe this tall, skinny boy was the angel Yvette had been praying for. She had followed him after he wandered away from his comrades after the hijacking.

This was her farm, the Fauxbourg farm. She would make it great again, but she needed help. A man. A woman on her own could never make it in this world, and she would never leave this place. She and the farm would be here when her brothers finally returned from the war.

Joey scratched the whiskers on his chin. He had not shaved since the hospital. He had hidden it at the time, but he had recognized one of the bandits, their apparent leader. "I know one of them. We crossed together on the same ship when we came over from the U.S."

"They are very dangerous. They are called the Chicago gangsters."

Joey stood and looked out a window. It had rained while he slept. He was now an outlaw, a deserter. Why didn't he feel ashamed or guilty? He knew he was unable to fight and kill anymore but maybe he could help this young girl.

Joey tried to remember the bandit's name. "Rico," he said aloud. "Rico Adduci. My friends call me, "Deuce." He turned and faced Yvette. "And he's not from Chicago. You think this black market has feed for your cow?"

"I think they have everything if you are willing to pay for it, but I have nothing."

"Help me find them."

Joey's memory of France was a blur of bombed out towns and frantic fighting. He'd seen little of the "real" France, only fleeting glimpses of gaunt faces peering from shattered windows – human skeletons compliments of German rationing. Yvette's cow and goat were skin and bones and she herself was just as thin. With the invasion underway, the Allies, like the Nazis before them, gave ration cards to the French people for sustenance, but it was still a limited diet. The millions of Allied soldiers in this devastated country needed food too.

Chapter 24

Captain John Jacob Myers's small office in Paris reeked of stale cigarettes and perspiration. Eight steel file cabinets in a shoebox room allowed very little space for a desk and two chairs. There were no windows, and ventilation was poor. Myers's chain-smoking did not help with air quality or visibility, but he had other things to worry about. He had the unenviable task of dealing with the mass desertions taking place in the fighting theater and the deserters who had gone rogue in the French black market.

Myers was only thirty years old, but the crow legs around his eyes showed a much older man. His once sharp eyesight had become poor from reading endless reports and documents. He kept putting off seeing the regiment eye doctor for prescription glasses. His once black hair was now peppered with gray and cut into a flattop that one could set a cup of coffee on.

His job was to catch the American deserters who formed gangs and were stealing mostly from the American Army. They were hurting the war effort. There was one particular gang that was the biggest and most dangerous. He had scant descriptions of the leader and did not know who he was. Whoever he was, he was very good at thievery and invisibility. Besides trying to catch these criminals, he also had to deal with the corruption in the ranks of the Army—US officers who were undoubtedly helping these gangsters pilfer war supplies.

Although they were deserters, the men in these gangs were not cowards. Nearly all had seen combat and were trained killers, courtesy of the US Army. With Paris just recently liberated, the French police were unorganized and ragtag at best. They had no desire to tackle these well-armed, military-trained hoodlums.

Corporal Peterson, with narrow eyes and a narrow head, knocked on Captain Myers's office door. He entered and saluted smartly.

"Stop with that saluting shit." Captain Myers was tired.

"Sorry, sir. I have some more reports here from several small villages north of Paris. Leschelle, Signy-le-Petit, Fresnoy-le-Grand. It's the Chicago Gang again."

"Who did they rob now?" The gang's thievery was insatiable.

"They weren't stealing."

Captain Myers lifted his head from his paperwork. "What?"

"They were giving food and clothing away to the villagers. Mostly stolen American goods. What do you think they are up to?"

Myers shook his head. "So, they are pulling some kind of Robin Hood crap. That's all we need. No wonder nobody wants to turn these bastards in." Captain Myers remembered Al Capone doing something similar in Chicago during the Depression, opening several food kitchens, giving meals away for free, swaying the public opinion to ignore his murderous activity. *Yes*, the captain thought to himself, *this bastard is very clever indeed.*

It was the end of another very long day for Captain Myers. He needed sleep more than anything. He gathered up paperwork to bring to his room at the relatively swank Hotel Lutetia where officers were being housed. But before he could escape, there was a knock at the door. Corporal Peterson entered and saluted. Captain Meyers looked at him angrily.

"Sorry, sir." Peterson sheepishly lowered his hand. "Captain, I think we might have a break here. A deserter turned himself in. Says he was with the Chicago Gang. Says he knows all about it. Says he wants a deal."

"Where is he?"

"In the interrogation room. He wants to make a deal."

Captain Myers scoffed. "He does, does he?"

"Would you like to see him now?"

Myers pushed his chair back. "Okay. Let's go."

A GI in handcuffs sat nervously behind a steel desk. A soldier with an M1 rifle stood next to the door watching. Myers and Corporal Peterson entered the room and sat in two chairs across from the prisoner. "Name?" Captain Myers demanded. He had looked briefly through the man's arrest folder and already knew his name.

"Private Eugene Fricke, 25327712."

"Desertion and theft of US war goods." Myers turned a cold eye towards the prisoner. "Frankly, Fricke, you are fucked." The guard at the door giggled. Myers turned angrily. "Sergeant, leave the room. Wait outside the door."

The guard stopped smiling. "Yes, sir."

"Fricke, if you don't face a firing squad, which is probable, you'll spend the rest of your life in prison. And a military prison is not a regular prison, which you will find out soon enough. There is no getting out for good behavior. There is no parole. Basically, your life is over one way or another."

Private Fricke straightened up in his chair. "I want to make a deal."

"There are no deals. If you help us find this gang of thieves, and most importantly, their leader, the judge may grant leniency, and I will request it for you. But only if we catch this mob. What's the leader's name?"

"I don't know. He goes by Deuce or Rico. Nobody knows his real name."

Corporal Peterson took notes.

"What does he look like?"

"I don't know," Private Fricke said, shaking his head. "He's short."

"How short?" Captain Myers stood. "This tall?" Myers stood and pointed his fingers horizontally below his own eyes.

"Shorter."

Myers kept moving his hand down until it was at his neck.

"There. That's about right," Fricke said.

"About five four," Myers said. Peterson kept taking notes. "Hair color?"

"Black."

"What's his face look like? Anything distinguishable?"

"I don't know. He's kind of funny looking."

"Funny looking? How?"

"He's got a single black eyebrow that goes all the way across his head."

"Unibrow." Peterson kept jotting notes.

Fricke went on to say the gang never stayed in one place for long.

"He's got a bunch of safe houses. I know that. He's even got an office somewhere in Paris, I think."

The prisoner sitting before Captain Myers thought angrily of the day Rico callously shot his friend Bruno and buried him in a hole behind the barn.

"He likes to steal gas," Fricke offered. "Most of the time he goes himself with two or three trucks with fake requisition papers. The depot at Chatou is an easy mark. He hits that every couple of weeks. Sometimes more. If you wait there, you can catch him for sure. But you better be careful. The gang is armed to the teeth."

"Sergeant!" Myers yelled. The guard entered the room. "Get him out of here."

As Fricke was leaving, he said loudly to Captain Myers, "Remember our deal. Remember."

Myers did not respond.

Chapter 25

Through village informants, word reached Rico that a tall American deserter wanted to meet with him, and Rico had a good idea who it was. He sent two Frenchmen in berets to a dirt crossroad a mile from Yvette's farm. They waited. Each man held an English-made Sten machine gun. They kept their stolen US Army jeep idling in case this was a trap. From a distance, Joey thought the men waiting might be American soldiers and hesitated to approach them. Joey, the deserter, had no plans of being arrested. He was done with this war and would not become its prisoner. Joey walked towards the jeep slowly.

"I assume you're waiting for me." Joey said.

The men did not reply, but instead they blindfolded Joey, and put him in the back of the jeep. Joey bounced and bumped for what was several miles until they lurched to a stop. In the distance there was a house with three large barns. From behind a nearby haystack next to the dirt road, two men emerged carrying American-made Thompson machine guns. The Frenchmen nodded to each. The only word Joey recognized was "Deuce." They proceeded down the road towards the barns.

When the jeep finally stopped, Joey was allowed to remove his blindfold. Rico Adduci came out the front wooden door of the farmhouse, all smiles. "I was wondering when you would find me." He motioned to the men with the machine guns to point their barrels downward. "They are used to shooting men who are blindfolded," he chuckled. "So, you want to join my gang."

Joey looked around the farm area. Young boys and girls, orphaned by the war, were hurrying in and out of the barns. Men were unloading trucks filled with crates while other men loaded trucks with other crates. It was a beehive of activity. "It looks like you have quite an operation here," Joey said.

"Let's just say business is booming," Rico replied with a wink. "C'mon. I'll show you around."

They entered the nearest barn, and it was filled with piles of K rations, canned goods, guns of different sizes and calibers, and bags of wheat, corn, and other grains. Joey could hear the whir of a generator.

Children, no older than eleven or twelve, were rifling through the enormous piles of K-tins.

"What are they doing?" Joey asked.

"They are sorting out the corned beef from the rest of the K rats. I have an order for one hundred fifty cans from some village south of Tours."

Joey took a deep breath. "I need a favor."

Rico stopped and turned his head sideways. He was no longer smiling. "A favor? And what do I get in return?"

"I don't have anything, but I did save your life back on the transport ship."

"And I saved yours. When I recognized you when we stole your trucks, I should've shot you."

"Why didn't you?"

Rico shrugged. "I don't know. Maybe I did owe you one. I guess I trust you. You did do me a good turn. I haven't forgotten that. Can I trust you?"

Joey looked at the children sorting through cans of rations. "Seems pretty inefficient," Joey offered. "All the K rats should have come separated in the crates. Why are they all dumped in a big pile?"

Rico looked up at the tall deserter quizzically.

"If you want my free advice, all that should be sorted out when it arrives and consolidated."

"Consolidated?"

"Yeah. Separated, so it is easy to find when you need it. All those guns you've got piled over there should be separated by weapon type. The ammo for each weapon should be consolidated near the weapon it is meant for."

"Consolidated," Rico murmured. "What do you know about consolidated?"

Joey's mind went back to the dime store and stocking the shelves he had built for the store's merchandise. "Plenty," Joey said. "Are those bazookas over there? Is that a forklift?"

"We got everything, and I plan on selling everything. We are making a bundle here. I thought I was doing good in New York, but we are just killing it here. I had some guys here a week ago from the Italian Mafia. They bought a tank. God knows what they're going to do with it," Rico laughed.

"I didn't come here to help you."

Rico's eyes became suspicious. "You're a deserter just like me. What did you come here for?"

"I need feed for a cow. It's skin and bones and won't give milk."

"Ha, so the kid from Chicago is now a farmer."

"It's not for me." Joey paused. "It's for a friend."

"Really? What's her name?" Joey didn't answer.

"Tell you what," Rico said. "You help me get this place organized, consolidated, and I'll give you enough grain for a whole ranch."

Joey was silent for a moment. "You got anybody here who knows carpentry? Can you get me construction lumber? Two-by-fours? Plywood?"

Rico smiled. "You got it."

With the help of two French carpenters, it took Joey only a day to build large shelves to house all the different merchandise that Rico's army had stolen. Pallets were built and the forklift was used to move stolen booty to waiting trucks for orders to be shipped out. All merchandise was stored off the ground to help prevent moisture, rodent, and mold problems.

Rico was impressed, and when he was impressed, he could be very generous. Nearly a ton of corn feed and wheat straw was delivered to the door of Yvette's farm. He even threw in two goats, and another cow. Rico didn't care much for goats. He was, however, reluctant to give up any cows as meat was a scarcity among the French. Meat drew an extra high price on the black market. The chefs at the Paris restaurants would salivate like wolves when Rico showed up with butchered meat for steaks.

But the real money wasn't mooing in a field. It was petrol. Gasoline. The Army supply system was so screwed up, Rico's gang could basically drive in and fill as many cans of gas as they wanted with fake requisition papers. Every business in the country relied on gasoline. It was scarce, and Rico's store was always open.

Chapter 26

One misty morning, Joey awoke at Yvette's farm to find she was not there. An unfamiliar pang of loneliness hit him unexpectedly. The ache was sharp and pricked at his chest until he realized what it was. He was falling in love.

Yvette had begun to smile and laugh more each day, and it wasn't just because he was able to get things to help the farm. She had let her guard down, and Joey found this girl to be smart, funny, and delightful without guile. Her dark, brooding eyes now sparkled, and it gave him some morbid hope that he was not dead inside, that he had something left in him that was worthwhile.

A broad grin raced across his face when he heard the clatter of bicycle wheels on the front cobblestone. Yvette leaned the bike against the barn wall, her face was flushed, and her hair plastered to her forehead with sweat. Several bulging sacks hung from the handlebars. Joey helped her carry items into the house.

"I didn't want to do it," Yvette said, "but I had to trade one of the chickens. We needed flour and other things. You need new clothing and I have no more buttons. You cannot stay hidden very well in that uniform."

Yvette imagined the day when the farm would be back to its old self. The cows would be giving milk to trade or sell. The goats would provide cheese. The fields would wave with golden wheat. The thoughts of the future overwhelmed her, and without thinking, she ran and hugged a surprised Joey. The warmth of her arms made him tingle all the way to his toes. His mind became a confused battle of unspoken desires. He held her tightly in his arms and then the passion hit a stop sign when he saw tears in her eyes.

"What's wrong? Why are you crying? Did something happen?"

"No. No. I am just so happy you are here." Yvette pulled away from Joey embarrassed and wiped her eyes. "You don't know what it's been like. You are an angel sent to me from heaven." She looked at him awkwardly and blushed at this lanky, bushy-headed boy and the aroused thoughts she found running through her mind and body.

Joey smiled. He felt good inside. His headaches were less and less with each passing day, and he rarely had nightmares anymore. He looked at Yvette's bicycle.

"Where do you go to trade?"

"There is a village, Tergnier, about eleven kilometers from here. The people are very kind."

"My transport passed a village. I think it was called Marle, a short distance from here. Why not trade there instead of biking so far?"

"I have my reasons. I am not welcome there."

"What reasons?"

Yvette sighed. "Monique Laurent. She is a miserable girl. I still have some friends in town. They warned me. Monique has accused me of sleeping with the German soldiers who stayed here in my house. I never did. We went to school together when we were children. She has hated me since we were little girls. I don't know why. Maybe she thought I was prettier than her. Maybe she thought I stole a boyfriend from her so long ago. It is all so childish, but I feel sorry for her. Her family was murdered by the Nazis. She is dangerous. Now that the Germans are gone, she has become more dangerous."

If only for a short while, Joey had forgotten the tremendous terror of the war, and now, listening to Yvette, he was jolted back to where they really were, smack-dab in the middle of hell on earth, and the deep wounds that had destroyed and bloodied so many.

Now that the farm had some livestock, thanks to Rico Adduci's thievery, Yvette and Joey mended fences to keep the animals from wandering. With shingles from the garage, Joey fixed the hole in the house roof that poured water through the ceiling of the upper bedroom. The two cows fattened up quickly. With winter fast approaching, the animals would stay mostly in the barn, but the land would soon become a farm again.

Joey enjoyed this new life. The work was hard, but he found himself worrying less and less about the war. Yvette worked as hard, or harder than Joey, and he found himself staring at her longer than he should. She had a strength and vigor that belied her slender frame.

Yvette had loved her brothers, and she liked to tell stories about them when they were young. Her brothers did not treat her like a girl, and they let her tag along with them when they were out playing. She remembered them dancing the Charleston in their kitchen to the radio, which the Germans had since taken. They played ping-pong on the dining room table. It wasn't the bad times that saddened Yvette; it was the good, wonderful, loving times she had with her family—the times now murdered by the Nazi invasion.

"Do you still have ping-pong paddles?"

"You have played the game?"

Joey smiled at the memory of playing that girl in ping-pong at the USO party a million years ago. Yvette went to her cupboard and took out a net, paddles, and a ping-pong ball. She set up a game on the dining room table. Joey lost again and again, and Yvette laughed at this big American who was so inept at the game.

At one point, they both crawled beneath the table in pursuit of a lost ball. On hands and knees, they stared at each other. An irresistible force pulled their faces closer and closer. It was the first time they kissed. Their kissing became intense, igniting a firestorm in their loins. Frantically they tore at each other's clothing and made love beneath the dining room table. The warmth he felt when she was in his arms made him forget the outside world. Joey felt a wonderful lightheadedness. *I belong here*, he thought to himself. *This is where I belong.*

After that, they made love nearly every day in a youthful, mad frenzy, forgetting all the horrors of their past. As they rested peacefully, Yvette ran her fingertips along the white scar on Joey's neck that ran beneath his ear down to his shoulder.

"Does it still hurt?"

"No. It tingles sometimes."

"Do you mind me touching it? It is so smooth."

Joey just smiled, rolled over and grabbed Yvette around her waist, and pulled her closer. All his fears vanished whenever Yvette smiled and held him tight. The soothing power of her breath against his body with her arms held tightly around him was indescribable. Yvette also felt a healing of her entire mind and body. She thought she could never feel real happiness again, but here it was in the gift of a tall American deserter.

Chapter 27

Rico and Henri rumbled down the dirt road in a jeep back to their hideout. Henri, chewing on a wet cigar, was the chauffeur. Rico had a lot on his mind. A member of Rico's gang, Eugene Fricke, had disappeared. He knew Fricke and the recently departed Bruno had been friends, and Rico had a bad feeling that if that weasel surrendered, he would betray him. Back at the barn, Rico had left Joey in charge to make sure things got done. He wanted all his people working double-time to clear out the barns so they could relocate to a new location.

Back at the barn, Joey and several young boys and girls had already loaded all the stolen contraband into six trucks ready to be shipped to an unknown destination. The goods were separated and meticulously categorized in an orderly fashion that Joey supervised—foodstuffs, weapons, ammunition, kitchen appliances, clothing. Rico decided they keep several stolen typewriters for forging ration cards. All they needed was the paper that they were printed on, and Rico knew he could get it.

When the convoy of trucks was ready to set out, Joey wondered where the hell Rico was. He then saw a speck approaching on the horizon. It was a US Army jeep coming fast down the dirt road, and Joey became nervous. Every time he came to the hideout, he made sure a motorcycle with gas was ready at the back of the barn in case he needed a quick escape across the countryside. The sentries should've opened fire on any military police. Were they asleep?

"Andre, binoculars." A boy returned quickly. Joey saw an officer in Army fatigues in the jeep. It was Rico, who was wearing the colors of a lieutenant. Joey laughed. He handed the binoculars back to the boy.

Joey saluted Rico when he stepped from the jeep.

"Oh, cut that out. How we doing here? All loaded?"

"Sir, yes, sir," Joey said mockingly.

Rico laughed. "I'm a lieutenant," he said proudly.

"I see. Where are all these trucks headed?"

"A village north of Montdidier. They have pooled a mountain of cash and are buying everything for resale."

"Ah, you're going wholesale. Good move. You don't have to charge sales tax." Rico did not get the joke.

"Listen," Joey said. "I need a few small items if you can get them."

Rico squinted his eyes. "Now what?"

Joey noticed blood splattered on Rico's pants leg. "Rico, are you hit? You got shot?"

"Ain't my blood." Rico smiled. "What small items were you looking for?"

"Well, it's a grocery list for a friend. I need enough fertilizer for two hectares of land. Don't ask me what a hectare is. A dozen steel buckets for cow and goat milk. And one other thing." Joey paused. "A mule."

Rico burst out laughing. "You stupid Polack. You fell for that dame. I thought it was just a temporary thing. Dumb. Dumb. Dumb. But I'm feeling very generous today. I took out my biggest competitor this afternoon. The Beaumont gang is history, and Lucky Pierre's luck has run out. That one-eyed Nazi bastard— well, let's just say that good eye ain't so good no more. Yeah, it's been a very good day."

Joey grimaced at the thought. "Well, can you get that stuff? I did a pretty good job of getting all this crap out of the barn in less than a day."

"Whoa, cowboy. I've already dropped off half a farm for you. I think that's payment enough."

"Gotta get the ground tilled and fertilized before winter."

Rico laughed again and shook his head. "You are a dope. Tell you what, tomorrow night if the weather's right, I'm going out and thin the Nazi herd. It's a little dangerous." Rico's eyes sparkled at the thought.

Joey's jaw clenched. "I'm done with killing. No more."

"I know you think what we're doing here is wrong, hurting the war effort and all." Rico's eyes became keen. "In the five months since I deserted Normandy, I've shot eleven Nazi officers. So, I'm helping the war effort and getting a little bit back in return. And I'm not asking you to kill anybody. Come take a look at this."

Joey thought about the road he had taken in the last year, from math scholarship to Army deserter, and now an outlaw in a land he hardly knew. Maybe Rico was right. Maybe the war did owe them after all they had been through. If Rico was killing Nazi officers, that had to be helping the war effort. If he and Yvette could get her farm going again, they could feed and emplcy nearby villagers, who were in desperate poverty. He and Yvette would be helping France get back on its feet.

Rico took Joey to the back of the jeep, where there was a large steel trunk. Stenciled on the top in white paint was:

US

SN 1PERSCOPE
INFRARED
SET NO. 3, 20000 VOLTS

Rico opened the lid.

"What the hell is this?" Joey recognized the M1 rifle, but there was also a large metal cylinder that looked like a bunch of coffee cans taped together. There were wires sticking out of it.

"It's a nighttime sniper's scope. We can see the enemy at night, and they can't see you. I was very lucky to get this one. Most are heading to fight Japs in the Pacific."

"It looks like something out of a Flash Gordon cartoon."

"I know. It does have some drawbacks. It only works within one hundred yards of the target. See those marks on the rifle stock? That's how many Nazi officers I've shot." Joey looked at the crude notches.

"Just like the Wild West."

Rico nodded proudly. "This thing is heavy. That's another drawback. Me and Henri can't be carrying this thing. Our guide needs to guide, and I need to shoot this thing when we get to the target. It weighs about fifty pounds, and we'll be traveling about ten miles if the info I have is correct. There are Nazis retreating from the south who aren't being chased by our main army yet. We'll go after them. You need a mule. I need a pack mule. I'll get you the stuff you want if you join me and Henri. We'll head out tomorrow after dark and hopefully be back before daylight. What do you say?"

Rico's offer was clear—a mule for Yvette's farm in exchange for his muscle. A trip under the cloak of night, a dance with death, and back before sunrise. Joey shook his head, but he couldn't refuse.

Only five months in this country, and Rico likely knew more about the battlefront situation than most US intelligence officers. Between his thieving informants in the Army, the local population, and the French Resistance fighters, he knew the condition of the enemy all too well. And Paris was now liberated, which opened a whole new avenue of revenue for the little gangster.

The Germans, unable to hold on to the city of Dijon, had begun a complete withdrawal from southern France. Their casualties were high, and their defense lines were thin. All veteran soldiers had been quickly sent north after the Normandy invasion. This left the south with a ragtag army of old veterans, and forced volunteers from various nations. The enemy's fighting morale was near zero. The weapons they carried were a mishmash of old, obsolete guns confiscated from all over Europe—Italian rifles, Czech mortars, Polish machine guns. Most of the soldiers had no training in any of these foreign weapons. There were virtually no trucks for evacuation, and, even if there were, petrol was scarce. Mules and horses pulled wagons full of soldiers and anything else that could be taken quickly. It was the officers in this retreating army whom Rico hoped to pick off while the picking was easy.

Later the next day, as the sun dripped blood-red on the horizon, Joey left Yvette and the farm. "It's just something I have to do," he told her. She was frightened.

Joey knew he had no choice. Rico had given him and Yvette so much, and he had grown to like and trust this dangerous little man. Besides, with healthy livestock and a harvest in the spring, he would be done with Rico's gang. A whole new life was ahead of him.

"I'll be back by sunup. Don't worry." After Joey left, Yvette went to the kitchen cupboard and took out a pistol which she brought to bed with her. She could not fall asleep.

A quarter moon cut the black sky like a sickle. Rico, Joey, and Henri packed their weapons in the dim lunar light.

"This is perfect," Rico said. He opened the green steel case and took out the infrared night scope and attached it to an M1 rifle. He removed the battery from the case and inserted two wires into the scope. A trigger mounted beneath the weapon activated the scope.

"Henri," Rico commanded. "Keep walking until you reach the end of the woods. Check this out." He handed the rifle to Joey. "Press the trigger here and look through the scope. Don't press the trigger on the rifle. We don't want to shoot Henri." Henri disappeared into the darkness.

Joey did what he was told and looked through the scope. To his astonishment, he saw the green figure of a man illuminated in the night. "Holy smokes. How does this thing do that?"

"I don't know. But it's the perfect thing for hunting Nazi bastards at night. They never know what hit them. Now, let's get moving. You lug the rifle and battery pack. Don't drop it."

"How the hell do we know where we're going? It's too dark."

"It's bright enough. Henri has been hunting these woods since he was a child. He doesn't need much light."

Rico had Joey open and close the case a half dozen times so he could noiselessly remove the weapon from its case when the time came. Rico had the steel case interior lined with towels. The case clasps were recently oiled. Silence would be paramount to their safety.

The air was icy, and the men coulc see their breath as they walked. Henri led the assassins through a wooded area that opened into empty fields. After several miles of hiking, the smell of manure and the tracks of animals pulling wagons showed that the retreating enemy was not far in front of them. Rico followed ten paces behind Henri. Joey carried the heavy weaponry and grew tired.

"Can we rest?"

"Not yet," Rico replied.

The ground was cold under their boots, and softly crunched as they moved with the furtive caution of animals. Joey could smell the pine trees and the earth. An owl hooted. It was too peaceful of a night for killing, he thought. The tiny moon disappeared behind clouds, and the darkness pressed in from all sides. They passed a small stream, and all the men drank from it. They scooped the cold water with their hands. Rico did not allow any canteens or cups that could rattle as they walked.

They moved quietly through rolling hills, staying hidden along the shadowy edge of the forest. Rico spoke not a word during their journey. Joey squinted into the murky distance and spotted a small, weathered cottage. There were no lights. No signs of life. Henri suddenly raised his arm, signaling the group to stop. Joey froze. Sitting against a tree, barely discernible in the dim light, was a lone German sentry. The soldier's rifle was propped against the trunk, and his head hung low.

"He is sleeping," Henri whispered. He removed a knife from its sheath at his belt and walked away into darkness. Joey could see nothing. Henri soon returned, wiping blood from his knife. He gave a hand signal for the others to follow him.

Soon they reached an opening in the trees and before them revealed a sprawling, haphazard scene of men and animals. German soldiers lay scattered on the ground, some sleeping while others sat upright, puffing on cigarettes. Joey made out the shapes of scattered wagons. The faint clink of metal and the occasional snort of mules broke the silence. The three assassins crawled slowly across the moist ground until they could hear men snoring.

"Joey, give me that gun," Rico whispered. He looked through the scope, which scanned the night in a ghostly green. Nearly every human being he could see was sitting, or lying on the ground sleeping. There was one image strutting in front of a tent. Rico knew it was an officer just by his arrogant swagger. He aimed the weapon and lined the crosshairs of the infrared scope at the middle of the man's chest. The German officer was lighting a cigarette when Rico's rifle cracked the night. The bullet drilled the man cleanly. The officer crumpled to the ground. Rico lowered the rifle and smiled. "Good night, Jew killer." He handed the M1 rifle to Joey.

The German camp came alive with shouting and movement.

"Let's get out of here." Henri was already trotting away. Joey was right behind him.

The first threads of dawn were seeping into the inky sky when the men arrived back at Rico's hideout. Rico watched Joey trot away in the dim light of morning. Each day was growing colder. Winter would soon be chewing on the land. Joey had told Rico he wanted no money from his help, that the farm supplies were enough, but this was a pittance as far as Rico was concerned. Rico knew it was important to take care of his accomplices.

Without Joey's knowledge, Rico had instructed his attorney in New York to send a cut of Rico's profits to the Kowalski Five and Dime in Chicago. Money bought loyalty where Rico Adduci came from. Even blood money.

Chapter 28

Yvette walked into her fields and could smell the chill of winter approaching fast. It was important to get fertilizer down before the ground became hard as a rock. As her father always preached, the autumn nutrients were crucial to prepare the soil for a vigorous spring growth. She could barely contain her excitement. It had been five long years since Yvette Fauxbourg had seen a mule plow her now ravaged fields. Plowing was tough business, and as strong as she was, she couldn't handle the beast and plow by herself. She needed to teach Joey.

"I will show you first how to harness Maisie."

"Maisie? You name all your animals?" Joey asked.

"Of course. Don't you?"

"Um. We had some mice and rats. Never named any. Mostly, my mom would just womp 'em with a broom."

"Maisie looks like a good worker." She kissed its neck. The mule had long sad ears and a sharp backbone. Yvette could see that this animal had done field work before. She wondered how this beautiful creature could have survived the war. The mule's jet-black mane glistened.

"Come here, Yank." Yvette said playfully. She had Joey remove a leather bridal hanging from the barn wall. She showed him how to attach it around Maisie's neck. Next came the horse collar, the hames, the trace chain, and then the steel plow, which was shaped like a rhinoceros horn that dragged along behind the beast. It was heavy.

"Ow. Shit."

"You have to make sure you watch out for the chains, or you could lose a finger." Joey sucked on the middle finger of his left hand.

"Thanks for the warning. You used to do this?"

"No, no. My brothers and father. I will lead Maisie to start. Make sure you hang onto the reins."

"Oh, Christ." Joey did not feel good about this, but he soon found that Maisie was an agreeable beast and did all the hard work. The ground turned coffee black as the steel gouged the earth behind Maisie. He only had to follow, and only fell on his face once. Yvette laughed.

"Not funny," Joey said. Yvette followed behind, tossing fertilizer from a steel pail with her hands.

It took three brutal days of work to till three acres as snow flurries began to dust the land. Yvette folded her arms with satisfaction. It was a good start.

"Joey, I need to show you something. It's been hidden," Yvette said, her voice low and serious. She led him to a dark corner of the barn and beneath a pile of rusted steel and tangled coils of rope she produced a bulky burlap bag. In it was a gun. Joey immediately recognized that it as a German MP 40, a lightweight sub-machine gun carried by the Nazi infantry. Joey lifted the weapon and could see that it had been taken care of by its owner, it's black steel well-oiled, no rust. With it were two magazine clips of ammo.

"Where did you get this?

Yvette hesitated. "It was given to me."

"Given to you?"

"Yes. As I said, the German soldiers who stayed here gave it to me. They worried for my safety. They were good men in a very cruel war. I have never fired it."

Joey only nodded. Joey studied the weapon resting heavy in his hands. A vague flicker of doubt brushed against his thoughts. Why would a ruthless enemy, men he had seen commit unimaginable atrocities, do such a thing? Did he really know this young French girl who had so quickly found a place in his heart?

He exhaled slowly, letting the questions pass. He was no judge and had no intention of becoming one. In this war, survival twisted morality into a thousand shades of gray. Whatever her past might hold, it could not outweigh the burden of his own sins. Joey placed the weapon back in the bag.

"Keep it hidden," he said.

Winter arrived. A sheet of iron covered the land. Joey had plugged every leaky window and mended the last hole in the house roof. With that done, he worked every day on the barn roof. Finally, frigid cold and snow blanketed the house and fields. They mostly stayed inside next to the buttery glow of the fireplace that burned yellow warmth. Yvette sewed Joey a shirt and pants, the shirt stitched from a salvaged parachute. She sewed burlap over his Army field jacket, so it did not look so obvious he was once an American soldier.

Yvette laughed at Joey's new wardrobe. "Now you now look like a proper French peasant."

Joey looked at himself in a mirror and smiled. "Merci."

Locked inside by the bone-chilling cold, they played ping-pong and card games. All the books in the house were in French, so Yvette translated stories by Flaubert and Maupassant to Joey each night. One passage in a book by an American author titled *Gatsby le Magnifique* resonated most deeply with Joey, a line in the story about chasing the green light at the end of the dock. The elusive green light harbored a future that Joey could not have dreamed of just months ago. He also remembered the book was Pops's favorite—the English teacher from Joey's squad who never made it off the beach at Normandy.

One evening, lying in front of the fireplace with Yvette in his arms, Joey gazed at the fire's hypnotic dance and began to believe the possibility that he could build a new life here, that he could somehow forget the violence that had killed his heart, that had smothered all hope. Shadows flickered against the wall. His thoughts were both exhilarating and terrifying. The wind outside howled. He held Yvette tightly.

PART VI

"The greatest battle that ever was fought—
Shall I tell you where and when?
On the maps of the world you will find it not:
It was fought by the Mothers of Men."
—*Joaquin Miller*

Chapter 29

Dorothy Kowalski strode confidently down Halsted
Street toward the First National Bank of Chicago, her
heels clicking sharply against the pavement. She didn't
wear a skirt like most women but opted instead for
pleated trousers with crisp creases that bisected the gray
wool fabric with a matching jacket that hugged her
frame. Dorothy had never been one to fuss over her
appearance, but that morning with her mother's help,
she had spent over an hour meticulously styling her hair
in the fashionable Victory style, and applying makeup
for the first time ever. The stunning results were
undeniable.

She caught the admiring glances of those
passing and felt a flicker of satisfaction. The rouge on
her cheeks and the bright red lipstick accentuating her
smile created a striking contrast to her sharp, masculine
attire. Dorothy swung her briefcase with an air of
purpose. She looked like a woman who meant
business—because she did.

Still, she couldn't shake the thought: *Makeup.*
What a waste of time. But she knew why she'd made the

effort. Today wasn't just any day. Today, she needed to impress. And judging by the heads turning as she walked, she had succeeded. Dorothy Kowalski was determined, and she wanted the world to see it.

She put out of her mind, at least temporarily, the recently certified checks that were being sent to the Kowalski Five and Dime from a bank in New York. The bizarre windfall was causing her and her mother unease, and it was a staggering amount of money. $9,800 in the first check, $14,200 in the second. The Kowalski's should have been happy, but the source of the money was an enigma that scared them. They did not deposit the checks. It was all so strange. Even without the mysterious money, with Mr. Dempster's inheritance, they had plenty of equity in their account to secure a loan from the bank. Whatever secrets the mysterious checks held, it would have to wait. For now, she had more immediate concerns.

Dorothy finally stood before the imposing façade of the First National Bank. She walked up the marble steps and entered the front door between tall Ionic columns. The floor was a cold, white-peppered marble, which matched the chill in her stomach. Her heart thudded in her chest as she gazed around the opulent banking hall, with its high vaulted ceilings and intricate plasterwork that seemed designed to intimidate. There were patrons waiting at dark oak counters with multiple tellers who chirped like birds behind brass cages. She went to an information desk and announced her presence. "Miss Dorothy Kowalski to see Mr.

Stewart." The gray-haired receptionist looked above her pearl-framed glasses. The young woman in front of her looked familiar. "Ah, yes, you are young lady who drops off deposits for the Kowalski Five and Dime." The old woman frowned. Who was this teenager pretending to be? The nerve!

"Mr. Stewart is quite busy."

"I'm sure he is," Dorothy answered curtly. "And so am I. I believe he is expecting me."

Mr. Stewart, president of commercial loans, met Dorothy at the door of his office. He would normally scoff at a woman asking for a commercial loan, but the amount of money in her account calmed any trepidations. He shook her hand. Mr. Stewart wondered at her age. She could not be more than twenty-five years old. Dorothy was seventeen.

"Good afternoon, Mr. Stewart."

"Good afternoon, young lady." Mr. Stewart knew why she was there. They had spoken on the phone. Ordinarily, he did not like dealing with women. They knew nothing about banking, loans, or interest rates. But the balance in her bank account was considerable. He also knew that she was the one who made the daily deposits for the Kowalski Five and Dime and was impressed that the deposits had dramatically increased over the last few months. She had a very serious face. Over the phone she sounded like a heady businessman, and he was impressed with her apparent business acumen. "And how can the First National Bank of Chicago be of service to you?"

Dorothy took from her briefcase a spreadsheet and placed it neatly on Mr. Stewart's desk, smoothing it out with a steady hand. Her serious demeanor never changed as she began to speak.

"Mr. Stewart, as we discussed over the phone, the Kowalski Five and Dime is in a strong financial position. This spreadsheet details our current accounts receivable and payable, along with our assets. You'll see that all debts have been paid in full, and our cash reserves are substantial."

Mr. Stewart glanced down at the numbers. He couldn't help but be impressed by the meticulous accounting. He looked up, his curiosity piqued. "And you're asking for a loan of forty thousand dollars. That's quite a sum. And your plans with that money?"

Dorothy met his gaze. "Expansion, Mr. Stewart. The demand for our products has grown significantly, and we're operating at capacity in our current space. With this loan, we plan to purchase additional inventory, upgrade our equipment, and expand into the vacant lot at Archer Avenue and Halsted.

"Ah, yes. The old Woolworth property. Tragic." He knew there were swirling rumors about the fire, and who was responsible, and now the Kowalski Five and Dime was conveniently taking over at the same location. He tapped his fingers on his desktop. But Mr. Stewart was not a policeman and that curious matter was of no concern to him. His business was money.

"Do you mind if I smoke?" Dorothy asked, her voice steady despite the whirlwind in her stomach. She took a cigarette from her cigarette case and tapped it several times to pack the tobacco. Mr. Stewart reached across the desk and lit the cigarette for her with a silver lighter.

The banker sat in silence for a moment, studying her. Finally, he smiled faintly. "You're quite the negotiator for someone your age. I'll review your proposal thoroughly, but from what I see here, I'm inclined to approve the loan."

Dorothy extended her hand, her grip firm. "Thank you, Mr. Stewart. I appreciate your consideration, and I look forward to working with the First National Bank."

Mr. Stewart was left speechless as Dorothy left his office. The audacity, the sheer nerve of this young woman! He had no doubt that the board would approve the loan. The numbers spoke for themselves. He did not need to tell anyone that they were loaning money to a business run by a woman. A young girl. Astonishing!

Chapter 30

Christmas and New Year's had come and gone leaving the gray days of winter behind. Spring was just around the corner. Now eighteen years old, Dorothy had quit school and never returned for her senior year. She was the full-time manager of the new Kowalski Five and Dime on Archer Avenue, and the success of the store was immediate.

Dorothy had decided to take the morning off and talked her mother into going shopping downtown. They also shopped at a furniture store and bought a new dining room table and chairs for their new house.

Ma, do you want to get some lunch?" Dorothy asked her mom.

"No. We have plenty of lunch meat at home. I don't want to waste it. And we've got to get back to the store."

"We don't have to hurry. Alice is handling thing perfectly. She is really turning out to be a good assistant manager. Come on, Ma, let's take a cab home for once. We're rich."

Zosha shot her daughter a sharp glance. "Don't talk like that."

The women were glad that they decided to take a taxi home as the skies grew dark, and the wind blew violently, bending trees and tearing branches loose. Fat drops of rain pummeled the street as the taxi pulled in front of their home. The storm seemed to be growing more ferocious by the second.

"My hair!" Zosha cried. She jumped from the cab and ran through the unlocked front door of their recently purchased redbrick bungalow. Zosha kicked past the letters scattered on the floor, which had been shoved through the mail slot. Dorothy quickly followed, pausing to pick up the pile of letters and junk advertisements. She froze when she saw a telegram that looked like it was from the US government.

"Oh, no," she murmured. She looked up for her mother, who was already at the back of the house in the kitchen, singing a cheerful Polish folk tune. Things had been going so well. Dorothy slowly opened the telegram, and her worst fears were confirmed.

Tears filled her eyes. "Oh, Mom," Dorothy said softly. "Oh, Mom."

C35 58 WMUA 19 44 GOVT= PXX WMU WASHINGTON DC DEC 30 1944
MRS SOPHIA KOWALSKI=
2531 SOUTH THROOP STREET CHICAGO ILLINOIS=

THE SECRETARY OF WAR DESIRES ME TO EXPRESS HIS REGRET THAT
YOUR SON PRIVATE SECOND CLASS JOSEPH KOWALSKI HAS BEEN REPORTED
MISSING IN ACTION SINCE TWENTY OCTOBER IN THE EUROPEAN AREA IF
FURTHER DETAILS OR OTHER INFORMATION ARE RECEIVED YOU WILL BE
PROMPTLY NOTIFIED=
                ULIO THE ADJUTANT GENERAL

Chapter 31

In the front row of St. Gerard's church, Zosha, clutching the rosary dangling from her wrist, rubbed the worn smoothness of the wooden prayer beads. She never stopped praying that her son would be found alive and unharmed.

The experience of attending mass had irrevocably changed for her since her lover, Tom Martin, had departed for the war. In his absence, the sacred rituals felt hollow. Father Martin's sermons had always been soothing and compassionate, with a quiet humor that all the congregants adored. He gave comfort.

With Tom Martin gone, Father Pembrook took on a bigger load of masses. The pastor seemed short-tempered and angry. He preached God as a punisher, not a helper. He was also not happy that he recently received orders from the archbishop that he was being transferred to another parish, although he did wonder what the altar boys at his new church were like.

She was not thinking at all about God. Knowing that Tom loved her gave her an inner strength she had not felt in a long time. Love offered unmistakable power.

Kneeling with her hands clasped together, Zosha always sat in the front row at mass, the better for God to hear her prayers. She arrived early. She preferred the church when it was empty and found a strange peace when she was alone. She felt like she could have a one-on-one with God. The cavernous cathedral ceilings and high arching stained glass windows somehow provided an inner calm. Besides prayers for Joey, she prayed to keep Tom Martin and her brother Chester from harm.

Other congregants began to arrive for mass, shuffling quiet feet, and soon the church was filled with murmuring, coughs, and the hushed sounds of reverence. At 8 AM, someone unseen rang a tinny bell three times which sounded the beginning of mass. Father Pembrook walked from the back of the church down the center aisle with three altar boys leading the way. The first boy carried a large gold cross, his small frame straining from the weight, while the two boys behind bore large flickering candles. Father Pembrook walked slowly in white vestments. He held the Bible in front of him, opened to some unknown page. The boys looked so young and angelic, and it reminded Zosha of her little boy, Timmy, who would forever be young and innocent.

Bellowing organ music filled the cavernous chamber of the church until finally the echoing blare of the brass organ pipes abruptly stopped. The liturgy commenced, spoken in an incomprehensible Latin chant, and then Father Pembrook walked slowly to the pulpit for the sermon. He spoke loudly and clearly.

"From the book of Isaiah." He took a deep breath and began. "How you have fallen from heaven, morning star, son of dawn!"

The solemn quiet of the mass was punctured by the cry of a baby and a woman softly whispering, "Hush."

"You have been cast down to the earth, you who once laid low the nations!" He raised a bony finger and pointed into the air. "You said in your heart, 'I will ascend to the heavens. I will raise my throne above the stars of God; I will sit enthroned on the mount of assembly, on the utmost heights of Mount Zaphon. I will ascend above the tops of the clouds; I will make myself like the Most High. But you!" Father Pembroke shouted, raising his voice to a thunderous pitch. "You are brought down to the realm of the dead, to the depths of the pit." The Bible in front of the priest snapped shut. The church hushed. No men coughed. No babies cried.

"Lucifer," Father Pembrook said, stabbing his finger at the congregation sitting wide-eyed in the wooden pews. "The son of the morning was Lucifer, once the most beautiful and powerful angel in heaven. He was second only to God. He was the most beloved of all God's angels. He was praised for his wisdom, strength, and beauty. But Lucifer was proud and began to think he was equal to God. He began to plot to overthrow God and take his place. One day, Lucifer gathered a group of angels who were also discontented with God's rule, and they rebelled against God. The battle was fierce, but in the end, God was victorious. Satan and his followers were cast out of heaven and into hell! So Satan began to tempt humans with sin. If we trust in Jesus, we can overcome Satan and his temptations."

"There is evil here today," he roared, sweeping his finger across the pews until it landed squarely on

Zosha. "Those who will try to lead you away from God with the temptations of the flesh must be thrown from our midst into the fires of hell." Father Pembrook walked away from the pulpit and stood in front of the altar. A ripple of murmurs coursed throughout the church. Zosha Kowalski's blood ran cold. Was he speaking and pointing at her? Her chest pounded. Did he know about her and Father Martin?

Father Pembrook stepped ominously down the altar steps and stood in front of the first pew. Zosha and others squirmed nervously. Standing in front of Zosha, Father Pembrook pointed straight at her. "Cast Satan from your heart! Repent!"

"You talking to me?" Zosha's voice, though trembling, held sparks of defiance.

"Repent, sinner," the priest cried.

Zosha stared back at Father Pembrook in disbelief, her stomach curdling. Then in a sudden surge of indignation and anger, she stood. She clumsily passed herself along the pew to the center aisle, stepping on feet along the way. "Sorry. Excuse me. Sorry," she whispered. All eyes of the church were upon her. Father Pembrook looked at her with astonishment. His lips curled in anger.

"Yes," she said loudly for all to hear, pointing a finger back at the stunned priest. "There is evil here today. And I am looking at it." She turned defiantly and walked down the aisle and out the front doors of the church, the heavy oak doors slamming shut behind her. Zosha gave an enormous sigh of relief, shocked at what she had just done. *What has gotten into me?* She smiled and didn't care that she would not be going to communion that day.

Chapter 32

Father Martin, now Lieutenant Thomas Martin, did not get his request to be stationed in Italy. *The US Army will send you to wherever they think you are most needed.* Instead, he was installed near the perilous front lines to console and attend to the fighting men near Belgium. He now saw firsthand the horrors the soldier must endure. The wounds were ghastly. Limbs torn away, eyes forever lost, faces mutilated beyond recognition, fingers and toes amputated from frostbite. Some boys with no apparent wounds sat mute and motionless, paralyzed with shock. Tom Martin had to wonder how he himself would hold up at the frozen war front. Europe, it was reported, was now experiencing the coldest winter in over fifty years.

Tom Martin never saw combat, only the human results of battle. Many of these boys, if they survived, had been entrenched in the gruesome cycle of killing and facing death for over seven months or more. The physical and mental endurance of the soldiers was extraordinary.

One bitter morning, while comforting and giving last rites to a wounded soldier who would never survive the day, who would never see another summertime, Lieutenant Tom Martin began to weep. He was not as strong as he thought, and he was ashamed of himself crying in front of these brave child soldiers. A chilling wind with no respect or sympathy rustled the green blankets covering the heads of the dead.

A corporal quietly interrupted Tom's thoughts. "Excuse me, lieutenant, I have orders here for you. You are to report to Captain John Myers in Paris."

Lieutenant Martin stood up and wiped his eyes. "Paris? Why would I be sent to Paris?"

"I don't know, sir. But I sure as hell would love to be sent there. They say if you can't get laid in Paris, you can't get laid anywhere." The corporal's face went red with embarrassment when he realized to whom he was speaking. "Sorry, sir."

This brought a smile to Tom Martin's face. "Forget it, corporal."

Captain John Jacob Myers sat in his cramped and claustrophobic office hunched over a stack of folders of the criminals and deserters recently captured. A knock on the door startled him. Corporal Perkins entered.

"Captain, a Lieutenant Thomas Martin is here to see you."

"Who?"

"The priest."

"Ah, yes." He had finally gotten prescription reading glasses, so the documents in front of him were seen more clearly. And he didn't know if that was a good thing. "Send him in."

Tom Martin entered the office. "Have a seat, lieutenant," Captain Myers said, gesturing to the lone chair across from his desk. He opened a manila folder with a red tag. "Your file here says you have a law degree."

"No, sir. Only one year of law school before I decided to enter the priesthood."

"Well, that's good enough for what we need." Captain Myers leaned forward and lowered his voice to a confidential tone. "Lieutenant , there are thousands of US soldiers in lockup for various criminal activities, but most are deserters. Military law requires them to have legal counsel in their defense. Right now, we only have you and two others." Myers coughed clearing his throat, "two other quasi-attorneys with similar credentials as yours handling this overwhelming caseload. And I assure you, Lieutenant Martin, there are going to be thousands more deserters captured before this is all over."

Chapter 33

A cool spring drizzle touched the black velvet fields that Joey and Yvette had plowed late last December. It was a soft rain, a farmer's dream. Raindrops, glistening like pearls, dripped slowly from the tines of a rake leaning against the barn. The young couple had planted seeds weeks earlier, and soon sprouts of corn and wheat would appear. Joey liked nothing better than sitting in a chair, beneath the shed roof over the back porch, and gaze upon the acres. It was a solace he thought he would never achieve. The vegetable garden had been securely fenced to keep out the goats. Soon carrots, peas, beans, onions, tomatoes, and other vegetables would be on the kitchen table.

The rain eased and became nothing more than a mist. Yvette walked from the barn and found Joey sitting at the back of the house. She folded her arms and frowned. "Nothing grows if you stare at it. And we got two dozen eggs that need tending to." Her voice wasn't angry but only a gentle chiding. Joey looked happy and that's all that mattered. His nightmares and choked sobs had disappeared completely. He had found a home.

"What kind of trees are those in the middle of the field?" Joey asked.

Yvette sighed. "Those are chestnut trees. They provide shade for the animals in summer. I was told my great grandfather planted them years ago. They are not common in this part of France."

"And those birds in the trees? There must be a thousand of them."

"Blackbirds. They are noisy."

"I like it."

Joey stood and walked over to Yvette and enveloped her in a hug. "I'll get to the hens when I get back."

"Do you have to go?" she said with a worried look. "When are you going to tell that gangster you are done with him? It is all too dangerous."

"I told you. I don't do anything dangerous." Joey looked out over the fields. "And look at what we have here, thanks to Rico."

Yvette sighed. "And thanks to you."

"I'll tell him today. I promise. He doesn't need me anymore."

"Well, don't forget, I need you."

Joey held Yvette tighter, feeling a blissful warmth. "I know," he murmured. He kissed her forehead. "I'll be back before dark. Love you."

"Love you, too."

Chapter 34

With the war finally grinding to an end, business for Rico and his gang boomed. The infrastructure of France had been ravaged from fighting. Roads, once arteries of commerce, were nothing more than muddy gashes. The outlying farms, liberated from the Nazi yoke, were now able to produce food and goods for the population without restrictions. However, getting these goods to the people of France was a challenge. Trucks and gasoline were gold, and Rico, with a nose for opportunity as keen as a truffle pig, was there to meet the insatiable demand.

The gang stole gasoline daily. Rico now had a fleet of twenty-two US Army trucks and thousands of gallons of gasoline to sell. Even with the new government of France and the United States in control, rationing was still in effect. Just like in the United States during Prohibition, the population of France was thirsting for items that had been denied them for so long. Rico purchased a two-story building in Paris at 32 Rue Blondel and a new kind of commerce was flourishing with gambling and a café on the first floor, and rooms for prostitutes and sexual pleasure on the second. He named the enterprise *La Belle Poule* (The Beautiful Hen).

At the beginning of the war, the British and United States Army had been using five-gallon gas cans, which were cumbersome and needed a wrench to open and a funnel to pour. They spilled as much as a third of their fuel when filling their vehicles. The US Army soon discovered that the Germans had superior gas cans called Wehrmacht Kanisters. The canisters were easily produced and had a spout that could pour gasoline without a funnel. The handles on the cans made it easy for one soldier to carry four cans at once. After much fudging and bureaucratic bungling, the Army wised up and stole the design. By the end of the war, the US had produced over twenty-one million gas cans appropriately named "Jerry cans." Rico's gang planned on stealing every last one they could get their hands on. With the war over, Rico's network thrived amid the chaos, ensuring that while the landscape of France improved, so, too, would his underworld.

In a cedar-lined closet at Rico's hideout hung a collection of United States Army jackets adorned with fake chevrons of whatever rank Rico chose for the day, from corporal all the way up to lieutenant general. Today, Rico would be a sergeant in the 120th Infantry Brigade. He and his cohorts were going to drive three trucks to a US Army gas facility with forged papers requisitioning gasoline for US vehicles stationed in and around Paris. Each truck carried sixty-five Jerry cans. They would haul away nearly one thousand gallons of gas which would be easily sold off in chunks on their journey home.

Such sales were netting Rico a fortune. Francs, British pounds, and even German marks were being covertly sent to banks in Switzerland and New York for laundering into clean US dollars. Rico and his "employees" were all wealthy stockholders in the shadowy "Adduci Corporation," which he had built with military precision. Unbeknownst to Joey Kowalski, he was also a silent partner in this illicit venture. Rico ensured it. For men like Rico, loyalty was a commodity—easily acquired with the right amount of cash.

What Rico did not know was that the US military police were waiting in ambush on the road out of Chatou. As the three trucks filled up with gas and left the petrol depot, two jeeps from Rico's gang emerged from the nearby forest and began escorting Rico's trucks with their stolen booty. The men in each jeep were armed with Thompson machine guns, and one jeep was mounted with the heavy menace of a .50-caliber automatic weapon which was usually mounted on tanks. If anyone was going to mess with Rico's stolen petrol, they were going to face some serious consequences.

Positioned at a strategic bend in the road, the military police weren't there to negotiate or arrest. They came to end Rico's black-market empire, and they came with overwhelming firepower. As the convoy passed, gunfire erupted. The truck Rico was driving bore the brunt of the initial assault, riddled with bullets from small arms and heavy caliber machine guns. The truck veered like a maniacal snake, crashing sideways and blocking the convoy's path.

The escorts in the jeeps reacted instantly, firing back with their guns. The forest echoed with the deafening cacophony of gunfire and smoke-filled confusion. Several MPs were struck by the gangster's return fire, their bodies crumpling to the earth, but the onslaught from the ambush continued without mercy. The trucks and jeeps following Rico's vehicle were trapped. A relentless hail of bullets shattered their windshields, killing the drivers instantly. Then came an explosion: one of the trucks, its tanks pierced by gunfire, erupted in a fiery inferno that lit up the surrounding woods. The blast rocked the convoy, sending shrapnel flying and covering the area in thick, black smoke.

Rico's world teetered on the brink of annihilation. Inside his overturned truck, he was dazed, bloodied, and pinned by the wreckage. Through the chaos, a wounded Henri emerged from one of the jeeps. Despite one arm hanging limp and bloodied, he pushed through the bullets and smoke. With sheer desperation, he smashed the truck's window, grabbed Rico, and dragged him across the ground and into the back seat of the still-functioning jeep. "Conduire! Conduire!" he screamed.

The jeep's wheels roared to life, as the driver floored the gas pedal. The barrage of lead continued as the attackers shifted their fire toward the escaping Rico and his two cohorts. Bullets pinged off the jeep's frame. Just then, another tuck filled with petrol exploded sending a maelstrom of fire into the sky that could be seen for miles. The thick shroud of smoke from the burning truck provided cover for what was left of Rico's gang. The lone jeep sped off, veering wildly around the smoldering carnage, and down the road as the sounds of the firefight began to fade.

Rico lay slumped in the back, his face pale, blood seeping from a wound in his side. Henri, held on to Rico's belt with his one good arm to keep him from being pitched from the vehicle. "Bouge-le vite," Henri screamed at the driver, his voice wracked with pain. Black smoke billowed like a cyclone into the sky as the jeep carrying the wounded Rico disappeared into the dense forest, leaving behind nothing but chaos and flames.

The battered remnants of the ill-fated heist furiously raced ten desperate miles back to their hideout. The guards on duty came out of their pillboxes with mouths agape when they saw the mess that was driving past them. They knew this was not good.

Joey came out of a large barn to see what the commotion was. Joey and the driver, another American deserter named Leroy, lifted Rico from the back of the jeep and laid him in a bed of straw inside the barn. Henri remained at the back of the jeep, his head tipped back. The Frenchman who was loyal to Rico until the very end was dead. Joey kneeled in front of Rico.

"What the hell happened?" Joey asked Leroy who was pacing back and forth in a panic.

"We were set up," Leroy gasped. "They were waiting for us. The whole fucking US army. We didn't stand a chance."

Rico's eyes suddenly opened, smiling, he looked at Joey. "What's new, Kowalski?" he joked and then coughed up blood. His body convulsed. "Oh, Christ. It looks like this is the end of the line."

"It's just a flesh wound," Joey lied. "You're just losing some blood. We'll get you patched up in a hurry. Fleishman is on his way with his medical bag."

Rico's eyes began to dim. He could no longer see Joey. He coughed again. "Did I ever tell you what my mother's name was?" he said softly.

Joey remained silent.

"You won't believe it. Cinderella. How about that? My mama bought me a bike when we couldn't even afford food." Tears mingled with blood on Rico's face. "I'd ride down the street with the neighbors watching from their windows. And they wouldn't say, 'There goes Rico, or there goes Deuce,' they'd say, 'There goes Cinderella's boy.' Can you believe that? Cinderella's boy."

Light slipped away from the eyes of the little gangster. Enrico Salvatori Adduci was dead.

Chapter 35

The juggernaut of war, having lumbered relentlessly for years across Europe resulting in nearly fifty million deaths, had finally turned against the Nazis. The enemy mounted a massive desperate counterattack in the frozen winter of '45, which became known as the Battle of the Bulge, but it failed. April 30th, 1945, Adolph Hitler and his wife committed suicide in their Berlin bunker, and within days, Germany surrendered unconcitionally.

A euphoric wave swept across the liberated nations. France erupted in jubilation, a riot of joy and relief. American and British soldiers were embraced with torrents of wine and kisses. Flowers rained down from the sky. Yet amid the celebrations, a darker current surged. The victory had loosened the chains of restraint, and a thirst for vengeance took hold.

With Germany defeated, France was gripped by a wave of executions and assaults. Suspected collaborators faced the fury of the liberated. Women accused of fraternizing with Germans were publicly shamed and humiliated. In the chaos, the lines between guilt and innocence blurred, and many fell victim to the mob's wrath.

Old grudges surfaced with brutal immediacy, none more bitter than in the small village of Marle. It was a time of reckoning, and collaborators who did not flee were dealt with ruthlessly. Marle's mayor who had betrayed French resistance fighters, and the town's only garage mechanic who happily repaired German vehicles, were taken into the nearby woods by Monique Laurent and other avengers, shot in the head, and buried in shallow graves. Others also paid the ultimate price, but the vigilantes were not through. Monique had one more act of vengeance seething in her cruel mind.

The cobblestone streets of Marle bustled with uneasy activity as Monique Laurent called for a meeting at the town's only tavern. The grim purpose of this drunken gathering was how to deal with one traitor in particular, Yvette Fauxbourg. The typical shaming of whores who slept with the enemy was to shave their heads in the town square followed by tar and feathering. This was going on in much of France. But Monique had more in mind.

"The traitors of our country must be severely punished. We, the living, must have justice." Monique had to shriek to be heard above the chatter of voices. It was noon, and half of those in the Flour Sack Tavern were already inebriated.

Monique continued to shout. Spittle ran down her chin. "Yvette Fauxbourg housed the enemy and was their whore while the Nazi bastards occupied our village. Murdered our people. Murdered *my* family! She must be punished!"

"Now hold on a minute," Anna Garnier, the shriveled and frail, seventy-five-year-old owner of the tavern croaked above the noise. "How do you know this? The Germans forced themselves into many of our homes. They stayed in rooms above my tavern. Does that mean I slept with the enemy?" Her remark elicited a roar of the laughter from the men. Anna looked around the room, bewildered by their mirth.

"I know in my heart that she is a traitor and a harlot!" shouted Monique.

A man burst through the front door of the tavern holding a bucket of black liquid tar. "Let's go. While the tar is still hot." A small boy followed him with a pillowcase filled with feathers. "To the Fauxbourg farm!" the man screamed, veins bulging from his neck. The drunken crowd surged through the door, crossing the bridge, marching the mile to Yvette's farm.

Yvette heard the voices of a crowd singing the *Chant des Partisans* well before she saw anyone. The voices grew louder and louder like a storm swelling in the distance until it was clear the tempest was coming up the road to her house. From the kitchen cabinet she drew a pistol and tucked it in her pants, the weapon hidden by her blouse. She walked defiantly to her front door and swung it open. The crowd, momentarily stunned, stopped and stared at her, the singing evaporating into an eerie silence. Tension vibrated the air like a wire stretched to its limit ready to snap.

Suddenly, from the back of the mob, Monique's voice erupted, sharp and shrill like a hawk's cry. "Punish the whore! Punish the traitor!" The dam broke. A man rushed up the front steps, tripped, and fell on his face. Others followed and grabbed Yvette by the arms and dragged her down the stone steps. Her pistol fell from her blouse.

"Look. The traitor has a German Luger." The mob surged forward, a frenzy of fists and kicks knocked Yvette to the ground.

"Why do you do this?" Yvette screamed. "Why? Please!" Her pleas were swallowed by the frenzied anger of the crowd.

Vicious hands tore at her clothes until she was naked. Her face was shoved into the dirt. "Lift her up!" Monique shouted. She slapped the bruised and bleeding Yvette across the face. "You are not so special now, are you?" Two men roughly pushed Yvette's head down as though she were ready for the guillotine. Monique began to cut Yvette's long chestnut hair. The sheers left large gashes in Yvette's scalp. Blood and hair fell to the ground.

Nearly all the hot tar had spilled from the pail on the march from Marle to Yvette's farm, so the best a small boy could do was brush a crude black swastika on Yvette's back. Feathers were thrown over her. Yvette fell heavily to the ground. Monique Laurent, her eyes bulging with maniacal satisfaction, gave Yvette one last kick to the head.

Yvette, half-conscious, heard her home being ransacked, and finally, the gay singing of *Chant des Partisans* fading slowly into the afternoon mist as her lifeblood oozed into the dirt and gravel.

Chapter 36

After the ambush outside Chatou, the military police wasted no time tracking Rico Adduci's trail to the gang's hideout. The shoot-out had killed and wounded many American MPs, but reinforcements arrived swiftly, and a small army of heavily armed jeeps and half-tracks closed in, tightening the noose on the Rico's gang. Rico's men scattered in every direction, some in jeeps, some just running aimlessly away.

Joey stood over Rico's lifeless body for a moment. He always knew Deuce would die violently. It was only a question of when. Joey, hearing the familiar sound of armored vehicles, dashed to the back of the barn and hopped on the motorcycle he always kept there for just such an emergency. With a quick kick, the engine roared to life. He shifted gears with his foot and frantically flew across a vacant field and into the nearby woods. The narrow forest path swallowed him, branches clawing at his face and clothes as he navigated the difficult terrain. Wind whipped through his hair, and for over an hour, Joey rode like a man possessed, weaving through fields and hidden trails, his mind racing as fast as the motorcycle beneath him. When he finally emerged from the forest, sweat-soaked and breathless, the familiar sight of Yvette's farm came into view. He slowed the bike as he approached. But something was wrong. The cows were no longer in the pen. Yvette never put them in the barn during the day. They had disappeared, and the familiar sound of the farm animals had vanished.

Joey found Yvette dead, crumpled like a broken doll at the foot of the farmhouse door. The flagstone steps were smeared with tar, feathers, and blood. Trembling, he knelt down next to her lifeless body. A pounding thunder filled his head like hammers as the claws of God and the devil together ripped his heart and soul in two.

Joey lifted his head and arms and screamed into the heavens. "Why?" he shrieked. A thousand blackbirds exploded from the distant chestnut tree, swirling above Joey and Yvette in a frantic storm of wild, screeching confusion. Sobs wracked Joey's chest.

"Why?" he softly whispered again. Yvette was dead because of senseless revenge. She harmed no one. He held her lifeless body, stroking her forehead softly. *Am I the angel of death?* he thought. *Is there so much horror and death because of me and my sins?*

Joey heard no chickens clucking in the barn. All the livestock was gone. The happiness he and Yvette had hoped for had been crushed with an invisible fist, shattering her life, *their* life. Just the day before, they had marveled at the spring seedlings pushing up tiny green sprouts through the black soil they had tilled together. Leaves were blossoming throughout the trees. Joey took a rag from his pocket and wiped away the blood from Yvette's face. He held her hand. The sun slowly faded. Joey found a torch and spade in the barn and dug a grave in the moonlight.

Prayers? There would be no prayers. He had said countless prayers his entire life and for what? For nothing. He was praying to a laughing clown. Joey shook his fist at the sky and began screaming. "You are not a God! Your heart is black. You are a God of no one! Take me now if you dare. Take me now." Shutting his eyes, he waited for the fire that would fall from the sky and strike him, but there was only the howling of the wind and the creak of the rusted weather vane above the barn roof. The crickets chirped a mournful metronome as Joey fell asleep next to the grave. He awoke at dawn with the first rays of light clearing the distant tree line, his clothing soaked from the morning dew. Gigi, the goat was chewing on his jacket.

Above the farmhouse door, in black, the word "traitresse" was hastily scrawled - a cruel, final judgment. Yvette had done her best to escape the horrors of the Nazis but could not escape the horrors of her own people. Joey found the inside of the house in shambles. Furniture broken. Mirrors shattered. Doors were torn from the kitchen cabinets. Gigi followed at Joey's heels like a dog waiting for a bone.

Joey walked to the barn and climbed the ladder to the loft and tossed the remaining bales of hay down to the ground for Gigi. "Here you go, girl," he said to the goat. "You are on your own now. I'm sorry."

He sat on one of the bales and put his face in his hands. An uncontrollable fury began to rise in him like a fever. He moved quickly to a cluttered corner of the barn, tossing aside rusted cans, and discarded rope, and

soon found what he was looking for, the machine gun
Yvette had shown him months ago. Joey's face became
a tangled mask of crazed menace. If the town of Marle
wanted revenge, he promised, they would get revenge.

The road to Marle was thick with the scent of late spring
- wet earth, blooming lilacs, and the faint, sour
 tang of something unseen. Joey, boots muddy, removed
the gun that had been slung over his shoulder and undid
the weapon's safety with an ominous click, making the
weapon ready for the destruction he intended. Oblivious
to the flowers sprouting stubbornly in the cracks of the
pavement and the gentle buzz of bees filling the air, his
anger rose like a viper. He scanned his path left and
right as he crossed the stone bridge into the outskirts of
the town, each step stirring memories of his murdered
Yvette – her laughter, her touch, her defiant strength. He
eyed his immediate target, a simple whitewashed
cottage with a garden overgrown with weeds. He
approached his victim like a rabid tiger, and kicked in
the front door, the thin wood bursting into splinters, his
face, twisted into a deranged, frenzied snarl. But he was
not met with a room filled with villagers, the blood of
Yvette still on their hands, only a terrified woman with a
wide-eyed barefoot child clinging to her skirt.
      "Ayez pitie! S'il te plait," the woman pleaded.
"Nous n'avons rien ici." She began to weep holding the
child tightly against her side.
      For a moment, time stood still, and then Joey's
rage froze and dissolved like mist from a tornado. In the
eyes of a frightened woman and the face of a child, he

saw that he had become the monster he had hoped to destroy. Joey sank to his knees. The machine gun slid uselessly to the floor as his shoulders shook with sobs. "I'm sorry," he cried softly over and over.

Joey left the cottage and walked away from the village, trudging several miles until he came across a contingent of American soldiers.

Chapter 37

Joey spent two weeks in what felt like purgatory, a barbed wire barracks crammed with about a thousand other GIs accused of criminal activity against the military machine. The air inside the temporary prison was thick with despair, defiance, and stale sweat. The first officer Joey met regarding his desertion was the rumpled division psychiatrist, Major James Thompson, whose weary demeanor suggested he had interviewed far too many broken soldiers. He asked Joey various questions about his mental state which Joey answered truthfully. A dull ache throbbed behind Joey's eyes, the same dull ache he couldn't shake after being wounded in battle, the same ache that had all but disappeared when he met Yvette. The diagnosis was that Joey had mild anxiety and a slight psychoneurosis but was still competent to face a court-martial.

The prison guards were harsh, pitiless men specifically chosen by the army because they had never seen the real horrors of war, men who had never faced the paralyzing fear of combat. The guards treated the prisoners as though they were all cowards, but to the prisoners, they were the true cowards, their cruel treatment of deserters a sign of their own moral emptiness. Joey endured their scorn in silence. These were not men who had watched their friends die or carried the weight of impossible choices. They wielded their malicious authority like a contemptuous weapon, and the prisoners hated them.

"Private Kowalski," a guard barked as Joey walked the dusty dirt next to the fence, a cigarette dangling from his mouth. He took one final drag and ground the butt into the ground.

"Up front. Now!" The names of two other soldiers were also called out. Each man had leg irons attached at their ankles before leaving the compound. The chains were only twelve inches apart, so running was impossible, and walking was a hobbled shuffle. They were led through a gate to a waiting truck. A prisoner from behind the barbed wire fence yelled at Joey and the two with him. "Break a leg, boys. We've been through hell. A firing squad should be a piece of cake." A guard ordered the man to shut up.

The prisoners arrived at an abandoned church just north of Paris, which would serve as the location for their military trial. The church had been miraculously pardoned by wartime bombing. A solitary schoolhouse, or what was left of it, jutted beside the church like a fractured tooth; all that remained was a single wall and a defiant chimney. Three officers sat on the church's altar with a crucified Christ hovering above. Thorns snagged Jesus's brow. A bloody gash forever bled from the statue's porcelain side. The stern looking officers would serve as judge and jury.

Joey was not the first of the three to stand trial. He sat in the back sacristy with his legs still shackled. A single soldier stood guard, his expression blank, and uninterested. Joey could not hear much of what was going on at the front of the church. He did hear "death by firing squad," and he began to tremble. He was the last of the prisoners to appear before the army judges, and was allowed a defense counselor whom he could talk with for fifteen minutes before he was tried. One of the voices at the front of the church sounded familiar.

Joey was stunned when Lieutenant Thomas Martin walked into the sacristy.

"Father Martin!" Joey blurted. Tom Martin was equally astonished. He had not yet looked at the file of the man he was about to defend. This kid did not look like the youngster he knew from only a couple of years ago, and then he recognized him like a curtain lifted.

"My God, Joey," Tom Martin stammered. "You're alive!" He crossed the room in two quick strides, lifted Joey to his feet and stared into his face. "Oh, my God. Does your mother know? Your family back home thinks you are dead, or a POW. Your mom is going to be so relieved." And then counselor Tom Martin pulled himself together and realized Joey Kowalski's grim situation.

"You are my lawyer?" Joey asked. A wave of relief washed over him as he recognized this familiar face from home.

"Well, sort of. I have one year of law school to recommend me," Lieutenant Martin called to the guard standing nearby. "Please give us privacy!" The soldier hesitated, then left the room closing a heavy wood door behind him. Martin opened a folder and looked quickly at Joey's file. He pulled a chair up close to Joey.

"Listen. We don't have much time. The men out there, your judges, have zero sympathy for deserters.

None of these stateside clowns have ever been in combat. They've never seen what you have seen." Lieutenant Martin sighed, running his hand through his short, cropped hair. "I've seen it. I know what you've been through. We can't plead 'not guilty' because you already admitted to desertion when you were arrested. The psychiatrist's report won't help you. The man before you had a similar psychiatric report, and he's been sentenced to thirty years' hard labor. I also know for a fact that General Fitzsimmons, who's in charge of this circus, has informed the panel of judges out there to produce guilty verdicts with harsh sentences. This is not good for you, Joey. It doesn't matter that you have medals for bravery, that you have fought heroically, but that will be part of our defense. I've also learned recently that General Eisenhower has provided amnesty to certain deserters if they agree to be transported to the Pacific Theater to fight the Japanese. If you are asked by the panel if you agree to this, reply, 'Yes, sir.' I think it is the only thing that might save you, but I can't guarantee anything."

Joey sat in a church pew and was then ordered to stand. He looked at the officers sitting on the altar, and then up at the crucifix looming above, Christ's face frozen in eternal agony. Joey stared at it, unable to shake the feeling that those sorrowful eyes were condemning him, judging him just as those officers sitting beneath it would. He felt a wave of guilt and despair, heavy and unrelenting, as if the weight of the cross itself had shifted onto his shoulders.

"May I approach the bench?" Lieutenant Martin asked. One of the officers nodded. A tired-looking, silver-haired colonel quickly scanned the papers in the manila folder that Martin handed him, and passed it along to the next officer.

"As you can see," Martin continued, "On September 1, 1944, a wounded Private Kowalski single-handedly repelled a German attack killing several of the enemy, destroyed an enemy tank, and heroically saved the life of one of his fellow soldiers. He consequently received a Purple Heart and Silver Cross for his bravery. We humbly ask the court for sympathy. Private Kowalski's errant judgment and fear of combat is gone, and he has agreed to be shipped to the Pacific Theater to continue the fight against the Japanese. And I believe you are aware of General Eisenhower's recent proclamation."

One of the officers on the altar asked the guard to remove Private Kowalski. Chains clanking at his feet, Joey was hustled back to the sacristy area behind the altar. Lieutenant Martin entered the room soon after, all excitement, breathing heavily like he had just run a mile. "They have agreed to drop charges if you return to the fight. I have papers for you to sign, and you will be released from the stockade shortly. You do agree to continue fighting as long as it takes to defeat the Japanese, right?

Joey didn't know if he could do that. "Yes," he blurted. His hands trembled uncontrollably as he scratched his signature on the document thrust before him, the ink from the fountain pen bleeding on the paper around his name.

Lieutenant Martin was elated. He had defended over fifty deserters, and not one of them was shown leniency. Private Joseph Kowalski had dodged a bullet, but probably not for long. The United States was ramping up for an invasion of the Japanese mainland with predicted casualties in the hundreds of thousands. Lieutenant Martin shuddered at the thought.

"I am going to send a telegram to your mother first chance I get to tell her the good news that you are alive." Thomas Martin became thoughtful. "I won't mention the desertion part. You know, she has had a pretty rough time since they reported you MIA."

"Please don't. I've already sent a letter home from the stockade," Joey lied. The truth was now a tangled mess he had to bury somewhere deep inside. He was adrift, caught in a tide of guilt. As far as Joey was concerned, he had died weeks ago next to a farmhouse outside the village of Marle. He didn't know if he could ever go back home.

"Thanks, Father."

A sad smile touched Martin's lips. "You don't have to call me Father anymore. I have resigned from the priesthood. Call me Tom. Take care of yourself, Joey. No more being brave. You are very loved at home." He sighed. A deep weariness settled over him. "You know your mother and I are very fond of each other. I write her often, but I won't mention any of this." He sighed again, heavier this time.

The boy who sat before him now was nearly unrecognizable, a shadow of the vibrant youth he had once known. Thin and gaunt, his sunken eyes were dark caverns of misery. This wasn't the same boy who had once laughed freely, became his high school valedictorian, who had fought through alleys, and boxed with reckless confidence in Saint Gerard's gym, an innocent who had, regrettably, helped him commit arson so long ago. Martin saw a stranger forever robbed of his youth, and a life cheated. *Where had the love of God gone in this world for His children?*

PART VII

"First Witch: When shall we three meet again?
In thunder, lightning, or in rain?
Second Witch: When the hurly-burly's done,
When the battle's lost and won."
—Shakespeare, Macbeth

Chapter 38

Joey Kowalski disembarked from a crowded transport ship in Boston, just another GI among thousands returning to the States. Only Joey's return would be short lived, two weeks' leave, then he'd ship out to the Pacific to face the Japanese. There was a train heading for Chicago at noon, and Joey would be on it.

As the cars rocked along the rails, Joey felt alone in a sea of khaki. He wanted to see his mom and sister but was afraid of what they would think if they knew the truth. A hero? A coward? He couldn't bear the thought of talking about the war. It had already killed something inside him. Joey never called or wrote to announce his return. The perpetual nightmares and headaches had returned. He found himself jittery at any sudden loud noise. He stared out the window at the blurred countryside, not recognizing his own reflection in the glass, his eyes sunken and dark like an emaciated ghost. Deep breaths were the only thing that kept him from crying like a child.

When he arrived at Chicago's Union Station, it was suffocatingly hot with a dense crowd of returning GI's running into the arms of exuberant, tearful loved ones. Joey felt crushed by the sounds of the cavernous depot with its impossibly tall ceilings yawning upward towards grimy skylights. Since he was still technically on duty, he wore his uniform and garrison cap, however, the relentless heat forced him to stuff his jacket and cap into his knapsack. Escaping the train station, Joey was suddenly afraid to go on. Some invisible force was stopping him. He had money to pay for a cab but instead walked east towards Lake Michigan, the opposite direction from home. He turned south on State Street, where he could hop onto a bus for five cents, but instead continued to aimlessly walk.

Flashes of the past and the future churned through his mind. A happy, contented home, a wife, children, were all now crushingly impossible. Yvette's spirit was following him everywhere in ways that didn't seem to make sense like a cloud suddenly missing in the sky, or she appeared as a reflection in a store window, and when he spun around, there was no one there. The feeling of being buried alive consumed him and thoughts of suicide became more and more real to end this misery. Speeding cars whooshed past. A simple step into the street could free him. He walked on.

State Street was a canyon of towering buildings. Traffic was relentless, and the exhaust choked Joey. Gone just two years, everything had changed. Car styles were now round instead of sharp and boxy. Women wore enormous hats, men black fedoras and white porkpie hats. The noise clawed at him. A car backfired, and Joey threw himself face down to the pavement. People stopped and stared. He blinked at the sun and the faces looking down on him. He stood up quickly and became dizzy and had to grasp the side of a building to keep from falling over.

"Are you okay, son?" a stranger asked.

Deep breaths. Deep breaths. Joey felt a little better. The world solidified momentarily, and the dizziness receded. He brushed off his pants and instead of taking a bus, he would walk the five miles to his old southside home.

He stopped next to a store with a red and white awning that advertised fifteen cent milkshakes and went inside. It was a dingy soda shop, but it was much cooler than out on the street, and offered a bit of shade and a quiet place to temporarily calm his restless thoughts. Since there were no customers, the young girl behind the counter was leaning against the cash register reading a paperback. She perked up when Joey entered. A name tag on her blue blouse read, "Beth." She had red hair and a bright smile, which immediately reminded Joey of Kathleen O'Brien. But that all seemed ages ago, like something that never really happened, like an old movie he had seen but couldn't really remember.

"What'll you have, soldier?" the girl asked. She eyed this boy carefully whose uniform hung so loosely on his tall frame, his face thin, his eyes a gray-blue shade of sadness.

"Chocolate milkshake, please. Do you have cherries and bananas?"

"Yup," she said cheerfully. "The bananas are kind of old. You want that tossed in with your shake?"

"Please." Joey had a craving for fruit, which was never part of the K rations in Europe. The men were only given sugar tablets for a supposed energy boost.

"Okee-doke. It's an extra five cents for the fruit. But I won't charge you," she whispered. "The boss will never know. And the bananas have seen better days."

"That's very kind of you." Joey devoured the milkshake, paid, and got up to leave. The girl giggled and pointed at his face. He looked in the mirror behind the counter and saw he had a white mustache. She handed him a napkin. "Good luck, soldier," she said. The girl watched Joey as he left the store. He might have been a handsome boy once, she thought, if not for his haunted, almost ghoul-like eyes.

The sunlight on the street was blinding as Joey continued walking south. He was suddenly tired. The skyscrapers had disappeared as he took a right turn at 26th Street and headed west. With the downtown behind him, the buildings became mostly a line of limestone tenements. Windows were open everywhere like gaping mouths desperate to catch a cool breeze. A young boy with a dirty face, his elbows resting on a windowsill, watched Joey pass.

Suddenly exhausted, Joey turned into an alley and laid down on the cool brick pavement, and fell asleep next to some garbage cans. He had slept in worse places. He was awakened by the filthy boy he saw in the window. The boy kneeled over him and shook him by the shoulder.

"Mister. Mister. Are you okay?" Joey had only been in Chicago a few hours, and it was the second time someone had asked if he was okay. He wasn't.

Throop and Hillock. With his hands on his hips and his duffel bag at his feet, Joey stood in front of his home, but the Kowalski Five and Dime was no more. The dime store sign was gone. The windows in front were covered with faded, yellow newspapers taped over the glass, and a sign reading *FOR RENT*. No one had told him his family had moved. He passed people he thought he recognized, but no one recognized him until a woman walked by on the sidewalk, stopped, and spun around. Her eyes bulged. It was his Aunt Sherry.

"My God. My God. *My God!* Joey. Is it really you?" She ran up to him and hugged him tightly. "Joey. When did you get home?" She began to cry. "Your mother. Oh, my God. Your mother."

"I ran into Father Martin in France. I mean, Lieutenant Martin. He said he would let mom know I was okay." Aunt Sherry could only shake her head. "Oh, Lord."

"Where is Mom? Where is everybody?"

Aunt Sherry grabbed Joey's hand. "Come on. They live in a house now. Oh, you won't believe what they have done with the Five and Dime." She stopped and grabbed Joey by the shoulders again. She looked up at his face. "We thought you were dead." She shook her head. "My God. My God."

Zosha Kowalski was at the back of the house doing dishes at the kitchen sink. They had moved into a red brick bungalow only a few blocks from their old place. The front door was unlocked, and Joey entered quietly. The home's hardwood floors and woodwork shone immaculately. He walked through the front room and dining room staring around at an affluence he had never known. He finally entered the kitchen. He stared at his mother from behind and could not speak. Zosha sensed someone behind her and turned around. She had a frightened look on her face. A stranger had entered her house.

"Mom," Joey finally said. His mother's eyes rolled to the back of her head, and she fell backwards, hitting her head on the kitchen sink. Joe immediately scooped his mother from the floor and carried her to a sofa in the front room. He could not find any bleeding, but a bump was beginning to form on her head. Aunt Sherry came through the front door.

"Oh, my God."

"She fainted and hit her head."

Aunt Sherry ran to the kitchen and brought back a dishrag filled with ice.

"Here," she said.

Zosha slowly opened her eyes. "Joey, is it really you? Am I dead?" Joey laughed. He could not remember the last time he had laughed.

"It's me, mom."

"Why didn't you tell us you were okay, that you were coming home? Oh, Jesus. Praise God. Ouch." She touched the back of her head. "Wait until your sister sees you. She's going to die. I'm not dead. Right?" This time they both laughed and hugged. She never wanted to let her little boy out of her arms again.

News traveled fast and Dorothy burst through the front door screaming, "Joey! Joey!" She ran into her brother's arms, nearly knocking him over. She began to cry. "I knew you weren't dead. I never believed it for a second. We . . . we . . . So much has happened since you left."

Dorothy tried to hide it, but she was horrified at how her big brother looked. His face was gaunt, nearly collapsed it seemed. The spark that had always been her big brother's eyes was gone.

They talked at the kitchen table over dinner, but there was much uncomfortable silence. Zosha had made meatloaf with gravy, mashed potatoes, and cooked carrots. She and Dorothy sat in stunned silence as Joey told them he wasn't home for good, that in two weeks to he would be shipped to the Pacific to fight the Japs. To Zosha, it seemed monstrously unfair. He had been wounded in battle. He had medals for bravery. He looked physically sick. How could they send him back?

Joey sat at the table struggling with his secrets, the eight months that he had deserted, the horrors he'd witnessed and committed. Joey cleaned his plate but ran quickly to the bathroom with stomach cramps and vomited.

Joey slept in his own bedroom, a far cry from sleeping on a cot behind a curtain at the back of the old Kowalski Five and Dime. The walls were wallpapered with pink flowers. In the middle of the night, he walked into his mother's room. She was sitting on her bed. She lifted her hand and pointed a finger at him. A brown spot of blood on her chest grew larger and larger. Joey screamed and jolted awake, drenched in sweat, his breath coming in shallow gasps. His mother was there beside him, holding him, rocking his head gently.

"Shush, baby, shush. It's only dream. It's only a dream. You are home now. You are safe."

Joey trembled.

Nearly every night, Zosha and Dorothy were jarred awake by Joey's nightmares. They occurred less frequently after a week, but his departure back to the war loomed near and cast a pall over everyone. The women felt helpless.

Zosha hoped for a miracle. She went to church every morning and stayed after the mass and prayed for her boy, Tom Martin, and her brother, Chester. She held her hands so tightly in prayer that her knuckles became white and lost feeling. She put a nickel in a jar in front of the Virgin Mary as a dozen vigil lights flickered on Zosha's pained face. She made the sign of the cross and lit one more candle for the poor and suffering.

Dorothy was anxious to show Joey the new store. Besides the Kowalski Five and Dime sign at the front of the building, the store looked very much like the Woolworth before the fire. Joey remembered acutely that night two years ago. It was something he never felt guilty about. So, unless Tom Martin confessed, no one would ever know their involvement in that fire, and no one ever would. Luckily, the police never pursued the matter after a few of weeks.

Dorothy proudly led Joey through the front doors. The inside was brightly lit with fluorescent ceiling lights. The floors were all ivory white ceramic, a mosaic of small hexagons. Everything shone like a new dime. A chorus of "Good morning, Miss Kowalski" rose from the uniformed staff as Dorothy and Joey strode through the polished aisles. She could not suppress her pride in all she and her mom had accomplished.

"Miss Kowalski?" Joey said incredulously. "Aren't you the fancy one?" He marveled at the rows and rows of miscellaneous items. And just to the right of the front entry door was a long, scarlet counter where a boy in a paper cap was serving coffee and doughnuts to customers while they read the daily newspapers. Joey eyed the menu above the counter: *Doughnuts – $.10. Hot dogs – $.30. Sliced ham sandwiches – $.40. Coca-Cola – $.10. Milkshakes – $.20.*

"Good morning, Miss Kowalski," a woman called from behind the counter.

"Good morning, Doris. That's Doris," she told Joey. "She comes in early and makes the donuts."

"Twenty cents for a milkshake? I had one on my way home for fifteen cents."

"Probably not as good," Dorothy laughed. "I pay all my employees fifty cents an hour, which is twenty percent higher than most wages. So, we charge a little more for our product. It's not hurting business. Come on, I'll show you our office. Mom should be here soon. She's in church, no doubt."

Joey looked at his sister with admiration. How could so much change in just over two years? Her looks, sheer confidence, the commanding tone of her voice, all defied her young age. It was though he had stepped into a different world. While he had been scarred by war, his family had thrived, and that was a good thing. He was mesmerized by the enormity of this enterprise. It had to be at least ten times as big as the old Kowalski Five and Dime.

They walked through a door that read *Employees Only*. There were shelves and shelves brimming with inventory. Joey's cousin, Otto, a familiar face from the past, was carrying boxes through the back door from the alley. "Joey!" he bellowed, a wide grin splitting his face. "Hey, ho! Welcome home!"

Joey had a flashback of the night Father Martin pried open the Woolworth back door to the alley with a crowbar. Joey was the look-out and from the alley door, he watched the priest disappear into its darkness.

Dorothy led her brother up a steel stairway to the office area. They walked a long gangway overlooking all the stock and inventory, rows and rows heavy with merchandise. *Consolidated.*

They entered the main office with black file cabinets and two female secretaries working at desks.

They kept walking and finally entered another office with two desks and more file cabinets. One desk was for Dorothy, and the other for Zosha. Another large window overlooked a flat roof above the store and out onto Archer Avenue. Dorothy closed the door behind them. Joey looked out the window onto the street.

"Boy, you've really got something here. I'm so proud of you."

"And we're proud of you."

"Don't be," Joey answered.

Dorothy gave Joey a puzzled look, and then her face became very serious. "Joey," she said, her voice dropping to a whisper. "I have to ask you something. And you don't have to answer if you don't want to. A lawyer in New York, his last name is Waxman, has sent Mom several checks. I don't know why. Forty-eight thousand dollars. That's an enormous amount of money. Where did it come from? Why was it sent to us? She crossed the room to a large safe in the corner of the office and opened it. She took out an envelope, which contained several certified checks. "We never cashed these. We work very hard here, and we don't need any trouble. Understand?"

She waited for an answer. Joey felt the weight of her gaze. He sighed deeply.

Zosha walked into the office smiling. She was happy to have her boy home, if only for a short while. She saw immediately that Dorothy was not smiling. Dorothy nodded to her mother. Zosha saw the checks in her hand and knew what the grave faces were all about.

She sat down in the chair next to Joey. There was silence.

"I . . . I . . ." Joey stopped. His loneliness came crashing in from all sides. He remembered the advice from Nurse Helen in the French hospital tent. *Deep breaths.* He inhaled and exhaled heavily. "I'm not a hero. I'm a coward," he finally said.

"A coward? You were wounded. You have medals for bravery," Zosha said. She looked at the long scar below Joey's ear.

"I deserted."

Dorothy and his mother looked at Joey in stunned silence. "I deserted," he said again. "There is so much more. I can't talk about it." He could not speak without choking. He was being crushed by something unbearable. He was ashamed of deserting, of helping criminals, of being a criminal himself. He would be forever tortured for killing a child.

Dorothy saw a man—a boy—sitting across from her desk crumbling before her very eyes. She reached across the desk and covered his trembling hands with her own.

Zosha hugged Joey. She whispered, "It's okay. It's okay. You are home now. You are safe." Zosha had been so happy when she walked into the office. And now the total unfairness of her boy leaving again for war was hitting her like a freight train. She would go to the War Office tomorrow and get this straightened out. She would go all the way to Washington and tell General Eisenhower himself that her boy has had enough of this war. She would beg President Truman on her knees if she had to.

Joey took deeper breaths. "Don't cash them. I told him I didn't want any money, but I guess he sent it anyway. And yes, it's dirty. I don't want to talk about it. It hurts too much."

Joey finally pulled himself together. "Clarence sent me a letter when I was in France saying he was enlisting. Have you heard any news about where he is? I guess I will be joining him soon."

Dorothy's face hardened. "I don't know why you would know. Clarence joined the Marines not long after you left. He was killed on some island in the Pacific called Iwo Jima. I'm told he died a hero." Joey was speechless and could only stare blankly, the weight of her words sinking into him like lead. He gave a slow nod of numb acceptance as if he had somehow known. He thought of Clarence, of his easy smile and kind heart, snuffed out like so many others. His old friend had just been too good for this world. *Clarence's father must be so proud of his son*, Joey thought bitterly.

Three days before Joey was set to go to the West Coast for deployment, a miracle occurred in the form of atomic bombs. The Japanese cities of Hiroshima and Nagasaki had been obliterated. News crackled through radios and newspapers blared giant headlines. Japan had surrendered! It was August 15, 1945. Joey could now be officially discharged from the Army, but there was no jubilation for him. The war would never be over.

Despite Zosha and Dorothy's pleading with Joey to come and work at Kowalski Five and Dime, or pursue whatever he wished, he knew he couldn't stay home anymore. No matter how hard he tried, his family and old friends had become strangers. Some invisible force, a malignant current in his soul, was moving him to an unknown destination. He was embarrassed by his frequent nightmares and excessive drinking during the day. The alcohol could not drown his pain. He was tortured at the constant worry he was inflicting on his family. He had to leave. Zosha knew he was sick but she didn't know how to help him. She prayed and prayed for her boy, and for Tom Martin who had yet to return from Europe, and Chester from the Pacific.

One morning, she entered Joey's room. His bed was neatly made, and on the pillow was a note.

Mom, I've been thinking long and hard but I can't stay here anymore. I don't know what it is but it's like I can't breathe. It's got nothing to do with you or Dorothy. I love you terribly and maybe that's why I need to go. It hurts too much to see you worry over me and nothing feels right anymore. Maybe I can figure everything out or maybe I can't. I know you worry about me, but don't. I'll be okay. I have to figure out who I am because I don't know anymore. Please give my love to Dorothy. Love you forever, Joey.

Zosha sank onto the edge the bed and wept.

Joey walked through the stillness of the early morning, the faint glow of dawn just beginning to edge the horizon. The night before, he had quietly made two sandwiches and took several apples in the dark of his mom's kitchen. He wore a flannel shirt and his Army-issued pants and boots. A hulking freight train with hundreds of cars groaned as it began to roll slowly out of the yard heading west. Joey jogged alongside, his boots crunching against gravel, and hauled himself up into the first boxcar he saw with an open door. There were two other men inside. Their lost, vacant eyes made Joey think he was looking in a mirror. As they rode along, no one spoke a word.

Chapter 39

Joey jumped off the train at a town called Fargo in North Dakota. The train yard was tiny compared to Chicago, with only three sets of tracks. Some of the railcars sat motionless like ancient and rusted beasts and probably hadn't moved from their resting place for years. He followed an abandoned rail with weeds covering his boots until a small town appeared.

The prairie city of Fargo basked under a crisp, azure sky, with the first hints of autumn painting the trees gold and crimson. A skinny stray bitch with missing patches of hair from some skin disease or a fight with a bigger beast emerged from behind a pile of rail ties and followed Joey out of the train yard. Joey stopped and stared down at the pathetic animal. He rummaged through his knapsack, kneeled and gave the dog half of his sandwich. The mutt decided to follow Joey, sticking to his heels like glue.

"So you want to hang with me, do you?" Joey said. "You got a name?" Joey thought for a moment. "You do now. Gigi."

The streets were alive with a gentle hum, where returning soldiers, their uniforms adorned with ribbons and medals, mingled with town folks whose faces bore the soft lines of relief and renewal. Banners proclaiming victory hung limp on lampposts, their once vibrant reds and blues dulled by the beating wind and sun.

Joey had run out of the little money he had when he left Chicago and hoped he could find a job somewhere. He passed several blocks of small wood-frame houses where elders sat on the porches nodding to each other with suspicion as he passed. Joey knew he looked like a bum.

Joey found work at a gas station near the center of town, a gray metal building with two pumps and a small repair bay. The owner, Art, was an old man with a weathered face, a steady demeanor, and a head that bobbed like a turkey when he walked. Art didn't pry into Joey's past but could see by his khaki pants and army boots that Joey, like so many others, had recently returned from war. And it was clear to him that the lanky kid with deep, troubled eyes had seen more than his share of hard times.

He handed the boy a set of overalls that were too short for Joey's long legs, and told him he could stay in the small room at the back of the station. "Just keep the place clean, and don't let the dog tear anything up."

The dog, Gigi, was content with her newfound friend. Joey fed her and let her curl up by his bed when he went to sleep at night. During the day, Joey spent his hours as a novice mechanic under Art's approving eye. He changed tires, worked the tow truck, and eventually tackled repairs like brake installations and tune-ups. His hands grew rough with grease and grit, and for the first time in months, he felt a faint sense of purpose.

There wasn't much to Joey's routine, and he liked it. Nobody talked to him, and nobody bothered him. He stocked the small refrigerator in his room with groceries and grabbed a meal at a place called Carl's Chicken Coop, whenever he could spare the change.

The days blurred together, filled with the rhythm of work and the quiet companionship of Gigi. Weeks rolled by, unremarkable but steady, and Joey began to settle into the small-town life, his mind slowly stitching itself back together, one day at a time.

"You ever spent a winter in Fargo, son?" old Art asked Joey. He spit tobacco through blackened gums into an empty soup can he always carried. "You got no coat? No cap? You don't know wicked till you spent a winter here, by jiminy. It gets awful cold sometime."

Art walked away and checked the steel lockers near the car lifts at the back of the garage and fished out a mangy, oily coat that could have been worn on an Arctic whaling ship. Joey had to admit that his flannel shirts were not going to hold up to the bitter temperatures that began to chew on the days.

"Sorry," Art said. "This coat has seen some days, but you can have it if you want. With all that motor oil on it, it's probably waterproof. Or you can throw it in the garbage."

Joey took the heavy coat from Art. "No. I like it just as it is. Thanks."

Hard work and long walks alone out into the endless prairie had a soothing effect on Joey's nerves. His migraines, which had once pounded his skull with relentless fury, seemed to dull in the presence of the whispering grasses and open skies. There was something narcotic in the vast plains, in the rustling leaves of the towering oaks and maples. He liked the smallness he felt. At the first kiss of snow, a restless ghost pulled at Joey's coat. Walking beneath a grove of cottonwood near the Red River, a black crow cawed from a branch far above shaking snowy dust onto Joey's shoulder. He looked up and felt the bird was speaking to him. It seemed to say, "It's time to move on."

Art had been good to him, but when Joey left one day, he never said goodbye. He found just disappearing like a shadow was the best way to leave. Art walked into Joey's back room and found Joey was gone. He had grown fond of this tall, sad boy. Art patted Gigi on the head. "I hope that boy ends up okay. Rotten war."

With a worn duffel bag slung over his shoulder, Joey pointed his thumb west into the teeth of the Dakota Badlands. The war had tried to kill Joey, but now after days of hitch hiking, it was the weather. While his heavy coat protected his torso, his legs and face became icicles tortured by the frigid wind. Just months ago, he didn't care if he lived or died, but there was a mystery budding inside him that said, *Live*. He didn't feel trapped. Maybe it was the clean, unscarred air, or the endless expanse of the sky, or the kind people he was meeting on his odyssey to nowhere.

Joey quickly decided hitchhiking was not an option, as few cars passed, and the sleet and ice were turning him into a walking snowman. To the north, the land was jagged, convulsing wildly from the earth, so when he left the road, he headed south through the flat, empty plains until he hit railroad tracks and waited. It wasn't long until a Milwaukee Railroad freighter passed. It was not moving slowly, and Joey had to sprint with all his might to barely catch the last boxcar, its inner refuge filled with crates of commerce. The cold became tolerable as he pushed some boxes aside and fell asleep.

Even with V-shaped snowplows at the front locomotive, the train moved slower and slower, battling through ever-growing drifts, each one a monstrous wall of white, some towering over the locomotive itself. Joey felt the train come to a complete stop and he heard banging on top of the boxcar and a conductor hollering, "If any varmints in there, get your ass out!"

Joey tried prying the side door of the boxcar open but could only move it a couple inches. It was packed with snow. Joey called out to the unknown man on the car roof. Each of the enclosed boxcars had hatches on the roof, and Joey soon heard scraping and the metallic screech of the hatch being opened. A pair of eyes, the only visible feature beneath a thick scarf and cap, peered down.

"Come on boy," he said gruffly. "We got some shoveling to do."

Joey soon discovered that he was not the only freeloader on this westward freighter. About a dozen other hobos of various sizes and in mostly ragged attire were given shovels. Anybody who did not want to pitch in would be left behind. Nobody refused. The makeshift crew began to shovel a tunnel in front of the train with snowdrifts well above their heads. The idea was to get enough room in front of the lead locomotive so that it could get a running start to plow its way through. After four hours of brutal shoveling, the train was on its way. All the bums taking a free ride were loaded into the same empty boxcar. One grizzled old timer sang a mournful ballad about "Ol' Kentucky."

Finally, the train was halted by Mother Nature at Miles City, Montana. The snow was not as deep as Joey had just witnessed, but reports said the tracks heading further west were impassable. The sun was a pale ghost in the hazy white sky, casting skeleton shadows across the brick buildings lining Main Street. Hunger gnawed at Joey's gut. He entered the welcoming warmth of a tavern called The Buckhorn. It was surprisingly crowded with patrons. Some locals sitting at the bar stared at the tall, shabby stranger with amusement more than suspicion.

The barkeep, a woman with eyes as sharp as a hawk and a smile as worn as Joey's boots, eyed him up and down. With a dollar and nineteen cents in his pocket, Joey ordered a ham sandwich and a glass of water. She returned quickly through a door from behind the bar and set the sandwich down on a paper plate in front of him.

"I hope you like white bread. It's all we got."

She turned her back to Joey and began to clean used glasses. She would dunk the glasses in dirty, sudsy water, and then dunk them quickly in more dirty water to rinse them. She wiped them down with a rag and set them up for the next round of drinks.

"Do you know where a fella might find a job around here?" Joey asked.

She turned and faced Joey with a quizzical look, apparently sizing him up. Her face, which years ago no doubt shone a beautiful young woman, was weathered like leather, a testimony to this harsh land.

"Well," she said, wiping down another glass, "the farms and ranches don't need much help this time of year, but I could use some extra help around here with all these thirsty souls. Lucky me, I'm the only bar that stays open in winter. You got a name?"

"I do. Joey."

"When can you start?"

"After I finish this sandwich."

She laughed. "I think I like you, Joey. The name is Mildred." They shook hands. "Come in back when you're ready and grab an apron. Pedro will show you what needs doin'."

The kitchen area was surprisingly clean, although there was a steel bucket on the floor filled with some kind of gravy. Joey made sure that he never ate anything at the Buckhorn that had gravy with it, although the patrons never complained of food poisoning. The smell of grilled onion made Joey think of his friend Isaiah Stomp who always reminisced about his days in front of his grill.

In just a few days, Joey was behind the bar serving drinks. He never touched a drop of alcohol, which Mildred appreciated. Her only instructions were, "Keep the glasses full and the fights short." But luckily there were no fights to break up. The only days he took off were Sundays, when the Buckhorn was open for food but no alcohol.

He kept an eye on the weather outside, but he was snowed in for winter and may as well have to accept it. Things weren't that bad. He stayed at The Squire for only two dollars a day, which included a hot bath once a week, and he was making over eight dollars a day working the tavern. Behind the bar, Joey became known for his steady hand and quiet demeanor. While he was easy with a smile, his eyes showed a grave intensity of a troubled past, but no one was there to hear the troubles of a bartender. The regulars were all too ready to spill their miseries on anyone who would listen. He nodded politely at the tales of cattle drives and prairie storms from the old ranch hands and helped the inebriated to the door at closing time. He played cards at the back of the tavern on breaks and usually won. When he did, he would buy everyone a round.

Before long, Joey was again feeling restless. On Sundays, his days off, he spent the time alone, mostly outside looking for some signs of a crack in winter, but there were none. His stay here in Miles City would be a bit longer.

He had gotten used to the cold. He would trudge knee-deep through the snow next to the Tongue River, entering a world enchanted. With each step, his breath hung in the air, crystallizing into tiny puffs. The infinite snow of the plains could be a blinding white or a soft pink depending upon the time of day and the capriciousness of the sky. Cozying beside Miles City, the Tongue River, an important artery in summer, was now a frozen canvas of blues and grays. The occasional cracks in the groaning ice sounded like gunshots which would give Joey a start, but other than that, it was delightfully peaceful.

Joey inhaled all the cold wonderment of this faraway land. The leafless cottonwoods along the riverbank stood naked and stark with branches etched black against the horizon like an ink drawing. Joey looked up and listened as the coyotes cried and moaned beyond the river to the west from a mountain range covered with a forest of lush green spruce and cedar, offering the only color to the winter tapestry.

Months passed. The river ice began to bubble from beneath and cracks began to appear in mid-March. Mildred sensed a sudden change in Joey's demeanor. He did not have to tell her. "You are leaving soon, aren't you?" she said sadly. Joey nodded. "You will be missed, and not just by me." She gave Joey a hug. "If I don't see you again, have a nice life. You deserve it."

Pedro wiped his hands on his apron and shook Joey's hand. "Good luck, amigo."

Joey stayed away from large cities, alternating between hitchhiking and hopping freight trains to nowhere. Big buildings, traffic, and crowds were not for him. He was breathing freely now. There wasn't a job Joey wouldn't take to make enough money so he could move on. He joined a crew of lumberjacks near Donkey Creek, Wyoming, where he worked a two-man saw, felling Poderosa Pine giants. In Trinidad, Colorado, he hauled coal onto conveyor belts, the black dust clinging to his sweat-drenched skin, and under a relentless sun in

Brewster, Kansas, he picked beans from sun-up to sun-down with a hundred other migrant workers.

Each job was just another brushstroke to his wandering. His gaunt face and thinness disappeared with the days. Tall and lean as a poplar sapling, Joey's skin browned, and his hair turned a sandy blond from the sun. His cheeks and nose glowed with youthful freckles, defying a continued sadness in his countenance. All the farm girls who swooned at his good looks were disappointed at his lack of interest. Any girl with a fetching smile sadly brought back the ghost of Yvette Fauxbourg, a wound still too fresh.

In June, 1946, Joey jumped off a train in Valentine, Nebraska, a cattle town. He easily found work at Jim Stanton's nine-thousand-acre Crooked Fork Ranch near Pelican Lake. Jim Stanton, whose frown lines looked etched in granite, didn't give a hoot that Joey had no ranching experience. He felt it was his duty to hire any veteran hobo who came along looking for work. Food and a bunkhouse to sleep in were free to all his ranch hands. Mr. Stanton found most of these drifters were hard workers and generally well-behaved.

Mrs. Stanton made sure her boys were well-fed, and Joey had never eaten so much food in his entire life. The hard work burned calories quicker than they could be consumed. The boss's wife made sure the tables were filled with vegetables and meat. Pancakes, fruit, eggs, and bacon every morning. Steak and potatoes filled the plates every evening at supper.

It took a while for Joey to get used to the gamy stink of so many cattle. The very air surrounding the ranch had a sepia tint from wafting dust, animal dung, and bovine flatulence. Ranch work was hard and nonstop, but that was what he wanted. The sound of the cattle was a continual symphony of baying, which could change from a roar to a contented soft bellowing at a moment's notice. Dust, dirt, and insects were Joey's and the other ranch hands constant companions. The harder he worked, the better he slept at night. The nightmares had disappeared. He repaired fences every day. Branding the cattle with a hot iron was nauseous work. The brand was, of course, a crooked fork. Joey had smelled burnt flesh before.

Joey took on all work the foreman asked of him. He fed and cared for the horses, and found himself talking to the steers like they were people. He apologized that they would someday end up in a Chicago slaughterhouse.

He learned that riding a horse around cattle was a dangerous business. He loved horses but had no interest in being on top of one. One of his fellow ranch hands was thrown into a fence post, splitting his head open. He was taken away in an ambulance. As was the case in the other towns Joey passed through, he made no friends or enemies at the Crooked Fork.

It was the Fourth of July, and the 3,219 inhabitants of Valentine, were set to explode in celebration. Mr. Stanton gave the cowboys at the Crooked Fork a full day off.

"Come on, Joey," a ranch hand named Butch encouraged him. "This is going to be a hell of a good time. Slim is in the bull riding competition, and I'm going to wrestle me some steer, and maybe a few little ladies," he giggled.

"Nah, I'll pass." Fireworks were the last thing Joey wanted to see. He would rather spend a quiet night with the animals. Joey was finally feeling better about himself and the world. He was no longer dead inside. Being around the animals soothed him. He much preferred them to people. Butch gave Joey a sad look as if to say, "C'mon, the war's over."

Joey put both hands on Butch's shoulders and looked down at him. "I'm okay. You guys go and tear the town apart. Stay out of trouble."

The Fourth of July victory parade started at 11 AM sharp, and wound its way past the red brick courthouse, the schoolhouse, and the general store. Floats were decorated with red, white, and blue bunting. The band played "The Star-Spangled Banner" over and over to a cheering crowd. The master of ceremony was ninety-eight-year-old Nehemiah Hicks, a former drummer boy in the American Civil War, wounded at Shiloh. He was dutifully pushed at the front of the parade in his wheelchair by his seventy-year-old daughter, Constance. They moved so slowly that the high school band eventually pushed past them which was fine with Constance as she was tired, and the old soldier, his brain addled with age, didn't know what was going on anyway.

Horses pranced. Children waved flags. Soon, the parade and the parade watchers were covered with the kicked-up dust from Main Street, which had not yet been paved. No one complained. In the town square, there were games and an enormous barbecue. There were steaks, hot dogs, corn on the cob, watermelon. The much-anticipated rodeo would begin soon. And the band played on.

The boss, Jim Stanton, appreciated that Joey was the only one who volunteered to stay with the animals instead of heading into town. He warned Joey that the anticipated fireworks, even though a half mile away, would spook some of the animals, especially the young ones.

The day turned into night. The sky was black. The stars dazzled. Suddenly, fireworks appeared in the sky over the town. Joey entered the corral with several horses and a young foal. The booms were soft but still made Joey shake. He hugged the neck of a colt born only a few weeks ago. It was trembling. He buried his face into the soft mane. "Shush. It's okay. Joey's here."

Well after midnight, the cowboys stumbled into the bunkhouse, most of them very drunk. Joey rose quietly. It wasn't until the pale light of dawn that the foreman discovered that Joey's bunk was empty.

Joey hitchhiked south and then east across central Kansas on Highway 10. Tiny towns that could hardly be called towns passed on the sides of the highway as mere dots on a map. McFarland, Paxico, Maple Hill.

Kansas was a vast, flat plain, dry and windy. The land was only beginning to recover from the 1930s Dust Bowl, the ecological apocalypse that killed off most of the vegetation, leaving the land barren and thirsty for any drop of moisture.

Joey sat wedged in the back of a rusted pickup truck with three children. He folded up his long legs and hugged his knees so he could fit between bales of hay and the gawking youngsters.

He had grown another inch since his army induction which now seemed ages ago, and was no longer a skinny stick of a teenager. Time and toil had thickened his shoulders, made his hands hard as oak.

Mom and Dad were in the front seats of the vehicle. A little girl stared at Joey, mouth agape, as though he were the oddest creature she had ever seen in her life. He smiled at the girl and made his face go cross-eyed. She giggled. An older boy in the truck bluntly said to Joey what Joey already knew: "Mister, you smell bad."

The truck rattled on. At the next highway intersection, Joey tapped on the back window of the cab and motioned he wanted off. He thanked the driver and jumped out of the truck. There was nothing around but a cloudless sky and dry prairie. He stood in the shade of a battered plywood sign that read, in white letters on peeling green paint, *Willard – 5 miles.*

Shading his eyes with his hand, Joey spied trees to the north. Trees in this wasteland meant water. He left the road and hopped fences until he finally saw grass and trees with green leaves. The landscape changed as he got closer to the Kansas River. The air became cooler.

When he arrived at the riverbank, Joey sniffed his armpits and grimaced. This looked like a lonely stretch of the river, so he decided to remove all his clothes and rinse them in the river. He rubbed his pants and shirt against a rock so maybe some of the stink would come off. The water was an electric blue, and the current was slow. Joey dove straight in headfirst. The coolness was delicious. He took a sip of the water. It tasted okay. He filled his canteen. There was a clean pair of underpants in his knapsack. He hung the rest of his clothes on a bush and lay naked in the grass. The sun and breeze felt good. He slept.

Joey opened his eyes. He rested his head on his knapsack and relished the tranquility. The sky had darkened to the west. Maybe a storm was coming.

He couldn't articulate the precise reason, but a new Joey Kowalski had emerged. The unexplained trembling, tears, and nightmares had completely disappeared. Hopelessness, his constant companion, had retreated. Perhaps it was the realization of how small he was in the vastness of this world that gave him comfort. He could not let the rocks of his past drag him to the bottom. What happened in the war was real but he did not have to turn his soul into a prison from which there was no escape. Yvette was gone. The seeds they had planted in the soil would never be harvested. It was a painful memory he would never forget, but he could still live in the now and find a sort of contentment. It was as though a veil had been lifted from his eyes, revealing a world he had been blind to since the war.

Far above, a half-dozen vultures circled the sky. Joey smiled. "You're a little early, boys," he said to the buzzards. "I'm not dead yet."

His clothing dry, Joey headed back to the main road reluctant to leave this idyllic spot. I wish I had a fishing pole, he thought, though he had never been fishing in his life. After a two-mile walk on Route 10, he saw a small house next to a lone church. The church was a stark white stucco against a bleached landscape. There was a small parking area of gray gravel and dirt, but no cars. Joey decided he would make a short visit. He could use the shade, and the water in his canteen was already running low. He pulled on the church's front doors. They were locked.

"Can I help you?" a man said kindly. A tiny priest in a long chocolate-colored robe with a hood came up behind Joey. Joey looked down at the little man.

"I guess not. Just looking for some shade."

"Sorry, we are all locked up. Repairs, you know." The priest looked up at the church and sighed. "This old building needs lots of repairs. See the cross you are standing under? The stucco is cracked and leaning out. That's going to fall on someone's head someday. Wouldn't that be a hoot?" The little priest giggled.

Joey looked up then backed away. The old priest's head swayed involuntarily from side to side. He was bald with tufts of white hair sticking out above his ears. He had a kind face and waddled when he walked. The man fumbled with keys he pulled from his robe and opened the doors. "The least I can do is give you some water and some shade. It's a lot cooler inside."

The church interior was humble and dim. It was tiny and drab compared to the ornate Saint Gerard's from Joey's old neighborhood in Chicago. No statues of saints lined the walls. No stained glass windows cast colorful patterns on the floor. The pews were wood benches with no backrests. The churchgoers would have to kneel on the floor. There were steel rods stretching overhead from wall to wall to reinforce the exterior walls and help keep them from collapsing outward. Yes, Joey thought, this place needed some work. There was a stepladder leaning against the altar. Off to the side, a large wooden cross lay propped against a wall.

The priest came from a room behind the altar with a jug of cool water. He filled a large, chipped mug and handed it to Joey.

"Christian?" the priest asked.

"No," Joey answered.

"Oh, well. God has no religion. Mahatma Gandhi said that." The short priest observed the boy towering above him. "You're sure a tall drink of water. Do you think you can help me with something? I got to hang this crucifix back up behind the alar. It's heavy. I can't manage it alone."

Joey heaved the wooden cross over his shoulder and carried it up the two steps to the altar. The priest was right. It was heavy.

The priest stood on the stepladder. "Lift it up. Just a little higher. I got to get this wire over this nail." Joey frowned and lowered the cross to the floor.

"I'm sorry," the priest said. "Too heavy?"

"No. It's just that that tiny nail ain't gonna hold this up. Is that a finish nail? Were you able to hit a stud?"

"A what?"

"That nail isn't gonna work. What else you got?"

The priest led Joey to a back room. There was an assortment of tools on a table. Joey picked up a hand drill and a three-and-a-half-inch lag screw. From the ladder behind the altar, Joey removed the tiny nail and piloted a hole for the screw. "This should do," Joey said.

Joey lifted the cross again. The little priest tried to guide the wire over the new fastener. "A bit higher," he said. "There. Perfect."

Joey rubbed his shoulder. "Thanks much for the water, Padre. I need to move along."

The priest knew a drifter when he saw one. "You're not from around here, are you?

"Not really."

"Do you know any carpentry?"

"A little," Joey replied.

"I got a couple weeks of work here. We don't have much money, but you can have free meals and a place to sleep. I'm a good cook."

"No, thanks."

Joey left the church, squinted through the white glare of the sun, and headed east down Highway 10.

Chapter 40

The Chicago sun beat down like a giant fist shattering Windy City heat records. Tom Martin, his shirt soaked in sweat, wrestled boxes from a delivery truck in the alley behind Kowalski Five and Dime. Mrs. Zosha Martin, formerly Zosha Kowalski, watched him through the door from the upper window of her office. She marveled at what a handsome, strong man she had married. Tonight, she would make spaghetti for supper.

Tom Martin had abandoned the priesthood but was on good terms with the new pastor at Saint Gerard's. He was allowed to use the social hall beneath the grammar school for meetings with war veterans. An overwhelming number of men returning from the war who had experienced combat were suffering traumatic wounds of the mind. The wartime world of the infantry man who had stared into the abyss was so far removed from anything normal that it was impossible for many to adjust to civilian life. Tom found that these veterans felt some comfort talking to others who had gone through the same horrors. War victory for many did not lead to peace, but to alcoholism, rage, hopelessness, and suicide. The loved ones of these wrecked souls suffered as well. Returning veterans needed help, but the US government was slow to develop programs that dealt with the psychological casualties of the war.

Tom finished unloading the truck. Zosha walked down the stairs to the dock and hugged the sweaty man. His earthy smell aroused a passion deep within her.

"Aren't you the most handsome man?"

Tom didn't answer. He was lost in thought; his eyes focused on something faraway.

"You know," Zosha said, "Otto or Billy should be the ones unloading trucks. They are supposed to be staggering their lunch breaks. Besides, you're management."

This remark made Tom laugh. "How bourgeois. Long live the proletariat. Hang the rich."

"Oh, God. A commie," Zosha exclaimed.

Tom stopped smiling.

"No, really. You've been distant. What's wrong?" she asked.

"The war isn't over. Far from it. These poor men I meet with twice a week in the school basement. I wish I could do more. They need real help. Trained counselors. Psychiatrists. Jobs. Guidance. This type of help takes money. A lot of money."

Zosha nodded. It was not just her son who had returned from the war a hollowed shell of what he once he was. She also saw it in countless others who had no doubt seen the searing horrors of war.

"Come with me." Zosha led her husband up the steel stairs to the office. She went to the safe and opened it. "Here." She handed Tom an envelope. Inside were several certified checks totaling forty-eight thousand dollars.

Tom was stunned. "Where did these come from? Are they real?" He looked at each check. "Who is Arnold Waxman?"

"He's an attorney from New York. When we contacted him, he said the money was from a distant relative and that's all he could say about it. When I showed Joey, he said it was dirty money and we should burn it. But that's all he said about it. I want you to take it." She sighed. "You know my Joey is one of these poor kids who needs help. You take it. Use it. Maybe good can come from this."

Chapter 41

Joey could see in the hazy distance a scattering of buildings. It was just another one-dog town like the hundreds he had seen on his odyssey. There were two streetlights to control the limited traffic. He walked along Main Street and passed a filling station, a two-story hotel, a hardware store with a pyramid of salt licks lining the front, a tavern, a hamburger joint, and a bank that looked closed. Small-frame houses scattered around this main strip. Cars were parked diagonally along a paved sidewalk. In front of a barbershop, old men in rocking chairs fanned themselves with magazines as they watched Joey walk by. Finally, Joey passed a small trailer park, and before he knew it, he was heading out of town.

Hunger made Joey turn around and head back. He stood in front of a single-story brick restaurant with a sign stretched above the door that read *Shirley's Shake Shack*. There were two red-buttoned Coca-Cola emblems at each end of the sign. Joey looked through the window. A couple of the booths had customers, and some more patrons sat at a long counter. He entered. Large fans hung at each end of the restaurant, creating a welcome breeze in the heat. Windows were open. The walls were painted yellow, the floor a checkered linoleum.

There were a few tables with chairs, booths along the windows, and a long counter with stools. A cook was frying burgers and onions with his back to the counter. He had long black hair tied in a braid that reached below the shoulders. Above the counter was a board with a menu and prices made with removable letters. Cheeseburgers. French fries. Milkshakes. A paper menu was stuck between the shakers of salt and pepper. Two old men, both with white hair, sat at one of the booths smoking cigarettes. One of the men was reading a newspaper. "I tell you, Archie, this world is going to hell." The other man nodded.

The cook half turned his head. "I'll be right with you, bub. Shirley!" he called out. "Customer."

Joey recognized the voice instantly, and a grin lit up his face. "I heard this dump has the best goddamned grilled cheese sandwiches in all of Kansas."

Isaiah Stomp snapped his head up. "Joey!" He spun around and stared at Joey Kowalski. "Shirl, take the grill." A short woman with dark skin and black hair emerged through a swinging door from the back of the kitchen. He handed her his spatula.

Isaiah limped along the length of the counter to the other side. Joey and Isaiah stood at arm's length apart, smiling. Then they both lunged forward and hugged so tightly that they nearly fell over.

"God, Joey, I thought you were dead." Isaiah's eyes became glassy with tears.

"I was," Joey replied. "I was."

The End.

Epilogue

Tom and Zosha Martin, with the help of Joey's "dirty money," created the Veterans Assistance Program to help soldiers transition to civilian life. The program offered counseling, psychiatric care, help with finding employment, and classes on how to navigate and benefit from the new complicated G.I. Bill. It served as a template for other programs throughout the country. Besides Chicago, centers were opened in St. Louis and Cleveland.

Warrant Officer Chester Kowalski, Zosha's brother, died July 28, 1945, along with forty-six other sailors on the USS *Callaghan* after it was sunk by a Japanese suicide dive bomber off the coast of Okinawa. The *Callaghan* was the last US naval ship to be sunk by kamikaze.

Jack "Fatman" Elliot went MIA during the Battle of the Bulge. His remains were never found. His CO suspected desertion.

Milton "Pops" Carmichael recovered from his wounds suffered on D-Day and returned to live with his mother. He taught high school English in Tallahassee, Florida until his retirement.

The Kowalski Five and Dime remained profitable, and another store was opened in downtown Chicago. Dorothy Kowalski's prescient eye for business opportunities foresaw the boom in women's fashions and she opened wildly successful boutiques just for women in downtown Chicago and Milwaukee.

Erskine "the Squirrel" York survived the war uninjured. He married his USO sweetheart, Irene Plunk, and opened a filling station near his childhood home in Tennessee. They had seven children.

Wilbur "Gorilla" Lafayette survived the war. He lost several toes to frostbite during the bitter European winter of '45. With over eight pounds of gold teeth and other pilfered loot extracted from dead Germans, he was able to start a lucrative alligator trapping business in Baton Rouge selling skins and meat.

Joey Kowalski settled in Topeka, Kansas and started Kowalski Construction. He fell in love with a Native American girl named Wild Geese and they had four children. He helped his friend Isaiah Stomp build a drive-through pickup window at the side of Shirley's Shake Shack. It is believed to be the first drive-through pickup hamburger joint in all Kansas.

World War II European Timeline

1939

September 1. Germany invades Poland. World War II begins.

September 3. Great Britain and France declare war on Germany.

September 17. Russians invade Poland. Sign a pact with Germany to divide Poland in half.

November 30. Russia attacks Finland. Demands substantial border territories. Fierce and determined resistance by the Finns.

1940

March 13. Russia ends war with Finland. Despite being outnumbered 3 to 1 in soldiers, 30 to 1 in aircraft, and 100 to 1 in tanks, the Finns persevere and retained sovereignty.

April 9. Germany invades Denmark and Norway.

April 10. Germany invades Holland, Belgium, and Luxembourg.

June 4. Trapped British and French forces miraculously evacuate more than 330,000 troops from Dunkirk.

June 10. Mussolini and Italy declare war on France and Britain.

June 14. German troops enter Paris. France surrenders.

September 7. The Nazi blitz of London begins. German aircraft bomb civilian targets.

1941

April 6. Germany invades Yugoslavia and Greece.
May 10. Germany briefly stops bombing England. London has more than 1 million houses damaged, and 40,000 civilians are killed.
June 22. Germany invades Russia with 4.5 million troops.
December 7. Japan attacks Pearl Harbor. United States enters the war.
December 11. Germany declares war on the United States.

1942

June 10. The massacre at Lidice, Czechoslovakia. 340 citizens are murdered by the Nazis in a reprisal for the assassination of a German officer.
August 19. About 6,000 Canadian and British soldiers launch a disastrous raid against the Germans at Dieppe, France, suffering 50% casualties.
November 8. Beginning of Operation Torch, the Allied invasion of North Africa lands near Casablanca.

1943

April 13. The Katyn Massacre. The Russian Army murders—under Stalin's orders—over 22,000 Polish officers and civilians and bury them in mass graves in the Katyn forest.

May 7. The German Army in North Africa surrenders to Americans and British.

July 10. Allied forces invade Sicily.

July 28. Hamburg, Germany's second-largest city is bombed by British and American planes. 37,000 civilians are killed.

1944

January 22. Allies land at Anzio, Italy. The landing is a disaster with 36,000 Allied soldiers wounded, 7,000 killed. A breakout from the beachhead does not occur until late May.

January 27. The Germans withdraw, and the siege of Leningrad, Russia ends after 872 days. Two million Leningrad civilians die mostly from starvation and disease. Cannibalism is discovered.

April 27. The Slapton Sands tragedy. Hundreds of American soldiers and sailors are killed over two days in southwest England in a training exercise preparing for the D-Day invasion.

June 3. The Allies enter Rome.

June 6. D-Day begins. 155,000 Allied troops land on the Normandy beaches, France.

June 10. The Oradour-sur-Glane Massacre—a town near Limoges, France—in which 642 men, women, and children are murdered in a German response to the local resistance activity.

July 9. Caen, France is liberated by British troops.

July 17. German Field Marshal Rommel is badly injured when his car is strafed from the air in France.

July 20. Attempted assassination of Hitler.

August 1. The Warsaw Uprising begins. It is defeated in 63 days by the Germans. The expected Russian Army halts outside the city and never arrives to help the civilians. 150,000 to 200,000 Poles are murdered mostly from execution during the Uprising.

August 8. Plotters in the bomb plot against Hitler are executed and their bodies hung on meat hooks.

August 25. Paris is liberated. The German military disobeys Hitler's orders to burn the city and destroy all bridges over the Seine River.

September 10. Allied troops enter Germany.

October 7. A riot takes place at the Auschwitz concentration camp when Jewish collaborators find out they are also slated for extermination. Over 450 are killed in suppressing the revolt.

October 14. Field Marshal Rommel, under suspicion as one of the bomb plotters to kill Hitler, voluntarily commits suicide to save his family. He is buried with full military honors.

November 7. FDR wins an unprecedented fourth term as US president.

November 26. The war in Italy is at a stalemate.

December 16. The Battle of the Bulge begins with German forces attempting a breakthrough in the Ardennes' region. The main object is to retake Antwerp.

1945

January 27. Auschwitz is entered by Soviet troops. Over 960,000 prisoners—mostly Jews—were tortured and murdered by the Nazis throughout the war.

February 9. The Colmar pocket, the last German foothold west of the Rhine, is eliminated by the French First Army.

February 13–14. The bombing of Dresden takes place. 25,000 civilians are killed.

March 20. Patton's troops capture Mainz, Germany.

March 27. The Western Allies slow their advance and allow the Russian Army to take Berlin.

April 10. Buchenwald concentration camp is liberated by American forces where over 56,000 prisoners are tortured and murdered throughout the war.

April 12. FDR dies. Harry Truman becomes president.

April 28. Mussolini and his mistress are shot and hanged by the feet in Milan.

April 29. The Dachau concentration camp is liberated by the Seventh Army. 32,000 prisoners died here. Hitler marries Eva Braun.

April 30. Hitler and his wife commit suicide.

May 1. Reich Chancellor Goebbels and his wife murder their children and then commit suicide.

May 7. Germany surrenders unconditionally.

May 23. Heinrich Himmler, son of a Roman Catholic schoolteacher, second most powerful Nazi next to Hitler, and organizer of the German extermination camps, commits suicide with a cyanide pill.

August 6. The Enola Gay drops an atomic bomb on Hiroshima, Japan.

August 9. The bomber Bockscar drops an atomic bomb on Nagasaki. The two bombs kill over 200,000 civilians.

August 15. Japan surrenders. WWII ends.